SECTOR 19

PART 3 OF PORTAL 106

SECTOR 19

PART 3 OF PORTAL 106

GEORGINA FATSEAS

CITIOFBOOKS, INC.
3736 Eubank NE Suite A1
Albuquerque, NM 87111-3579
www.citiofbooks.com
Hotline: 1 (877) 389-2759
Fax: 1 (505) 930-7244

Ordering Information:
Quantity sales. Special discounts are available on quantity purchases by corporations, associations, and others. For details, contact the publisher at the address above.

Printed in the United States of America.

ISBN-13: Softcover 978-1-963209-86-0
      eBook   978-1-963209-87-7

Library of Congress Control Number: 2024904478

EDITOR'S NOTES.

This book uses some Australian expressions. British spelling is used.

AUTHOR'S NOTES.

For the purpose of the story, the names of stars and constellations have been used as names for planets. Other named galaxies and planets are fictitious.

Over the last ten years, astronomers and people working in related fields have made incredible discoveries. Some of these discoveries have been utilized in this story.

As proof for the existence of parallel or multi or string universes go, it is currently in the field of theoretical quantum physics. Proof may be in the distant future.

The possibility of time travel is much further into the future unless quantum physics can speed up the research.

We are turning back the clocks to the eighteenth century when people became spectators to a war. They considered it a form of entertainment.

But for now...

Please be seated. Put your seats in an upright position.
Please do up your seatbelt. After lift-off from Earth, you will be advised when it is safe to undo your seatbelt. However, should we enter an area with turbulence, you will be advised to buckle up again and place your seat in an upright position.

We would appreciate if you take a minute to go through this checklist.

[ ] Turn off your phones and other electronic devices. They will still be there with a list of missed calls, messages and emails.
[ ] As this is a budget flight, food and drinks are self-serve in the kitchen.
[ ] For your comfort, the restrooms are down the hallway.
Additional things you may need to do to ensure there is no disturbance on this flight are:
[ ] Give the dog, cat or other pets to someone else to mind for the duration of the journey,
[ ] Place a do not disturb sign on a door of the room you are using or on the coffee table beside the couch you are using,
[ ] Wear noise blocking earphones,
[ ] Have someone prepare you snacks or meals and fetch you drinks and leave them on the coffee table for you if you do not wish to prepare your own meals.

[ ] Please tick the box if you have read and understood the waivers and the insurance policy of this journey through the universe. If you haven't read them, please refer to the sales receipt.

When you have completed the journey, you can snap back to reality and attend to all the delayed chores and missed calls and texts. But, most important, tell other readers about your sightseeing tour through the galaxies in this make-believe universe.

Now, enjoy the journey as a war observer.
Thank you for your attention.

CHAPTER 1

The Lords of the Universe – The Council of Five.

Meeting Room.

Councillor Sigma broke the awkward silence. Like the others, he knew things had already gone from bad to worse. Now it was critical. His figures concerning the destruction of mankind were devastating and the death toll was climbing daily.

"When is Zindel coming?" he asked.

"He should be arriving any minute. He was examining the galaxy of Julos in sector 19," said Azna, the only female councillor.

Xetron turned to the massive glass door behind him. Beyond the door was a large landing pad. In the distance he saw an illuminated speck coming towards them. "He is coming now. Just a few more minutes."

Zindel landed his craft softly on the landing pad. As the engine wound down to a stop, the doors directly to the meeting room slid open without a whisper. "Sorry for the delay. A Draconian mother ship made things slowed me down. I had to dispose of it."

"In what sector was that ship?" asked Jose.

"Twenty. It was heading for Lyria, in the White galaxy or as the locals call it, The Milky Way. My new toy managed to blow it up."

Sigma looked puzzled. "New toy?"

Zindel turned to his craft and pointed. "That black box on top of the fuselage and just slightly back from the cockpit is the new addition. It is a test model. I will report to my research team on its effectiveness after this meeting."

Sigma asked, "If you destroyed a mother ship, then it works."

"The range needs improving from a quarter to half a light year. Those ships make one giant mess with flying debris. I would prefer the debris to completely evaporate. Less mess in space."

"What is the technology behind this …." Jose searched for a word but settled on an inadequate term "Canon?"

"The actual mechanics were explained but that will take too much precious time. Put simplistically, it shoots out balls which consist of gamma, delta rays and every other ray you can think of including electrically charged light, dark matter, anti-matter, sonic and assorted radio waves. It is basically replicating black holes regurgitating star-like matter; the materials which make new stars."

Thuma nodded. "Normally, I would be horrified at such a weapon. Since it is ours, I give my approval. Just make sure the Draconians don't acquire it and make copies."

Zindel smiled. "They can't operate it. My vessel has been modified to only permit my biometrics.

If anything is touched or removed, the entire craft blows up."

Thuma looked shocked. "Have we stooped so low? That is awful."

"It is only awful to the person, robot or creature trying to pull it apart." Zindel walked further into the room to begin his report.

"Most of my news is bad but there are some minor elements of hope. I will start with the bad items first. Firstly, we don't know where the rip in the universe is. We don't even know what it looks like. However, my research teams have analyzed the data. Draconian ships seem to be concentrated in one area. As suspected, the concentration is in sector 19. But we must also consider it could also be a decoy. Draconians love decoys.

"Secondly, the Draconians have taken over the following galaxies - Amada, Oberon, but that is not new and have started attacking planets in the Normaria. Xion has been attacked and I fear Segma will be next. The refugees who created new colonies are not ready to fight. The low population is one area of concern, and not all new planets are generous with food and mineral resources.

"Thirdly, the Lyrians in the White Galaxy, are also struggling. They have endured many years of battle. I believe it is now close to 25 years. My research teams have been trying to track the paths of the Draconians going to Lyria. It appears they use several paths and use each of them at random. My research teams have discovered a corridor going from inner Oberon close to where the old Pleiades and Sirius B used to be. Then it comes out

200 million light years from the centre of the White Galaxy's major black hole. When the Draconians discovered this corridor, yhey have ised it and found their way to Lyria. We currently believe, the Draconians don't know the exit of the corridor in The White Galaxy is almost dead centre of a triangle where Lyria, Earth and Genesis are located. We believe the Draconians are using the remnants of the old corridor first discovered by the Pleiadean, Siriusian and the Andromedian nations centuries ago. We are double checking that with ancient records. It will only be time before Genesis and Earth will be discovered."

Sigma who had looked over the death tally of the human race across the universe, closed his eyes. "We can't sustain these losses. We can't continue this battle. Earth must be defended at all costs. Do we send a delegation to Earth and retrieve the DNA files stored there?"

Zindel was quick to respond, "Many Earth people are not ready for anything like an intergalactic delegation. There has been minor progress by some government officials and a small amount of the general public, but not enough. I believe there is an important United Nations meeting which will occur on Earth in a matter of days."

Zindel looked around the room trying to gauge their reactions. This was one of the few times, he couldn't read their thoughts and gestures. He put it down to them being stunned. He coughed to gain their attention. "The good news and a slight hope. We all know Alcyn died on Earth after fighting the Lacertians. Previously, he was born into a royal family on Daraxon. This time, however, he was reborn on Genesis. His mother, Zantha, was initially sent to Earth to be a part of the guardian-protector team but decided to go to Genesis siting her diplomatic skills were needed there. She met Commander Patrum while in the middle of a battle in an attempt to save Amada. They met up again in Genesis. About three years after, Patrum and Zantha with their toddler son and with a few from the original crew went to Earth. Baby Alcyn was able to recognize his staff from Daraxon. Zantha had always said to her husband, they were raising Prince Alcyn but he didn't believe her until they arrived on Earth. I will have you note, many parents on Genesis also called their sons Alcyn. To stop confusion at school or other social settings, they were called, for example, Alcyn PZ, Alcyn AH and Alcyn LB. Over time their friends and teachers just used the parent's initials attached to their name. Now, Price Alcyn is called PZ. It has kind of stuck and he doesn't mind. To call him by his first name, he believes he is in trouble of some kind."

Azna smirked. "Has PZ retained the essence and the training from his last life?"

Zindel hesitated before answering. "Much is coming back and is now more powerful than before. His mind powers did a massive jump. He only needs the cranial neurotransmitter for distances between two or more galaxies. He is making social contact with a few Pleiadeans refugees based on Earth some twenty plus years ago. One of the new Pleiadean additions to Earth is Ashton. I am training him. His wife Kora shows potential but is being held back a little with the first Pleiadean naturally conceived and born child in 800 plus years. Also, she is in charge of looking after about 400 unborn Pleiadeans in cribs rescued from Beta Cancari. She is a bit busy. I think she will achieve level three over her lifetime, but her husband is bounding ahead in some areas but need strengthening in others. Then there is a young lady called Tanke. A Pleiadean rescued from Beta Centari, the main Pleiadean colony. Her two friends, Wilbut and Milay, and Tanke herself are being trained by Patron and Dalmon to be peacekeepers-com-liaison for whatever is required on Earth. Patron and Dalmon are dying from old age. I very much doubt they will last another five years. Tanke carries essence as well. PZ has telepathically seen Tanke and is totally smitten."

Thuma sighed. "Well, if those two do get together, I would hesitate about what power their offspring will have. Where is PZ now?"

"Somehow, he managed to get on a ship going to Earth. He has tossed his studies into neutrino physics. But then again, he did that subject before. He should be doing gamma technology. There is a shortage of those technicians."

Jose brought the group back to the purpose of the meeting. "I hear whispers that some Lacertians are sympathetic to the humans. Is that true?"

"Yes," said Zindel as he flashed a holographic image of Kyrina. "Kyrina is the granddaughter of President Kyros. Kyros and his elected members of parliament and their families were rounded up and dumped on a planet that we still have not located. Kyros was able to send a distress signal to a Pleiadean ship. That ship relayed the message to the other presidents and Alcyn who were in a war planning meeting. Kyrina survived the home invasion as she was being child minded by a neighbour who claimed the child was one of her litter. The neighbour brought up Kyrina as her own. The others in the litter never betrayed her.

"As she grew up, she became appalled by the treatment humans were subjected to but was also becoming equally angry as the controlling Draconians began to mistreat Lacertians. With each passing year, she noted penalties against Lacertians were becoming harsher and harsher. She formed a rebel group that helps both humans and Lacertians.

"Some Lacertians just want to help other Lacertians while others will help both parties. Her people have been feeding information to our spies, human and Lacertian spies, and trained 'rebels or 'terrorists'. Terrorists or rebels is a description the Draconians and the faithful Lacertians have given to anyone carrying out missions to free slaves and those destined for the dinner table. Just over a year ago, Beta Cancari was attacked. The elimination of the remaining Pleiadean people was almost complete. Kyriana's efforts saved the remaining Pleiadean survivors. Captain Keka evacuated the planet and gifted it to Kyrina. The human survivors on Xion and Segma drew up a trade and defence agreement with Kyrina. The agreement has been honoured by both parties. On Beta Cancari, Kyrina and her so-called rebels, fight the invading Draconians and at times Lacertians. They also protect the original inhabitants, the Mammalians, a race of mini humans."

Azna leaned forward. "Mammalians were only placed on Earth in two locations; one in what they call Africa and another on some island in what is called Indonesia. Just how did they get to Beta Cancari?"

Zindel shrugged. "In the past, Earth was visited by many different humans – Pleiadeans, Siriusians,

Centarians and Nubians to name a few. All went there for mining. The companies which formed guarded their area of Earth so viciously, they would wage war against each other. But that was thousands of years ago, well before the federation was formed. Earth was abandoned when the planet-like comet passed by and nearly collided with Earth. It is pure speculation, maybe some sympathizers smuggled these people on board. Then maybe they were set free on Beta Cancari when the sympathizers found the planet was suitable for them to live their lives in peace. Who knows? Rebels or sympathizers are rarely in footnotes in history. Very few history chronicles acknowledge them as being major shakers and movers. They become myths at best. Kyrina is our biggest asset. She wants the Draconians out of Lacertian lives. She wants Lacerta and its colonies back under Lacertian rule. She is unaware of the White Galaxy and its human populations. It is best she remains ignorant of that point."

Zindle gave a slight bow. "If there is nothing more to hold me here, I must go to Earth."

Jose, Azna and Sigma nodded back. "Good luck on Earth," said Thuma.

Zindel bowed deeper. "I need all my skills for that place. A great place but I can't figure out what we did wrong."

"Nothing," chorused Azna and Xetron.

"We guided the Pleiadeans in genetic manipulation. They did everything perfectly. In some fields of science, earth people are like our six-year-old children just starting their education on complex theories of science. In other areas, they are like a group of toddlers who have just discovered adult work equipment and are mishandling it in their self-assertion in the form of war. They will soon learn war leaves no winners; just rebuilding on both sides." said Jose.

CHAPTER 2

Earth.

New York. United Nations Head Quarters.

Four police helicopters circled a one-kilometre radius around the U.N. headquarters in New York. The streets for two blocks around were sealed to the public. Sniffer dogs with their handlers paraded in the closed off streets. Extra security cameras installed the week before were having final adjustments; the instructions came from hidden observers in the secluded area.

The first arrivals were the heads of state from nearly every country. Then followed a string of advisors and translators. As each vehicle pulled up to the entrance, the passengers hastened to the front door. Each was briefly checked as the cars quickly disappeared into the empty carpark underneath the building. The car park was cleared a day before of all vehicles and sealed as sniffer dogs searched the area. More and more heads of state arrived. The procedure was repeated. In just over an hour, all of the world's leaders were seated inside.

A bell rang. The doors were locked. Two guards were stationed inside at every door and two more outside.

A stage had been set up with a lectern on each side. Coming on to the front stage were a line of directors from Daraxon Technologies Incorporated. Intergalactic diplomats who had been living on Earth followed. All took their position on the seats on stage.

Jed Lawson was the first to introduce himself and gave a small background speech about his life and meeting the people from Daraxon and how Daraxon Technologies was formed.

"I was working on an extension of my home nearly twenty-six years ago. I heard a noise and went to investigate. I found myself being sucked up into a vortex which took me to lower space. I passed out due to the lack of oxygen.

I woke up in a hospital bed which I later learned was in a palace belonging to Prince Alcyn. When I landed on Daraxon, I was close to death. Prince Alcyn and his people nursed me back to health. When I recovered, I was permitted to move around the palace but always under escort. However, I saw it as my mission to escape. My escape attempts kept the guards occupied and amused Prince Alcyn when he read the reports. Alcyn admitted later, he admired my creative attempts. He also admitted these attempts endeared me to him," Jed looked up when he heard a few chuckles.

He continued, "I didn't know it at the time, Prince Alcyn and his team were trying to make a safe method for me to return to Earth other than using the royal spaceship. While this was going on, I was working with their linguists to device the first Daraxon-English translator." Jed pulled the translator out and quickly showed the crowd before putting it away. "Over the months of my stay on Daraxon, Prince Alcyn's team did succeed in making the increments where a transporter could return me to Earth. On that first journey, Prime Minister Pyram, his advisor, Ryder, General Tayee, and Alcyn's right-hand man, Hammond visited Earth. On that journey, they saw opportunities for trade. Unfortunately, that would never occur due to the impending war looming in the two galaxies of Amada and Oberon against the Lacertian occupied Julos. Instead, they acquired information, some equipment and techniques of war. Oberon and Amada had been at peace for over a thousand years and found their societies had lost the passion and skills of war. Earth provided what they were looking for. Help. The politicians of the time could and would not assist them, so Prince Alcyn and his crew left payment for equipment that they thought necessary to take to war". Jed displayed the film clips caught on security cameras at the time. "This included the 'buying' of three jets and kidnapping their pilots who were returned safely to Earth." Jed displayed the photos of the three pilots who were considered as heroes on Daraxon at the time of the first defence assault.

"While Prince Alcyn was here on his first diplomatic mission, he asked permission to send no more than 300 refugees to this planet. Like the initial refusal of equipment, Prince Alcyn ignored the negativity he received and just sent the refugees in the transporter. The last to arrive was Prince Alcyn who was escaping a bomb explosion at his palace. The explosion followed him to Earth. The transporter blew up. Prince Alcyn and the refugees became isolated from the rest of their society. Prince Alcyn's palace had been previously emptied of all personnel and he alone fought the enemy using techniques learned on Earth." Jed broke off as he looked up and gave a slight smirk. "These techniques included some old war-style computer games as well as documentaries about World War One and Two." Jed heard a few more chuckles. "His attempts were successful as he single-handily took out ten mother ships. Unfortunately, it didn't stop the war which has continued to rage. Now, I will introduce you to Patron, a person many of you know and know of his mediation works on Earth." Jed turned and gestured for Patron to stand up.

As Patron stood up, he was applauded, and a few gave him a standing ovation. Patron looked around the packed room and nodded his acknowledgment. He waited for the crowd to settle down.

"My dear Earth friends, I address you with a number of important messages. But first, I will give you a little history about myself. I am from the planet of Pleiades, a planet which I learned last year, no longer exists." There were gasps around the room. "I was for over twenty years, the only refugee from my planet to be on Earth and I was tasked to continue my diplomatic work to help bring peace to countries on this planet. I hope I have succeeded." Patron stopped talking when there was a standing ovation. He wiped a tear trying to escape his eyes. "As Jed has mentioned, we were cut off from the rest of our kind – isolated with no means of communication. We could have built a communication system to reach our kind, but the protection of Earth was far more important. Our enemies had devised a technique which identifies and tracks communication signals to their source. Earth would have been exposed to the horrors our people endured over the last twenty-plus years.

We couldn't expose Earth. Earth is our home and your home. Incredibly important to all of mankind in the universe. We remained in isolation but were accidentally discovered last year. Yes, it was an accidental discovery.

"The ship that arrived was from a Pleiadean colony which we have since learned, has been attacked.

The attackers are moving through the universe slowly overtaking any liveable planet and eliminating people. Many people are for their consumption. Some are farmed to keep the stocks going. Others are enslaved. My people have abandoned their colony on Beta Cancari. In fact, it was given to rebels among our attackers. These rebels do not know of Earth's existence. It will remain that way. Now, slight change away from the doom and gloom." Patron turned to look at Tanke.

"I am training this young lady, Tanke, and two of her companions, Wilbut and Milay." From their seats, the three stood up and gave a shallow bow. Milay and Wilbut sat down. Tanke walked to the lectern closest to her. She didn't speak immediately knowing Patron had one more thing to say. Patron gave her a warm smile. "Ladies and gentlemen, some of you know Tanke, but many do not. I am training Tanke to take over my duties. I am phasing out my workload and handing this to Tanke and her two friends.

I will be around the edges, but not for much longer. I am retiring. Tanke will be able to contact me for advice as required." Patron stopped talking. He could see the crowd before him were shocked. Some were giving the slow rhythmic protest clap. He held up his arms trying to quieten down the room. "Please. Please, I assure you, Tanke and her assistances will be very capable." He waited for another minute. "I need to hand over my duties to a new generation. My health is slowly declining. That can be expected from a person who is over 160 Earth years. I give you Tanke." Silence filled the room.

Tanke looked around suddenly feeling inadequate. "I was living on Beta Cancari with about 200,000 Pleiadeans. The evacuation from Pleiades was supposed to be one million. That never happened. We learned our planet along with Andromeda and Sirius B were destroyed. The government of the colony decided to send, what would be your equivalent, seals or special forces to our once home galaxy of Oberon where humans still existed. We were assisting any human rebels with attack missions, food, clothing, medicine and anything that was required. Unfortunately, the war continued much longer than anyone expected and is still raging. Our people were becoming war weary plus the planet we settled on wasn't kind in resources.

"President Findlee ordered a research spaceship to be built. It had orders to seek other vacant planets in this galaxy which we call the White or Spiral Galaxy. Also, the crew was given remnants of an ancient maps to find, what was considered, to be the mythical planet of Tiamat. Just how they found Earth from the scanty information was a miracle. The maps were only rediscovered when the President of Pleiades ordered staff to search the historical records for techniques in battle. Some techniques were found. That was when they discovered the ancient map. The information contained little more than that Tiamat was on the far side of the Milky Way on a spiral.

"There was some information that a space corridor was used to take our ancient astronauts from Oberon to the White galaxy in two weeks rather than a few months. We were sure that the corridor still existed to some degree. The explosions of Andromeda and Pleiades caused disturbances; other planets shifted, tilted or spun to a new orbit or any combination of that. The corridor may no longer exist. If it still exists, we don't know where the entrances or exits are. All we knew was the entrance was, maybe still is, smack in the middle of enemy-occupied Oberon. It was much too dangerous to explore that option, and it may lead our enemy to Earth. No one wants that.

"When the Pleiadean ship, The Explorer, which first visited Earth, was returning to Beta Cancari was under the command of Commander Jalon.

Commander Jalon was warned that the Beta Cancari was attacked. We learned the elected President Findlee used to command a spaceship and was familiar with war emergency situations. He fought the circling enemy ship. However, the enemy ship crashed into the centre of the city, the main part of the colony. President Findlee died in the battle from radiation poisoning, but he made sure our evacuation into the caves in the nearby mountain was complete. Unfortunately, radiation did seep into many caves destroying water, food supplies, medicine and killing many Pleiadeans. Some caves, like the one I was in, were unaffected but our food and water supplies were perilously low by the time the Explorer returned and saved us.

"The commander and captain of the returning ship, The Explorer, Keka received word of the planets in the Normaria Galaxy. Two colonies were established on two different planets, Xion and Segmar. Then luck would have it, we made contact not only with Xion and Segmar, the main refugee planets for Oberon. Much later we came in contact with another colony in this galaxy, on a planet called Genesis. This was the main colony for refugees from the galaxy of Amada. Genesis is in a direct line from Earth but on the other side of The Milky Way as you call this galaxy. We are expecting either a Pleiadean ship or a ship from Genesis to visit us in the next few days. The ship is expected to land at Daraxon Technologies. I ask, please assist us with supplies which will be bought. I will assist with such negotiations." She gave a nod to the crowd and turned to Dalmon, the only Sirsiusian who escaped to Earth.

Dalmon also received a warm welcome and a standing ovation from the crowd. He waited for the clapping to stop and gave a slight bow. "Many of you may not like what I have to say. Like Patron, my life is coming to an end. I will be helping Wilbut and Milay to take over my task." He glanced over to Patron. "My dear friend, it is about time we went fishing after the next ship leaves."

Patron nodded and said, "It's a go. Do you know how to fish?"

Dalmon replied, "No. It is about time we learned some earth pass times." Dalmon continued.

"What I am about to say, is from a second source. I hope I got all the facts right. Patron's nephew, Ashton who has some notoriety in Australia, has informed me to expect another emissary from… I am not sure if it is a place… or is it an organization. The man's name is Zindel. I was warned this man is on a recruiting drive to fight this war. He may headhunt your finest brains and train them up. He has a number of other skills which I was told but not privy to any specifics. He has recruited Ashton. And I think he may have or will recruit others on any human spaceship. Locking up your astronauts is not going to save them. This man will sniff them out. I was told he is eccentric but annoying right. He cares for humans of all colours, shapes and sizes. When he arrives, you will immediately recognize him." Dalmon was going to continue when an image formed on the screen.

"Hello, everyone. I'm Zindel." He gave a cheeky grin. "I will be joining you in a minute or two. Dalmon please continue." Dalmon was speechless for a few seconds. "That is one of Zindel's habits I was told. He pops up unexpectedly and any place and any time." Before he could say more, Zindel suddenly appeared on stage. Everyone gasped.

Zindel wore his typical black outfit. This time he added a cloak. He spun around to make his cloak spin at right angles. When he stopped, he stood at the other lectern. He gestured for Dalmon to continue. Dalmon was still searching for words. "Do you always make such an entrance?"

"No. I was just so excited about my new cloak and wanted to see if could do the work like the old one. ...Nice eh?"

Dalmon was starting to recompose himself. "Very nice indeed. I suggest you take over this meeting. Please introduce yourself and where you are from. I wasn't given such details."

"Sure. I'm Zindel as I said on your screen just minutes ago. I'm from.... the dawn of time, from a place, called.....Okay, I don't know what the place is called but I meet with some really powerful people who call themselves Lords of the Universe. They overwatch mankind on all planets in this universe. As Dalmon said, I am on recruiting drive to help me get rid of the enemy who is taking over human-occupied planets. They are greedy, not nice, clever, strong, very ugly, and very technologically advanced. They are your nightmares all rolled into one package. Do I need to describe more?" Zindel looked around the room to see a silent stunned audience.

"You may ask what the enemy looks like?" Zindel clicked his fingers to show a hologram of a Lacertain. These guys are on average about two metres tall. When Prince Alcyn was alive and before the war started, the elected president of the Lacertians and all of his ministers, their families, and friends were rounded up and dumped on an unpleasant planet in the galaxy of Julos. The new dictatorship was a puppet to the more advanced race of humanoid lizards, the Draconians. They convinced the Lacertians war was preferable over diplomacy. They convinced the new puppet leaders to force Lacertian parents to hand over all newborns and inject them with fast-growth chemicals.

"In this rapid growth period, their brains were wired to certain training programs. The babies grew up fast devoid of any understanding of emotions. They did not understand the concepts of socialization. The Draconians were making disposable soldiers out of the Lacertians. There was one side effect that was quickly noticed. The drug changed the digestive system of the Lacertians. They also became meat eaters. This did not bother the Draconians. However, the second side effect didn't show itself until five years later. All the newborns were sterile. This meant, over time, there would not be enough Lacertians to be used as pawns. This caused a change of policy. Now each Lacertian had half their litter taken to be converted into flesh-eating disposable soldiers and the other half were assigned to be breeders. This split the Lacertian society into two groups: the vegetarians and the meat-eaters. Over time the vegetarians were given limited education and limited job opportunities. They were gradually

"Over the years, the vegetarian groups began to sympathize with humans. Some were being relegated to slave labour. In the past, humans were reduced to slaves doing hard labour and menial tasks or assigned to breeding stock. They were upset with the way they were being treated. There are two groups of rebels. Those who only want to save their own kind and the other who want to save humans and their own kind. One such rebel is the granddaughter of the kidnapped President Kyros. Kyrina only escaped because she was being cared for by a neighbour who declared Kyrina was hers. Kyrina is an ally who was gifted the planet of Beta Cancari by Captain Keka. She earned his trust and respect. The planet is also under attack.

Kyrina's rebel group fought the Draconians who want to settle Beta Cancari. Kyrina's group. Also, she defended another human species who are like your pygmy population. They are called Mammalians."

Zindel showed a hologram of Kyrina before she was tortured, "This is Kyrina before she was attacked." He showed another of her sustained injuries. People in the room gasped at the transformation. Then Zindel showed a hologram of a Draconian. "Human enemy number one. This is a picture of one of their commanders. I had the satisfaction of blowing up his ship in this galaxy. That was two of your days ago." There were more gasps from the captive audience.

He continued. "This is a Draconian. It is about three metres tall. He is your nightmare. We are hiding Earth from Draconians. This may sound a bit like science fiction to many of you. I hope I can make it simple. This universe is for humans. The other universes are for other creatures. They are kept separate and as a rule and cannot cross over from one universe to another.

"But the Draconians have discovered a way in. We suspect there is a rip or tear. Initially, they were dumping their so-called deformed or handicapped on the planet of Lacerta in the galaxy of Julos. The handicapped, the Lacertains, were supposed to die out, but instead, they flourished into a very formidable civilization. Then the Draconians decided to capitalize on their advancement and use them as pawns to do their bidding. Over the years of the war, the Lacertains were being ill-treated and robbed of any high-standing jobs in their community. It was Draconia of old resurfacing."

Zindel showed a holographic picture of the universe. The giant hologram floated up for the people could see. He pointed to the marked-out sectors. "Earth is here in sector twenty. This is waste space, a galaxy still in formation. Nothing of interest there." He slid the pointer over. "This is Amada just beside the waste space. Here is Oberon beside that." Zindel pointed to Normaria where Xion and Segmar were. "That is in sector eighteen. Julos is in sector nineteen." He pointed to the close proximity of the Lacertian planets. "Somewhere here is the rip. Sector nineteen stretches from Lacerta in the galaxy of Julos, to the next three galaxies, galaxies yet unnamed. We leave the naming to the settlers or other intelligent life which may evolve in its own time.

"The Draconians have spread through Oberon and Amada because the two galaxies have had contact with Lacertiains. Lacerta became the stepping stone to attack and exploit the two galaxies of Amada and Oberon. Now they are slowly exploring other galaxies. They are already in this galaxy." Zindels heard gasps from the audience. He waited until that was exchanged with a number of questions.

Zindel waved his hands around. People were immediately silenced. Those who were standing suddenly felt a force pushing them back into their seat. When he saw the room calm again, he added, "There is a race of people called Lyrians from the constellation of Lyria. They have been fighting the Draconians; stopping them from further exploration of this galaxy. They are protecting Earth. They have visited Earth in the past and consider Earth like a baby sister or brother who needs protection." Zindel created a holographic image of a Lyrian. "Look at these people. They are wise and very, very spiritual. They are your friends and not to be feared. They may visit in the future. When? I don't know. It is up to them. In the past, they were sending observational missions but that has stopped thanks to the Draconians. They have been monitoring human progress on Earth and every so often, drop a hint or two to some citizens. Unfortunately, you people have a bad habit of keeping your mouths shut when important information is divulged. And those who do divulge such information are ridiculed or placed in a hospital.

Oops, they tried sending messages telepathically to individuals who are positioned to do something. That has worked better. Sorry. Some of you thought it was your idea or brain wave. It was a big chance it was a brain wave from a Lyrian. The same Lyrian who guided that person to achieve their goal." Zindel waved his hands around anticipating another outburst.

"Now, I must leave this meeting. Please be mindful, these wonderful people on stage may not be able to answer questions you may have. I will inform you if any Lyrian arrives." With a blink of an eye, Zindel was gone. Silence filled the room as people turned around to see if Zindel relocated himself somewhere else in the room. The silence was broken by a chorus of phones ringing.

Jed nudged Patron and Dalmon. "A spaceship has been detected and is coming this way. We better get back to Daraxon Technologies as soon as possible."

Tanke leaned over. "You three go. Wilbut, Milay and I will do our best to handle questions. I suspect the room will empty quickly if everyone got a similar message. They will all be star gazing tonight."

CHAPTER 3

Earth.

Daraxon Technologies Incorporated. Australia.

The Explorer hovered over the Daraxon Technology complex for two minutes waiting for permission to land. Slowly the ship settled making a sound not louder than a soft whoosh. The ramp doors opened silently. Slowly people emerged. Those who had landed on Earth before walked with a steady gait and smiled at the familiar people they met before. Those who were new walked tentatively down the ramp while looking around.

Tayee and all his family who were part of the initial refugees stepped out first to give a warm greeting to the new arrivals. The others on Earth slowly came forward to embrace the arrivals. One by one, introductions were for the newcomers. When the entire crew emptied out of the ship, the ramp went up. The ship was remotely locked.

The crowd was directed to the mess hall which was now fifty percent larger than a year ago. The expansion included a major refurbishment. It now was capable of handling such events as this. Captain Keka introduced Captain Darius from Xion. The crew from Segmar, Xion, and a handful from Genesis. All were guided to the mess hall. For the benefit for the new people, there was a short orientation.

Ashton, his wife Kora, and their son, Ashra, sat to the rear just in case Ashra who was now in an advanced state of teething, decided to let the whole hall know of his discomfort. The door was just a few metres away. Ashton looked around the room searching for Alcyn PZ. His brain picked up a signal. Alcyn PZ responded to the invasion and went towards Ashton and Kora. "Nice meeting you in person," said Ashton.

Alcyn PZ, stretched his hand to shake Ashton's and Kora's. "Please call me PZ," said Aston. "There are two other Alcyns here. There was a spate of boys being named after Prince Alcyn. I just happen to be one."

Ashton smirked. "I will go along with that."

Alcyn PZ gave a broad grin. "How many people here know?"

"Your old friends such as Hammond and his wife, Jed and his family, Tayee and his adult children but Tayee's grandchildren only know of Prince Alcyn through stories they were told by Patron and Dalmon and others from Amada."

"Vestele and Beechum. Where are they?"

"I was informed they passed away," said Kora. "Are you one of Zindel's students?"

"Yes. I didn't complete my mission last time round so I'm back and with a bit more mind reading power."

Ashton was curious. "What was your mission that you failed to complete?"

Alcyn hesitated. "I'm not exactly sure. I was in the Hall of Records reviewing my life when I was called up. I never got to that bit. Being in the Hall of Records is an experience and a half. I think I got to my twentieth year of life when I felt myself being sucked out and into Zantha. Zantha is now my mother. Before she was a diplomat for all of Amada. I was informed I really got to like her in the war. She was supposed to have saved my life and the ship's crew by flying through enemy lines to deliver supplies. Ah! That is all history now. What changes have occurred on this planet?"

Kora thought for a moment. "Patron and Dalmon are going to retire. Well, let's say they will be on standby to assist their replacements."

"Who are they?" asked Alcyn PZ.

"Tanke, Milay and Wilbut," said Ashton.

"Tanke? The beautiful Pleiadean refugee from Beta Cancari?"

"That's her," said Ashton.

"I've got to meet this babe. Where is she?"

Ashton sighed. "On the other side of the planet. I think New York or London. Somewhere about there."

"How do I get to her?"

"Slow down," said Kora. "If you rush things, you will scare her away. Take a deep breath."

"Are you busy tomorrow?" asked Alcyn PZ.

"No," said Ashton.

"Then we go tomorrow. When is the next spaceship leaving?"

"No planetary spaceships yet. It is not that advanced here."

Alcyn grimaced. "What has Hammond been doing all that time? Not advancing space travel!"

The speaker whistled through the air. Instantly it grabbed everyone's attention. Tayee introduced himself and his family. Then he went on with the main part of the message. "Tomorrow, my family will be conducting tours of this complex. Anyone who wants to see the place should meet here at the front door at ten in the morning. The tour will last about two hours but that is variable as it will depend on what people want to see. Please enjoy your first Earth meal and have a pleasant stay."

Alcyn PZ said softly, "I better do the tour first and see what this place has been up to over the years.

Then we go looking for Tanke."

Kora smiled. "She is very matter of a fact. No funny business with her. A tip if you want her attention, think with your brain."

Alcyn PZ gulped. "I will take that on board and try to keep it in mind, so I don't make a fool of myself." *Keep it professional and business like*, he thought to himself.

Exactly, replied Ashton in thought transmission. *No prizes for idiots.*

Butt out of my thoughts, said Alcyn PZ.

Then don't think so loud, replied Ashton as a grin started to turn into a laugh.

Kora looked at both men and rolled her eyes. *Kids.*

"We heard that," echoed Aston and Alcyn PZ.

The next day just about all of the crew wanted a tour of the facility. They were broken up into five groups. Alycn PZ was placed in a group with Hammond and Tayee. The group of twenty was led to the research and development section. Hammond pointed to the semi-made structure in one room. "The rebuilding of the transporter using neutrino travel has been slow. The slowdown occurred with the microchips. The plans were accidentally left behind and were blown up with the Daraxon palace. I wasn't in the development of the microchips, but I was doing everything else in the construction. We have made faster progress since one of the original seats was uncovered a couple of years ago. The seat was in bad shape, but it did hold some microchip solutions. The chairs are complete. We have created thirty such chairs. We are still developing the control panel. Some of it works perfectly, that is, the self-destruct button if it came under attack." The small group chuckled. Alcyn PZ asked, "May I take a closer look?"

Hammond shot a glance over to Tayee who nodded. "Yes."

Alcyn PZ walked closer to the structure and sat on one of the four inserted chairs. "Nice, very nice. He looked at the test control panel and noticed the chip inserted was ready for testing. "May I?" he asked Hammond.

Hammond went into protective mode. "May you do what?"

"The chip is upside down. Can I put it the right way?"

Hammond walked over to Alcyn PZ to see the chip Alcyn PZ was referring to, "Go ahead. Flip it."

There was a distinct click followed by a short buzz. "Perfect," said Alcyn PZ.

Hammond was surprised. "I didn't know you knew about microchips on the transporter."

Alcyn PZ said matter-of-factly, "In the past, and even this time round, I do microchips. How about I help out and get this thing running the way it should be. Would two days-time be, okay?"

Hammond and Tayee gave a surprised look. Tayee spoke, "If you can get the chips sorted out, that would be great. Then we can add all the co-ordinates for Genesis. Travel between the two places will be so much faster, just an hour or so rather than two to three weeks. It's a date."

The crowd moved on to other parts of the facility.

They were at the hangar when another past memory came flooding back to Alcyn PZ. "The horses are gone. Is that old shed still in use?"

"It largely houses the remains of the original transporter. Mind you there is not much left. The explosion did a thorough job. The staff now uses a part of the shed as a rest area." Hammond pointed to the new hangar. "This hangar will interest many of you. Come." The crowd followed Tayee and Hammond.

Inside was a series of jets going from the original two-seater to a four-seater and then the largest, an eight-seater. There was another the same size as the four-seater but only held two seats. "This is the cargo jet or spacecraft. It is capable of ferrying supplies from Earth to the moon. There are six of these scattered around the world. Each major agency has one. All maintenance is done here. There are a few eight-seaters stationed on the moon. They are emergency crafts. Moonquakes do happen so crafts are needed there for quick evacuations. One camp was hastily evacuated. All lives were saved. The scientists were able to return and repair the damage. Supplies are sent up in the cargo jet. There are no plans to develop larger vessels yet. Mars is next but there are a few issues to overcome. It won't be that far away before settlement can begin."

"How long do you think," asked Captain Darius through a translator he was wearing like the others.

"I give it a year," said Hammond. "However, I will be leaving that to my son, Titus, and Jed's son, Mark. My generation is phasing ourselves out for retirement. We will be keeping an eye on things. It is time we all stepped down."

Alcyn PZ met up with Ashton the same afternoon. Ashton spoke first. "Hi. I got in touch with Tanke. She is in Paris. She can see us tonight at her apartment. About eight. She said if she is late, keep waiting. There is always some delay in Paris."

"Tonight? Do we take one of the crafts in the shed?"

"We have permission for the four-seater. Titus will be our pilot. No Titus means, no ride. Here he comes now," said Ashton.

Alcyn PZ looked at Titus. His memory of Titus came back. The last time Alcyn PZ saw him, he was a child. Now he was an adult in his thirties. Alcyn shook his head trying to make a quick mental adjustment. Titus gave his passengers an instruction to wait until the craft was out of the hangar.

"Climb in. Headphones on. Seat belts on," said Titus. "We should be in Paris in about forty minutes.

It will be close to seven in the morning, smack in peak hour traffic. We will do a bit of sight seeing before we meet up with Tanke."

The jet landed on the outskirts of Paris at the special landing pad on air force grounds. They were met by a small contingent of soldiers who escorted them to the main building. In the building, Ashton and Titus handed over their documentation and one which was hurriedly drawn up for Alcyn PZ. When the formality was completed, they were ushered to a waiting vehicle. The black car with blackened windows drove them to a station where they caught the train to the city heart. The first thing they did was to buy a coat as the early autumn winds were making their presence felt. Titus said, "I purposefully left my old jacket at home. It was starting to look a bit shabby." He pointed to a department store. "In here."

Alcyn PZ's eyes kept wandering. He vaguely recalled going to a small shop when he arrived on Earth in his old body so many years ago. *This place is huge, and huge by Genesis's standards.*

Now rugged up, Titus let them wander down the streets. Ashton pointed to a casino. "I need to get some cash out." He slipped on his wrap-around glasses and walked in. He passed two machines before he spotted a person inserting a coin into a slot. Ashton watched the coin fall. The man pressed a few buttons. Ashton said, "Green," in Pleiadean. The machine's internals spun around. The man grinned at the sound and display of a jackpot.

Good, thought Ashton, *the glasses still work*. He walked over to a higher paying machine and slipped in a coin. "Green." The bell rang loudly. Two casino assistances appeared. They guided Ashton to the teller where Ashton converted some of his winning to cash, but the bulk went into his card. He walked out to meet the others. "Okay, I'm loaded up now. One day I just might get kicked out of these places. Cheaters are not welcomed. But they cheat the customers, so a bit of their own medicine won't hurt."

Titus asked, "Just how much did you put in?"

"Five euros and came out with 20,000. That should be enough for us to live on for a while. Us being, Kora and Ashra."

"Does Kora know this?"

"Yes. It is always in and out. The longest and biggest binge was with a group. We had to raise money to buy supplies for the Explorer a couple of years ago. A team of us raided the casinos in different countries. The winnings paid for the goods the Explorer needed. Casinos are our private ATMs."

"Don't tell me more," said Titus.

"It was for a good cause getting supplies. Now I am a good cause. Zindel keeps me training so much, I don't have time for a proper job. Kora does some training too. His training generally interferes with jobs. I do a bit of security work for Daraxon whenever I can. They know Zindel is training me up. Sometimes I use the new skills for Daraxon Tecnologies."

"Like what?" asked Titus.

"Finding lost stuff in space. Finding lost property. Finding lost staff and collecting them."

Alcyn PZ asked, "Lost staff?"

"Sometimes new people get lost in the place. Outside the facility, I have been called in by police to find lost or kidnapped children. It is good public relations for Daraxon Technologies. Since I have been around, the rate of kidnapping, which is largely caused by disputing parents, has decreased by twenty percent."

"What happened to the other eighty per cent?" asked Alcyn PZ.

"Some kids turn up by themselves or are returned by a relative. Some find themselves overseas where I am not permitted to work. I only state where the child is being kept. I can only go in if police or parents request it and diplomatic procedures are completed."

After spending the day sight-seeing, it was nearing six in the evening when the group sat down for a light dinner. Titus ordered the meals which were washed down with wine. He looked at his watch, Tanke's apartment is twenty minutes away. By the time we get there, it should be close to eight."

A cab dropped them off at a coffee shop that fronted the ground level of the apartment block where Tanke lived. They went to the narrow entrance and pressed the intercom system. Titus spoke his name. There was a click. The door opened. Titus guided them to the lifts. "She's on the sixth floor." The lift doors opened. The group stepped in. Seconds later the doors opened to a wide passageway. Titus knocked on the door. When Tanke opened the door, she immediately recognized Titus and Ashton. She was formally introduced to Alcyn PZ.

Alcyn PZ smiled as soon as he saw Tanke. She looked at him from head to toe, assessing every aspect.

Where I have seen you before, she thought.

He stared back and replied in thought, *I saw you a few weeks ago when I was still on Genesis.*

Ah! That's right. The guy who was having mind control issues, thought Tanke.

I was. I have control now, replied Alcyn. *Like now.*

Tanke burst out laughing, *Not exactly. Mind control has improved significantly. Impressive. The rest, well, let's say is all over the place.*

Ashton coughed. "Okay, you two, talk. Titus is being left out and I am slightly embarrassed by what I am hearing."

Titus asked Ashton, "What are they saying to each other?"

Ashton slowly shook his head. "Assessing each other's mind control." He looked at Alycn PZ and Tanke, as he overheard more thoughts, "Enough you two. Save the growing barbs for the Lacertians and Draconians."

Both snapped out of their conversation. "Sorry," both said simultaneously.

Through the rest of the evening, Ashton felt like a piece of conduit with wire transmitting electrical pulses back and forth. He was exhausted by Alcyn's and Tanke's conversations. Titus knew they were communicating telepathically. *They couldn't help themselves*, he thought. He watched their faces and body gestures. He took out his mobile phone to record what was going on. Alcyn PZ asked, "What are you doing?"

"Recording the conversation. It's amusing to watch."

Tanke looked at Titus. "Amusing? They aren't vocalizing anything."

"True," Titus replied, "But the facial expressions and gestures say a lot is going on."

Ashton stood up. "Titus we both need to get out of here. How about a coffee downstairs and let these two battle their brains out before they reach some kind of truce?"

At the coffee shop in the same building, Titus showed the recording to Ashton. Both laughed so loud at the faces and gestures, they started to draw a crowd. A young lady approached and asked, "I like watching humorous You Tube clips. What is that called?"

Titus looked at the young lady who would not have been older than twenty, "I just recorded it. It is not on You Tube and never will be."

"Why not?"

"It is none of your business," replied Ashton. Titus put the phone away. The lady strutted away telling the others in French it wasn't going to be shared on any media platform.

Titus asked, "Is the battle finished?"

Ashton went quiet. "Okay. It has, but we still can't go up to pull Alcyn out and go home."

"Jesus! How long do you think?"

"We better find a motel," replied Ashton.

"That says it all," smirked Titus.

The next morning at the air force base, the trio went through exiting procedures. Alcyn PZ stopped and grinned like a cat in a fish shop. He picked up on Tanke's thoughts. The processing officer said, "You obviously had a good night with your girlfriend. That look says it all."

Alcyn PZ felt himself come to Earth in a thud and looked a bit embarrassed. "Yeah. A good night."

Titus nudged Alcyn PZ. "Okay lover boy, we have a jet to fly home. You can dream away on the flight. And for Ashton's sake, keep your brain in check. He doesn't want to hear what happened."

Alcyn PZ clicked his heels and gave a salute. "Aye, Aye captain."

The Daraxon Technologies jet stopped on the landing pad to allow Ashton and Alcyn PZ to alight. Titus taxied the craft to its storage position. Service technicians were ready to prepare it for any new sudden flights. "How was France," asked a technician as Titus climbed out of the cockpit.

"Very good, if not entertaining this time." Titus gave a nod towards Alcyn PZ and Ashton who were standing at the door waiting for him. Titus led them to the mess hall where lunch was nearly at an end. "We get the scraps," he said.

"We barely made it in time. Alcyn do you want to eat here or on your ship?"

"Here. I am tired of ship food."

Hammond approached the late comers. "When you have finished, I want all of you to come to my office. We had word that Zindel was coming again. He only wants to talk to a select group."

The room was crowded. About fifty people were seated. Ashton asked Kora, "Where's Ashra?"

Jenny and her new husband, Mitchel are looking after him. How was France besides the extra funds going into our account?"

"Funny. I will tell you later," he whispered when he heard the doors open.

Hammond introduced Zindel. Zindel looked at the crowd before him and appeared to study each person as his eyes flicked from one to another. "I will get down to business immediately.

I was at the U.N. two days ago. A mixed reaction of near panic to disbelief. The rest of the planet with their individual governments can sort out what they believe, can and can't do. But here, I will give you an in-depth explanation and some strategies. Tomorrow, we talk about execution."

CHAPTER 4

Earth.

Daraxon Technologies.

Zindel showed the group a hologram of the Milky Way. Using a red light beam, he pointed making a line coming from an outside location to a position that was below the central black hole. He drew a triangle joining Lyria, Genesis, and Earth.

"The Draconians come through this space corridor and attack Lyria. The Lyrian people know of Earth and recently of Genesis. The Lyrians have been visiting Earth to check on its progress. They have never landed or taken Earth people for study for 10,000 Earth years. They did have a colony here but abandoned it at the time of the great biblical flood. Since then, they have been quietly watching and saving Earth from invasions including smashing comets and meteors on a path that could have damaged or destroyed Earth. Lyrians are your allies. Don't forget that. They are becoming exhausted – physically, mentally, and in recourses. They need help just as much as you will need help if the Draconians come this way or to Genesis."

Zindel showed the galaxies going from the Milk Way through the waste space, through Amada and stopping at the far edges of Oberon. He pointed to the red line leaving the Milky Way and stopping where Pleiades and Sirius B, once were. "In the combined history of Andromeda, Sirius B ,and Pleiades, your ancestors used this corridor to go from Oberon to Earth in a matter of weeks, not months. I am aware, the exit orentry point in Oberon has changed with the demise of several planets. That did not stop the Draconians from finding a new entry point. I estimate it about here." Zindel shifted the light beam between the central black hole and a supernova not far from the planet of Medac.

Alcyn PZ smirked at an event of his past life. *I set a Lacertian ship in that direction with a killer gorilla on board. The gorilla was lost and commanded the ship into the supernova.* Zindel, Ashton, and Kora heard the thought. Only Zindel replied, "Yes you did. Where did you get that beast?"

"Affen-Welt. It's near Genesis." Zindel nodded.

Zindel continued. "The galaxies which you have seen are in sector twenty." He showed the Lacertian planet of Lacerta and its colonies, Turbia, Sufus, Marnef, and Indulos. "This is a part of sector nineteen."

"We know the following. The Draconians dumped what we call Lacertians on Lacerta because they were considered deformed members of their species. Instead of dying out as expected, they thrived and built their own society. They expanded onto new colonies. The attempted purification of the species by the Draconians was a failure. The Draconians decided to use Lacertians as pawns twenty-five years ago. The initial perceived failure was now converted into an asset. Some of you know the Dranconians convinced the Lacertian military who took over the government, to use a drug that made the Lacertians grow fast. The drug was discovered to have side effects. The first was converting Lacertians to become meat-eaters. The second was not discovered until much later. The Lacertians forced to have the drug were sterile. The Draconians controlled the Lacertian's government by de facto. They made it a policy for half of each litter of newborns to be kept as breeders and those who had the drugs were wired up to programs. Those given the drug were programmed to such a degree that they were mindless biological robots, and that suited the Draconians.

"However, over the years, some of the non-altered Lacertians realized their so-called victorious invasions were nothing more than mass exploitation of their kind. Females were subjected to have more litters than they could physically cope with. Both males and females who held high positions in all aspects of society were replaced by Draconians. All Lacertians were slowly converted to slaves or doing low-paid tasks. At the start, humans were both enslaved and farmed. Now they were only being farmed and lived in more diabolical conditions than the current enslaved Lacertian. This led to small groups of Lacertians revolting against their masters and some also assisting rebel humans. We are in contact with one such Lacertian rebel leader. We have been advised there are two groups of Lacertian rebels. One group just helps Lacertians and the other will help both Lacertians and humans. The leader who we are in contact with is called Kyrina, a granddaughter of the disposed elected Lacertian nation. All in this room already know of her. Just a reminder, Kyros was democratically elected and all the elected politicians, their families, and their closest friends were rounded up and dumped on a planet. We never found that planet." Zindel saw Alcyn PZ and a few elders in the audience nod their heads.

Tayee asked, "Just how trustworthy is Kyrina?"

Zindel showed two pictures of Kyrina. "This is what she looked like before severe interrogation. She never broke down to disseminate any information. And here is what she looks like now. Disfigured and semi-crippled. She now lives on Beta Cancari which was gifted to her by Captain Keka. The planet has Draconians trying to occupy it. She is also protecting a race of humans called Mammalians.

They need all her help as they only know how to farm. That just about completes the most recent developments over the last twenty-five years."

Zindel looked around the room looking for any questions. He was grateful when no one asked for further information or clarity. Maybe it was a swag of information they were still digesting. He pushed on.

"How has the transporter going?" asked Zindel.

Hammond replied, "We may finish it with Alcyn's help."

"And the jets?"

Hammond replied again. "They are not designed for war, only to transport people and cargo. It will cost a lot of money to convert or redevelop them into fighters. We don't have that much in resources…or time."

"I can speed that up." Zindel pushed a button on an armband. A shadow appeared before his craft hovered just outside the window. "Copy my ship. The black box thing on top can only be built by my research and development team. They have already constructed five hundred of these."

"What exactly does it do?" asked Tayee.

"As Earth people call it, a zooped-up cannon. Instead of shooting out missiles carrying whatever destructive material, it shoots out a mix of waves that resemble material spat out by black holes. It incinerates everything in its path." Zindel pushed the button again. The craft suddenly shot up vertically and out of view.

Hammond looked worried. "What materials do we need to manufacture this craft?"

"I will give you all the required material and specifications."

Mark stood up. "One problem, we don't have pilots for this craft. Who will train us and how many do we need?"

Zindel replied. "It takes half a day to learn and a lifetime of practise. But we don't have a lifetime. Learning the controls is simple. The hard part is thinking about what is ahead before you get there is the skill. That will sort out who can fly and who can't."

"How do you test for such pilots?" asked Mark who was not liking the idea of going to war in space.

"I can sort them out in a matter of minutes," replied Zindel with a smug look on his face.

Kora asked, "Will the Lyrians have these crafts?"

"They are manufacturing them now. But I supply the cannons. Some technology should not be manufactured by those who don't have the capabilities or facilities."

Hammond asked, "Buying the materials will be costly. It will be well beyond our budget."

Zindel was thoughtful for a moment. "Yes. I can fix that up. Not an issue."

Hammond looked at the time. "Okay everyone, be here tomorrow at ten."

There was a sigh of relief. Soft chatter was heard from the small groups as they filed out of the room.

Alcyn PZ was silent as he focused his attention on Tanke. Tanke stopped eating her breakfast.

What's up? she asked.

When can we meet again?

How about in three days? I can be over that way. Zindel is training me up, she replied.

Zindel training you?

I didn't know. What level are you up to? He asked.

I'm halfway to level one What are you up to?

Level three and a half.

Wow!

Do you need help with practice? he asked seeing this was a possible way to extend his time with her.

At times I could do with some help. Self-defence is what I suck at, she replied as she placed another mouthful of cereal into her mouth

Okay. I will see you in three days. By the way, I think you are cute and cuter without those pyjamas.

Tanke put the spoon down and stop chewing and blushed. *I did say your brain was all over the place. It has slipped out of the skull and is occupying your dick.*

That's low, he retorted. *I feel crushed.*

Pull my other leg, as they say on this planet. Then she jumped back hitting her legs under the table. The remains of her cereal were scattered across the table.

How did you do that? She asked.

Alcyn grinned, *something to look forward to when you get to level three*. Alcyn planted a kiss on her forehead and disappeared.

She rubbed the spot gently, *that felt so real.* She shook her head.

Alcyn PZ drew his attention to his surroundings. Kora was holding Ashra when he snapped out of the trance. She warned, "If you get too friendly on this planet, you get one of these." She placed Ashra in Alcyn PZ's arms. Alcyn looked shocked as he intuitively held the toddler.

"He doesn't bite," Kora added.

Alcyn handed Ashra back as fast as he could. "I will keep that in mind."

Hammond approach Alcyn. "Don't go anywhere. I need your help with the chips for the transporter.

As soon as we get the chips sorted, the faster we can get the final touches finished."

Alcyn followed Hammond to the lab where he had altered the chip's positioning.

Hammond pulled out the chips he and his team had constructed, catalogued, and since coated with crystals. Alcyn PZ examined each one carefully under a powerful microscope. A couple held his attention. These he checked against the current construction. He slipped one into a spot well away from the location where Hammond previously tried and failed. "Fire it up," he asked Hammond. It worked. The machine was switched off again.

Then he took another chip from the catalogue and placed it where it was designed to fit.

"Another fire up, please," instructed Alcyn PZ. Nothing happened. Alcyn PZ took the chip out and re-examined it. While his eyes were focused down the barrel of the microscope he said, "I see the problem. The design is right, but the power is insufficient. It needs to be three times more power."

He handed it back to Hammond.

Alcyn PZ examined the rest of the chips before closing the volumes of catalogued designs. "For a person who has never studied this technology, you did an excellent job. I have identified a number of chips that need boosting in power and some others need a bit of tweaking. For now, just focus on the main chips, the main ones to make the transporter work. Boosting the power is not as simple as it looks. I will give you a hand."

Alcyn PZ worked through the rest of the day on the chips. When he knew it was right, he gave it a test. He smiled when the part activated as it should have. He turned to Hammond and the rest of the research team. "Job done for the day. I'll see you all again tomorrow morning." As he walked out of the door, he said to Hammond, "The viewer is really needed."

On board the spaceship, the two captains were discussing plans. "The plans Zindel gave us for the new fighters look deceptively simple. It appears the technology is in the exterior materials and just a handful of control panels."

Darius drummed his fingers. "We don't have enough people to fly these crafts." He flipped through the specifications until he reached the final page. He looked at the heading: Simulator.

"We build the simulator first and then sort out which of our defence pilots can fly these crafts. What did he mean by saying he will sort out those who would be the most capable?"

Keka blew a breath. "When we were going to Segmar, he placed his hands on people's heads and told them which future job they will excel in. Somehow, he taps into some deep-seated talent or psyche source and says where people are most suited. He is annoyingly right."

"Will you ever see the day when you will reclaim Beta Cancari?" asked Darius.

"No. A gift is a gift. But it is also tainted with Draconians," replied Keka. Both men again poured over the plans of the simulator.

CHAPTER 5

Beta Cancari. Same Time Period.

Head Quarters of the rebel Lacertians and home of the Mammalians.

The leader of the Mammalians, Brondie, had assembled his and the remainder of other tribes.

All tribes had taken a battering; many had disappeared, many injured when frequent overhead battles between the Lacertian rebels and the Draconians occurred. Brondie saw his people and the remainders of the surrounding tribes as collateral damage. He was very concerned.

The Mammalians had observed the smaller lizard creatures would not harm them and would protect them from the larger lizards. To them, the war and rage that occurred in the sky were non-sensical. Explosions saw debris fly through the air to destroy their homes and injure or kill their people.

Once they lived in huts above ground. Now, they live in caves or dug out caverns to hide from the invaders. It was in one of the natural caves this meeting was taking place.

Brondie looked around counting the survivors. The numbers had dropped by ten over the last month. Sadness filled his heart. Every loss was a disaster to the well-being and survival of all Mammalians. Smaller numbers meant more work had to be taken up by the now overworked survivors. Young children who once wandered free and played without any fear were given simple tasks. The children rarely complained but Brondie was saddened by the necessary childhood deprivation. It was necessary to alleviate some of the workloads by the dwindling adult numbers.

"The fighting in the sky by the creatures is diminishing our numbers. Our farming land is littered with debris. As we have all seen, the metal and other bits of items we have never seen and have no idea what they are or how to use such items, are destroying the soil. They block us from attending the fields. They destroy plants on impact. Crops are failing. If this continues, we will starve. Our water supply is also becoming undrinkable. The water is slowly becoming bitter or sour. We cannot continue living here."

One of the farmers, Popish, now turned warrior asked, "Where do we go? Our few remaining neighbours who have not joined us and act as our spies, tell us the larger and more aggressive creatures have taken over their lands and eat whoever they capture. They are many and powerful. How do we leave here without many of us or all of us dying?"

Brondie hesitated. "This will be unpopular. Remember it is only a suggestion. We ask the smaller creatures to guide us to another place to freedom." Immediately there was an uproar.

Popish signalled for the others to calm down. "In theory, it may work. We cannot fully trust these creatures. They could lead us into a trap, and we become their meal or something else they desire."

Brondie nodded. "That has crossed my mind. I have two other suggestions. First, we stay and clear the land of the pieces of metal and other objects which fell out of the sky. Then we begin farming again. The rubbish collected will be stacked to make a wall around our crops. It also becomes a hiding place for attacks where hand-built caves and holes are not close by or ready." Murmurs filled the cave. Brondie allowed the discussion to continue. After twenty minutes he brought the meeting to order.

"My final suggestion is we borrow more and link the caves. It will be time consuming and very dirty work. But we still need people to attend the fields or what is left of them. That is equally dangerous.

What do you say to that?"

A teenage girl, Jama, stood up to address the crowd. "I cannot speak for others. I speak for myself.

I think we can clear the land but not in a circle. It will look like a target like we do with spear practice. The creatures will know we are contained within the walls. We will be food. We have holes in the ground we go into when a flying machine comes our way. We jump into the holes to hide. Some holes have covers. Other holes need replacing. We build the walls going east west and have our hiding holes hidden inside and under the rubbish like a cave made of these strange metals. Then we line up the new hiding holes on one side to another. Each hole or tunnel provides shelter from the skies. When a flying machine passes then each person can run from one metal tunnel to the next. These tunnels run go north and south heading to this cave. We can go from the tunnel in the metal rubbish to the next to leave the farm.

A person will be exposed to the sky in the run from tunnel to tunnel. Can I draw on the wall to show what my idea looks like?"

Brondie stepped aside to let her access the blank earthen wall. She dipped her fingers into the yellow moist pigment which was normally used for ceremonial decorations. She said as she drew the first lines. "This needs more thought and refinement." Jama proceeded to draw horizontal lines. "This is how we stack the rubbish. We plant our food between these lines. We can leave gaps every so often so we can go with our farming tools from one crop area to the next."

Then she dipped her fingers into the red pigment and drew spots on the appropriate existing holes designed for people to hide in when an attack was imminent. "These are the underground holes that are already there." She dipped her fingers again but into the blue pigment. "We are here." She continued with the blue ink pigment lines running right angles to the intended rubble walls. Still using the blue ink she said, "We join the existing underground tunnels we made to come up to under the tunnel made in the rubbish. We link the holes with small tunnels going through the rubbish. Where we have no underground holes, people can run from one tunnel hole to the next. They will be exposed to the sky for a short time, but no one runs until the flying machines pass over." When she was finished, she turned to the tribe. "What do you think?" Silence filled the cave. Some people approached her diagram to consider it in detail. Brondie stood back to listen to their comments.

After a short discussion, the tribe had organized themselves. Ten people with some young children would tunnel through the walls of the existing cave. Some would attend to the farm as best they could. The six men kept watch and listened to the sounds of crafts approaching. The remainder gathered the scattered pieces of metal and dumped them into organized lines. For one week the work progressed without interruption.

The alarm sounded when Popish saw a glint of silver flash in the sky. The people on the land disappeared into the nearest holes or caves. The craft swooped low and circled. It moved on but the all-clear signal didn't sound. Popish wanted to make sure the craft didn't return. The craft did come back and hovered as if studying the land clearing below. It zoomed away. Popish waited longer.

Two crafts came. One hovered while the other landed on a section of the cleared area. The Draconian pilot climbed out of the cockpit and looked around. He examined the ground for footprints hoping they would lead him to a hiding place. He walked a short distance looking like he was following a trail. Then he stopped and turned back. He climbed into the craft again and looked around once more before joining the other hovering craft. Both flew away. Popish still didn't sound the all-clear. Something bothered him.

In the distance, he saw more flashes of light. More crafts were coming his way. These were the crafts belonging to the smaller-sized creatures. They flew low over the farm and then disappeared.

Then to his horror, the original crafts came back. This time they were at a short distance from the farm where a new air battle raged. Taking advantage of their distraction from the farm, Popish gave a signal for people to evacuate their holes or caves and head for the main cave.

While in the main cave, the ground shook. It was a clear sign to the Mammalians another craft had crashed; which one was immaterial. There was always a mess; a body or two and debris.

Brondie ventured to the opening of the main cave. He hid behind a bush to see what had landed. The craft belonging to the large creature had landed heavily on their farm. There were cracks and thick smoke emanating from all sides of the craft. One injured creature had crawled out and began firing his lazer gun at random. To Brondie, the creature couldn't see what he was shooting at. The creature had blood pouring out of his head and going into his eyes, mouth, and into one ear. Brondie stayed behind the bush to observe what the creature would do next.

Another craft landed. This one belonged to the smaller creatures. The creatures in the smaller craft opened a door and shot the larger one with beams of light. The body lit up like a candle before lying burnt and exposed in the field. The smaller creatures from the second craft climbed out of his craft and stole some items from the downed craft before flying away. The broken craft which had landed in the nearly cleared land remained spewing small random flames and fumes into the air. Brondie went inside to report what he had seen.

Brondie knew others would come. Maybe they would take the craft away. Maybe they would comb the area for his tribe. He felt evil was ever present in this location. The farm was now totally ruined. His people had to leave but it had to be a tribal decision whether to stay or leave. Whatever the decision, he would lead the tribe. The tribe agreed the farm was not able to be saved.

The tribe decided to leave their cave and move into the next cave they discovered years earlier but never ventured in. One of the survivors from another tribe, Mundo, led them south for three kilometres and into the new cave. The cave opening was about the same size as the one they all left. The inside was vastly different. Natural tunnels formed by ancient lava flows riddled the cave system. Mundo pointed to the smallest opening. "We crawl through here. There is water. I can hear the drops and smell it."

One by one the tribe filed through the small opening. As they went, the sound of water guided them to a cavity full of stalagmites and stalactites. Mundo said, "We should make this our main camp." Brondie nodded. "We rest. Then a small group will explore one tunnel at a time."

Two hours later Mundo requested Brondie to select a group of five people to go with him through the most distant tunnel. The group set out with a rope tethered around their waists. An hour later they returned. Mundo reported, "It's a dead end with a dangerous drop going deeper into the earth. We will try the next tunnel if these people are willing to try again." One of the younger men shook his head. "I am out. Someone can take my place. Two women similar in age stood up. Brondie selected one. To the others, he said, "Next time you go." The second attempt began.

The group returned in two hours. Mundo reported, "There are many turns in that tunnel. We just kept going straight ahead. We found this." The group held up their arms loaded with edible weed. "Food. There is more in there. Maybe enough for one week. Light enters that cave through very small holes. It is worth exploring in the future." The food was rationed out.

The next morning, another team led by Mundo entered the third tunnel. This time they returned four hours later. "We have found the other side. We found the day light but there are many creatures, small ones. We watched them. They eat the same food as us. They had a larger one tied to a post and guards surround their camp. We watched for a short time to see if they would do anything to the captured big lizard. Then we came back."

Brondie and the rest realized they were trapped in the cave system. "We must explore the other tunnels. The other group which went to the food source has returned with enough food for two more days. Tomorrow, we explore the other tunnels".

Luna, one of the children, who was playing with other children came running over to Brondie. He puffed, "There was another small tunnel." Luna pointed to that direction. "Behind the small wall. It is hard for adults to climb into."

Brondie was led by Luna to a small hole at ground level. *Luna is right,* Brondie thought. *It is hard for adults to squeeze into the gap.* Luna went down on his stomach and wriggled until his body was only halfway through.

He saw something shine and grabbed it before wriggling back out. He held up a crystal. "There are many such stones there." When Luna and Brondie walked back to the campfire, the only source of light, Brondie examined the crystal. A rainbow shot across the cavern. Audible ahs was spreading across the cave.

Luna walked up to Brondie. "Can I have my pretty stone? I want to try something."

Brondie squatted down. "What do you want to try doing?"

"Make the rainbow stay. This place is so dark. That stone makes pretty colours. I want to put it around the fire. Around, not in. I don't want to burn myself." Brondie indulged the child's request and handed over the crystal. The light from the fire magnified that tiny location. Beaming with pride, Luna yelled out, "It works! More light." He ran off to the wall of stalagmites. Two others followed. They gathered as many as their small hands could hold before coming back to the fire. Luna organized the crystals around the fire.

Mundo and Brondie went to the area. At the end of the small passage naturally formed between the cave wall and the rows of stalagmites was another cave. Realizing there was no way they could enter this cave, they called Luna over. Luna was directed to crawl inside, but he didn't go far. The torch he was carrying lit up the area. Large crystals magnified his light. He crawled back. "Giant pretty stones. Just giant stones. So beautiful." Brondie laid on the ground at the entrance. He slipped his arm holding the torch through the opening. His head barely was inside the new cavity. *Luna was right. It was a cave of crystals, very big crystals.* Some towered like pillars which had fallen in every direction. *Beautiful*, he thought. He wriggled back out. "We take these small stones to the campfire. We build a bigger wall around the fire."

Mundo and Brondie built upon the existing circles around the fire. The light in the cave extended further, giving a twilight effect to most of the cavern. Mundo stuffed a few into his crude cloth bag. He would test the crystals even more when he will lead the next exploration.

Mundo left the main cavern with two other people. This fourth tunnel twisted but there were no offshoots. It opened to a clearing. The trio smiled. They found to a gorge that had some of their edible plants and weeds similar to the one in the second cave. The small u-shaped clearing offered a place for cultivation. The surrounding gorge walls offered some protection. The attackers could only fly through. There was no place for them to land and circling to turn back could only take place well above the gorge. The trio headed back and gave their report.

The tribe settled into the gorge with its small clearing. They explored the area noting where larger trees offered some protection from the sun and the crafts flying overhead. They searched for a suitable location to settle down. Members of the tribe kept their eyes open for animals which they could herd and later keep. No animals were found.

Mundo noticed another but smaller horseshoe-shaped area nestled on the western side. He directed his team to that location. When they explored this alcove, they found a spring which had water dropping no more than a metre into a lagoon. From the lagoon, the water travelled a very short distance before it disappeared behind a boulder and then into the earth below. "This is where we settle. Look!" he pointed to a series of cave entrances. "We will look at these caves and see if they are big enough for shelter."

The small group separated to explore the caves. Minutes later they met. The caves were no more than entrances going no deeper than six metres. Mundo said, "The Gods are kind to us. We have pre-made homes for our people. I will stay here, and you bring the others here. This is the best place for us now." The others departed. Within minutes, from where Mundo was standing, he could see the rest of the tribe, coming towards him. He greeted each group as they arrived.

*

At the rebel base, Kyrina viewed the recordings of the attack. When the craft fell on the farm but didn't immediately explode, it put her deep into thought. She turned to Nage, her second-in-charge.

"They have changed their technology. Obviously designed to let the pilots escape." She timed the time of impact and the spasmodic burning. It was just ten minutes. "Let's flip back to the first flyover." She studied the ground where the Mammalians had worked their farm. "The little humans were clearing their land of debris. Then that landed on top destroying their efforts. Are there any pictures of where they went?"

Nage shook his head. "We believe they went into a cave. They hide when any craft flies over. We will have to send a group to explore the area to see where they went. I have a hunch; they have left the area after that craft smashed into the clearing."

Kyrina nodded. "Send a group in. Maybe we can find them. They can't have moved that far. They are a group on foot. No vehicles of any kind would allow them to cover vast distance is in a short time. Send a team out tomorrow morning. Remind them, these humans are scared and that makes them unpredictable."

The next morning a group of five landed on the farm between the mountains and smouldering Draconian craft. The group checked the downed craft to see what other items were salvageable and loaded them onto their craft. They conceded they would have to come back; the booty was impressive. They turned their attention to the mountain.

"Over here!" called Nage who decided to lead the expedition himself. "A cave!"

The others ran to join him. They moved slowly with their led-light torches beaming as if it was like daylight. They studied the surroundings. "They have been living here and looks like it for a while. Look they left a drawing on the wall. It looks reasonably fresh." The others studied the drawing but couldn't quite make any sense out of it. "The lines go east-west. That looks like the intended rubbish collection. What are the spots and other lines? Any ideas?" asked Nage. The others shook their heads.

"I'll take a picture of it. Maybe someone at the base can work it out," said one in the group. "Regardless, they left this place. They must have left when they thought it was safe or under the cover of darkness. Check the outside to see which way they went," said Nage. "I just hope the Draconians didn't get to them."

The group searched the surroundings for clues. Nothing. They went back to the cave. "Search this again. There could be a way out," ordered Nage. Nage looked at the drawings on the wall again. Something about it bothered him. *They were planning something. Forming a strategy, we have a choice, we go either east or west,* he thought. He went outside again and studied the directions.

It was confirmed, the long lines were walls of debris. He smiled. *Yes, they were clearing their farm and placing the rubbish into lines that ran east and west. That problem was solved. Now the other blue and red markings. What do they represent?*

He walked along one of the lines of rubble. He slowly examined the forming structure hoping to find a clue. Nothing. He went to the other side of the downed craft and examined the broken lines on each side. He was now close to the nose of the craft. The lines were now more defined. Nothing.

He climbed back into the downed and burnt-out Draconian craft near the cockpit, a place he and the crew had not entered before. He studied the cockpit controls. "Nice," he whispered to himself. When he decided to leave, he slowly opened the buckled door. It squeaked its protest. He jumped. Instead of hitting terra-firmer, his body sank into a hole cleverly disguised with natural plants. He cursed at first and then laughed.

He ran back to the cave yelling, "I know what the spots are." He looked at the drawing again and explained to the others what he discovered. "We still don't know what the other lines are?"

One of the group members looked at the details again. "Just suppose they were under attack. They disappear down the holes. The lined-up rubbish offers some protection in one direction. Poor protection but it was just the start of the construction. They see a craft coming. They go down the holes. Invisible to anyone flying above. Just suppose, these holes are linked in pairs. The links go under a wall of rubbish going to the other side. If a break occurs, they run to the next hole and go under the rubbish again. Each time they do that, they reach the safety of this cave." He looked around. "Shall we try the theory?"

The Lacertians went outside and looked for the escape holes. They were so well disguised. It took a while for the first one to be discovered. They dug it up. This was just a hole with no links. They tried the other side. Just another hole. Now knowing what they are looking for as a tell-tale sign, they went to another area. They found a new hole, and this had a small tunnel going under the line of debris. Directly on the other side was another hole. The tunnel in the middle with the two holes could allow up to five Mammalians to hide together." Nage walked across to the next line of rubble. He found another hole linking one on the other side. He grinned as he walked back to the other

"Clever little people. It takes about ten seconds to get out of one hole and run to the next. There would be one person escaping at a time. Let's head back. They have left the area. "We will drop off supplies at the next camp just minutes away. We will let them know the Mammalians are on the move."

CHAPTER 6

The Draconian Command. The Reptilian Universe.

Same Time Period.

"The domination of Oberon and Amada is now one hundred percent complete. The humans now only speak, or the best their vocal cords will permit, Draconian. The elders over the age of forty no longer exist. They have no knowledge of their history and culture.

"There has been an attack after the discovery of humans on a planet they call Xion in the Normaria Galaxy. We are certain there is only one major settlement. Small ones may exist, if so, our detectors did not locate them. The people will also be harvested. Going by the structures of their buildings, it seems to be a mixture of refugees from Oberon. There appears to be no sign of any Amada refugees. Our ships are exploring other planets in the same system. We are certain more planets have been settled."

Commander Landryk turned on the hologram of a path going from Oberon through Amada, around the waste space, and to the White galaxy. "Years ago, when we started our expansion, Commander Jarke who died in the first battle – killed by Prince Alcyn, discovered this incredible corridor." He pointed to the path highlighted in red. "The idiot who blew up some Oberon planets and shifted others, caused a massive time delay in relocating this entrance, not to mention it caused a massive food shortage. The entrance had shifted some fifteen thousand light years.

"The White galaxy has humans called Lyrians. They are tenacious fighters. We can't seem to get past them. However, I do believe we are wearing them down by exhausting their resources and tiring their people on such a prolonged war. Where there is one human based planet, there will be others. It is a matter of finding them. Easier said than done. I suggest we send exploration ships going through the void on the edge of Amada and slowly and systematically search each spiral of the White galaxy."

"That will take months and months to cover the area," replied General Sanyana.

"True. We must secure our food supply for our rapidly growing population. Humans are plentiful, cheap and tasty. Other animals are not as prized, cheap or readily available. Our population has developed a taste for humans and each race has a different flavour. That makes them an interesting culinary dish. No one knows exactly what their flavour will be unless told of their origin and race. The farmed humans with controlled diets are regulating the flavour for the market. The flavours are very successful as it offers consumers consistency to some degree," said Commander Landryk.

Reluctantly the general gave in. "It is against my better judgement that I will give permission for exploration, but it will be restricted to the side closet to the waste space and only for two years.

No more than two crafts searching the region and don't ask for more crafts at any time. I will not permit it. This will only go ahead if the government approves it."

Commander Landryk nodded knowing full well he had already lobbied most politicians beforehand.

The general turned to his head of army intelligence, Colonel Yuma. "What is happening with the rebel Lacertians?"

Colonel Yuma opened his file and pressed a button to show a hologram of Kyrina. "Sir, the leader of the rebels, Kyrina. She is the daughter of the ex and now dead last elected president of Lacerta, Kyros. She has her friends scattered everywhere on all planets. We simply don't know which vegetarian Lacertian is with or against her. We have a bounty on her head."

"How much?" asked the general.

"Ten million credits," said Yuma as if it wasn't enough to bring out a traitor against Kyrina. The general nodded. "Continue."

"We believe Kyrina is on Beta Cancari. Our people have been attacked by Lacertian crafts. Only Kyrina would have the ability to organize craft theft and carry out very organized attacks." Colonel Yuma flicked a switch. A picture of Nage appeared. "It is unconfirmed, this is her second in command. We don't know his name and from which planet he originated." Colonel Yuma flicked three more pictures of Lacertians. "All these are suspects. Suspects only at this stage. No one talks. Everyone is deaf, dumb and stupid when these faces appear."

"Now, I have something a little more interesting. Humans on the wanted list have magically disappeared." Colonel Yuma flashed up four names. "These are all Pleiadeans who have assisted the local humans to escape.

Murder, sabotage and bombings, you name it. This group has had its fingers in everything. We have no pictures, no information just names. Ashton, Eraton, Garyth, and the only female in the group, Kora.

"Since this quartet disappeared, the attacks have not been as savage, but the Lacertian resistance has taken over. The Lacertian rebels are slowly becoming more aggressive. We do know the resistance is in two groups. One is only assisting Lacertians. Apparently, this main group hasn't been thrilled about job changes. They encourage a lot of sabotage in all fields of work. No one speaks, sees or hears anything. Sabotage happens by magic. Before the Lacertians were highly educated, skilled and held assorted high positions. When the government decided to limit their aspirations, that was when this group formed. The politicians created this problem. Only they can break this group up by reversing the laws. That will stop a lot of problems. Many are also the breeders for our disposable soldiers, which we injected with drugs at birth."

The general sat back in his seat. "The politicians dumped these deformed Draconians on Lacerta. They were supposed to die out. Their intended demise and misery turned into happiness and prosperity. They still serve a purpose as slaves and disposable soldiers doing the most dangerous of work. Human slaves are now rare; most are food supply. That was another political decision. The slave gap was filled with Lacertian breeders and soldiers doing the worst of jobs in the armed forces and doing other worst jobs in our society. If we find humans in other parts of the White Galaxy, the converted Lacertians go as the sacrificial lambs. They test the waters out for us to see what we are dealing with."

Yuma sighed. "We have problems with the unaltered Lacertians. They are still vegetarian. They are not wired up for brainwashing. That is exactly the problem. They recall they had a position, a good income, social life, and some status in everything. That was taken away from them. Frankly, if I was in their position, I would be rebelling too," said Yuma who sounded to the general like he was about to defect to be a rebel.

Commander Landryk commented, "This debate can go on forever. I have repeatedly asked that the drug given to Lacerians be re-examined. We need some clever Draconian to block out the infertility side effect. Then we just breed Lacertians to be our disposable robots. No one is listening."

General Sanyana rolled his eyes. "You were not told, were you?"

"Of what?" asked Landryk.

"In Nubia, the research was progressing to fix that very problem. Some self-righteous Lacertians sabotaged the near-perfect details of the new drug.

They installed a pile of variations in the formula at the manufacturing level. When it was tested, all the Lacertians died. It was so well executed, that the new genuine formula automatically deletes and is overridden for new wrong ingredients. It smacks of Pleiadean interference. They did that to the water supply on Nubia. We had to rebuild everything to get over the problem, and that included tossing out all electronic controls. We had to do the same with this drug manufacturering. A brand-new lab was built on a different site. What do you think happened to that lab? The bastards burnt it down one week after completion. Then there has been a series of industrial accidents. Eventually, we banned all Lacertian workers including the ones wired up from birth. Then another building site was selected. Same thing. It goes up in smoke,"

said General Sanyana in a frustrated way.

Colonel Yuma shook his head. "Did anyone check the electronics and the electrical wiring?"

General Sanayna frowned. "I don't know. I will check that out. Who manufactures those electronic bits?"

"They're manufactured on Genobola B, a place filled with Lacertian workers doing dangerous and often mundane work. Someone may have been slack with security or gave Lacertian access believing they were trustworthy," comment Colonel Yuma.

"I will check out the manufacturing of components," said Yuma.

"Now back to the exploration of the White Galaxy. I want the two latest long-haul ships. Plus, one hundred jet fighters on each. Also, I want to hand-pick all staff," said Commander Landryk.

CHAPTER 7

Earth.

Daraxon Technologies Inc. Australia.

Zindel placed his small recruited group in the most comfortable recliners he could find on Earth. They were arranged in a semi-circle. Zindel looked at his recruits hoping the training would advance each person.

He looked at Kora and Tanke, "See the balls in the middle of the floor? Kora, you have the red ball. Tanke you have the blue one." Both nodded. "Your task is to use mind control to lift your ball off the ground. The higher the better. Start. Remember to focus."

He looked at Ashton and Alcyn PZ. "You two are going to see what is on the other side of this planet.

I will give you the same co-ordinates and show you this ancient-looking school kid's globe. He pointed a finger to the western side of the Gobi Desert. Tell me what is there." Zindel gave the co-ordinates. He sat back watching the small group and checked their levels of concentration by jumping into their minds. Telepathically he coached each in turn.

Kora, Zindel said softly using his telepathic powers, *Focus. Ashra is asleep. You can give full attention to this task.* Kora heard Zindel and responded in the same manner, *I will start again. I want to do this.* Zindel gave her a sensation of a comforting pat on one of her shoulders. *Good. I believe you can do it, but you must believe in yourself.*

He looked over to Tanke after overhearing some disturbing thoughts and laughter, *Tanke,* he said in a firm voice, *focus on the task of lifting the blue ball. Stop playing around with Alcyn.*

Tanke apologized as she said, *It is easier stirring Alcyn than the blue ball.* Zindel glanced across the room to see Alcyn trying hard to ignore Tanke's attack. Alcyn was squirming and fighting himself to focus. He mentally sent Tanke a message, *Later, not now. Get out of my pants. Don't make me embarrass myself. What will Zindel think?*

Zindel thinks you two should not be in the same galaxy. He turned to Tanke, *Enough! There will be consequences!*

Such as, she asked.

Zindel gave her a sensation of a punch to her stomach. *That was your final warning.*

Instantly, Tanke sobered up.

Ashton drew Zindel's attention, *I think I see something in the desert. Not at the location where you mentioned. About fifty kilometress south is a massive structure. Only some of it is above ground to be entrances and exits. Can I go inside?*

Zindel replied, *Go. See what is there. No more than ten minutes.*

Alcyn saw the same structure, *I see it too. Can I join Ashton?*

No. Scout for all the entrances and exists. See who or what is at this facility, said Zindel.

Zindel turned his attention to Kora. He noticed a grin across her face. The red ball was now almost to the ceiling. *Perfect. Now see if you can make it go up and down.* Kora focused. At first, the ball went slowly down and then up. She repeated the action. *Can I make it fly around the room*? she asked Zindel.

Make it fly, he replied, *but don't knock out the lights or windows.*

He looked at Tanke. The ball had lifted ever so slightly off the ground. Suddenly it whizzed around the room going faster and faster. Zindel intercepted it and made it fall to the ground. *Not so fast young lady.* Tanke mumbled *sorry. I got excited.*

Zindel looked at her. *You need more self-discipline. We will do some of that training tomorrow.*

Zindel called out, "Stop"

Everyone snapped out of their trance-like states. He handed each a tablet. Draw or write a report on your experience. What you felt... I don't mean the playfulness between Tanke and Alcyn. You have one hour to put it all down.

As they wrote about their experiences, Zindel listened to their thoughts. *Interesting* he thought as he made comparisons between the two women and their set tasks and the two men and their task.

Kora is more cautious and in control. Tanke is so energetic, and her control of the ball was incredible. He paused. Tanke and Alcyn were in conversation. He tuned in but they suddenly stopped when they noticed Zindel was listening in. They directed their attention to the task at hand. Zindel sent them a message, *Leave the social organization for later.*

Footsteps were heard from outside the room. Hammond walked in, he whispered to Zindel, "Send Alcyn to the lab. I want him to check all the microchips."

Zindel nodded. "Thanks for the loan of the room. I will give you a report when I have read their experiences." Hammond left the room. Ashton and Kora returned their tablets. Alcyn and Tanke soon followed. "Alcyn," said Zindel, "Hammond wants you in the lab to check the microchips." Alcyn walked out and went to the lab he had been in for nearly two days.

Hammond asked, "How did that mind training go?"

"Good," Alcyn didn't offer more. He looked at the semi-assembled transporter and the semi-assembled viewer. "I think it will work. Because it is not linked to the transporter, it can only spy on parts of this planet. Just have the fire extinguisher ready just in case something goes wrong."

Alcyn PZ flicked a switch. The familiar soft sound of the motor began. It hummed for five minutes before Alcyn PZ flicked a second switch. The viewer screen came on. He tapped in some coordinates, the place he and Ashton viewed from their seats just an hour ago. He stared at the structure.

"I saw that. Zindel asked us to focus on some coordinates. Ashton looked inside. I was sent to look around the perimeter. We saw some very advanced stuff going on. Well, advanced for this planet."

Hammond stared at Alcyn. "That's some Chinese facility which the Chinese say doesn't exist. It is like their version of area 51."

"What's area 51?"

"A U.S. facility but over the years the U.S. has decided it does exist, but they never say what is going on in the place," replied Hammond.

"Do you want to know?" asked Alcyn.

"Not yet. I have a good hunch. There is a possibility you may be detected even in mind travel. Help me put the exterior cover onto the viewer part. We will test the transporter part tomorrow."

"Is there another transporter station on the planet?" asked Alcyn.

"No. I am not sure who or where we could build one," said Hammond.

"We need to set up a temporary place. How about in Tanke's apartment in France? Make a copy of the transporter. Then we fly it over and set it up. I am sure she won't mind the thing in her place. It will save us both time and effort going back and forth."

"You have an ulterior motive. Have you asked her?" asked Hammond.

"Just a minute, I will ask her now. She is somewhere in this building." Alcyn focused his attention on Tanke. She quizzed him about the transporter. *I'm coming up to see it and I know what space I require should I say yes.*

"She is coming over," replied Alcyn.

Tanke walked into the test laboratory. She looked around briefly before she walked over to Alcyn and Hammond. For a minute, she studied the small viewer beside the semi-built transporter.

She ummed and arrhed before measuring it. "Too big. I see this is a four-seater. How big will it be if it were a two-seater?"

Hammond did a few calculations. "Same height and width. The length would be half a metre shorter."

Tanke thought about the size. "It needs to be a bit smaller. Height down by five centimetres. Width down by four and length down another ten. Then it will fit on my balcony. My apartment is too small for this at any size. *It looks like Dr. Who's T.A.R.D.I.S.*"

"*Who is Dr. Who?*" asked Alcyn PZ.

"*A fictional character on this planet. Zindel is the closest thing to this invented character. Zindel zips around in a controlled pod. Dr. Who goes to places in an uncontrolled box.*" replied Tanke.

Hammond completed his new calculations. "We can get it a bit smaller, but we sacrifice speed.

It will run about much slower. Instead of here to Paris in five minutes, it will take ten."

"Only five minutes different?" asked Alcyn who was expecting a larger time delay.

"What will the new measurements be?" asked Tanke.

"One point five high metres and two metres wide and three metres long. A two-seater," replied Hammond.

Tanke smiled. "It will fit on the balcony. Umm, What is the weight? I forgot about the weight factor?"

Hammond did some more calculations before replying. "About the weight of six people – 600 to 800 kilos."

"Damn. Too heavy. The balcony was designed for four people, maybe five" said, Tanke.

Hammond drew in his breath. "Another recalculation." He tapped away.

"Okay. A one-seater. That brings the weight down to 500 to 550 kilos. I can't reduce it anymore. The time will be twenty minutes."

Tanke nodded. "It is just on the edge of maximum weight-wise. Still a bit risky."

"Alternatively, "said Alcyn, "We place it near the building or in some other location that is not too conspicuous."

"Like where?" asked Tanke and Hammond.

"On the roof. Hardly anyone goes to the roof. But the access is always locked so we need to get a key. The advantage is it still can be a four-seater."

Tanke gave a broad grin. "That is a very good idea. The transporter can then be any size. There is ample space beside the enclosed steps. For safety and from prying eyes or unauthorized usage, it will need to be locked and add some biometrics. Also, some safeguard just in case some caretaker tries to dismantle it as an unauthorized roof item."

"That can all be arranged. A four-seater transporter with full power."

Titus with a few staff loaded parts of the transporter onto a Daraxon Technologies cargo jet.

He sought air traffic control clearance in the two countries. Tanke accompanied him on the flight.

Titus touched down at the regular air force base in France and allowed the inspection to take place before landing on top of Tanke's apartment block. Together they set up the first stage of the transporter before flying back to Daraxon Technologies. The trip was repeated three times.

The transporter was now fully installed.

Tanke spoke to Hammond on the phone. "Titus is on the way home. Are we ready for a test?"

Hammond placed a box of food in the transporter at his end. "Test one. A parcel of food. It should reach you in five minutes."

As Tanke waited for the parcel to arrive she looked over the city. On one side the view was blocked by a taller apartment block. She wondered if any person there saw the new construction going up.

She walked over to that side and looked at the matching floor level and then at each level above. Nothing looked out of place. She focused her attention on each person she saw and in every room. Her mind drew a blank. She only picked up by telepathy one comment about a Daraxon jet on the roof but nothing about the unloading of any items. She gave a sigh of relief.

She heard a thud behind her. She waited until the motors had come to a stop. She punched the code for open and turned the lock. She was surprised just how heavy the door was. She looked inside for the box and dragged it out. "Oh, bugger. Mush," she whispered to herself. She phoned Hammond.

"Hammond. We have a box of mush. Is that supposed to happen to food?"

"Send me a photo. I want to see how much mush we have," he replied feeling a bit disappointed at the results. When he received the photos he said, "We need to do some adjustments. It's too powerful."

Three trials later, Tanke reported back on the condition of the food. Finally, a shipment arrived in perfect condition. She was thinking the testing was over when she heard Hammond say, "Let's try it on some animals."

"What?"

"Go the pound. There are lots of animals there that need homes. One small, one medium, and one large. By large I mean between 50 and 70 kilos. What arrives safely will be housed here. Most likely trained up for security," said Hammond.

Half a day later Tanke walked three dogs into the foyer of the building, into the lift, and then lead them to the roof. "Do I put all three in or one at a time," she asked Hammond.

"One at a time. We need to calibrate each size. Start with the smallest. We have a vet on standby just in case anything goes wrong."

Tanke put the smallest dog in first. "Test one. A chihuahua."

" I was expecting something slightly bigger," said Hammond.

"You did say small," retorted Tanke.

Back at the Daraxon Technologies test room, Hammond opened the door. He looked at the chihuahua. The animal looked back. He picked it up and handed it to the vet.

"It looks a bit sick," said the vet. "I'll run some tests."

Twenty minutes later, the vet gave a nod. "It is still sick, but it should recover. The vitals are becoming stronger. It is standing on its own feet, and it drank some water. What do you want to do with it?"

"Keep it. Tayee's granddaughter would love it. I am not sure what Tayee and his wife would say. The child has been asking for a pet for two years now. Her birthday is coming up in two weeks. Just make sure in that time it has a perfect bill of health and all the necessary shots." Hammond phoned Tanke, "We're ready for the next dog."

Tanke put a red-setter cross into the cubicle. Minutes later it arrived at the laboratory. Hammond opened the door. The dog was standing up and showed no side effects. The dog rushed out wagging his tail. Hammond bent over and for some unknown reason, he took an instant liking to the animal. "Hello," he said as he patted the dog. "You're a nice boy, aren't you?"

The vet coughed. "It's a girl."

"Oh, sorry. The young lady from Paris has won my heart. Okay. You're going to be called Paris."

The vet smirked. "I better give you some lessons on dogs."

Hammond gave Tanke the signal to put the largest dog in the transporter. Minutes later when Hammond opened the door, he stepped back. Staring back was a great dane. The vet laughed. Tanke found the biggest breed. It's a full adult great dane."

Hammond froze as the dog slowly came out and sniffed both. The dog rolled over and waited to be patted. The vet obliged. "Gentle giants. Great pets for kids."

Hammond retorted, "I've seen horses smaller than that." The dog rolled over, stood up on his hind legs, and placed his paws on Hammond's shoulders. The dog gave Hammond a sloppy lick across the face. Hammond recoiled. The vet laughed. "The dog has selected you as a friend."

"What do you mean?"

"Sometimes animals select their owners. You have just been selected."

Hammond was flustered and pushed the animal down.

The dog nudged at Hammond's knees. "What now?" asked Hammond.

"Pat him," suggested the vet.

Hammond gave a short pat on the head. Then he phoned Tanke, "All animals have arrived safely."

"Good. I'm going to be busy at work for the next few days," said Tanke.

Hammond and the vet went to another room where the vet had set up a mini surgery. The chihuahua was now walking around sniffing at the unfamiliar smells. Paris went to socialize with the small dog but the great dane just stayed by Hammond's side. Where Hammond moved, the great dane went. The vet chuckled at the situation. "You are not going to get rid of him." He nodded to the dane. "What are you going to call him?"

Hammond shrugged. "Denmark, I suppose. I don't want two dogs. We will need to find a home for Paris. I'll put a notice up for staff." Paris joined Denmark. Both nestled together in a corner of the room. The vet said to Hammond. "Those two have decided to be friends. Like it or not you have two dogs."

"Denmark is more than enough. They will be okay when separated. "

"Not always," replied the vet. "They can be like people and pine for a friend."

Hammond was getting frustrated. "Denmark picks me and Paris picks Denmark. Really?"

The vet nodded as he began packing up his equipment.

 "Alternatively, give Paris to Tayee's granddaughter and the chihuahua moves on. When the families meet, the dogs see each other. The chihuahua can come with me. Someone will take it for a pet."

Alcyn came into the room. He stopped dead in his tracks when he saw the three dogs. He stepped sideways around Denmark. "The tests look like they were successful," said Alcyn as he eyed the three dogs.

"Tanke said she will be working for the next few days," said Hammond.

"Ah," he said in a disappointed manner. "I was going to test out the transporter with me in it. It looks like another time."

"I recall from the last time, you always used yourself as a tester as the first person to use the transporter," commented Hammond.

There was a buzzing noise coming from Alcyn's hand communication system. He read the message. "It looks like the ship will be leaving in a couple of days."

"Where are you going?" asked Hammond.

"Back to Genesis."

Hammond almost went into a panic. "That means we have only 24 hours to build a transporter."

He called home to tell Stella, his wife, stating he would be working late. Then called all the staff connected to the transporter. "The ship is not going without a transporter. Get Keka and Darius. I need the co-ordinates for Genesis. Alcyn left the room to head back to the ship. He looked down to see Paris was following him. He walked back to the laboratory, pushed Paris through the door and closed it firmly before trying again to go to the ship.

CHAPTER 8

Genesis.

The Explorer landed on Genesis. As most of the equipment was unloaded and people disembarked, Alcyn was left in charge of the transporter. He directed it to be installed just inside the doors of the government's Administration office. Zanthe and Patrum, his parents, ran down to greet him and were stunned to see the transporter in parts.

Partum looked worried. "You can't build that here. It takes up half the space. Outside, now."

Alcyn glared at his father. "No. It stays. This was done in a hurry, and tests need to be done. We can't risk anybody using it. When it is safe, we have a direct fast link to Earth. That just doesn't mean our people, it means resources and ideas. How else are we going to communicate when the Lacertians and Draconians can track our signals? Look. This is a twenty-seater and if half the seats are removed, it becomes a cargo carrier, a two-way cargo carrier."

"The Draconians are in this galaxy."

Partum was going to say more when he felt Zanthe's hand pull on his arm.

"Well, this is not the best location. If this place comes under attack, the transporter will be the biggest prize the Draconians could ever have. You are right. It needs to be less conspicuous, but also readily accessible. Placing it too close to the space station or in here is not an option," said Patrum.

Alcyn looked around studying the street. Zantha followed his gaze. "How about over there?" She pointed to a new building going up. "It's a new motel," suggested Zanthe.

Alcyn grinned. "Perfect. It is just a matter of permission to see if the owners and the builders would accommodate such an idea. People coming and going would be seamless." Alcyn gave his mother a kiss on the cheek. He walked over to the building site.

One week later, the transporter was installed on the left side of the motel. A corridor no longer than three metres joined the transporter to the motel. A camouflaged door ensured the access was not immediately visible. It was the only part of the building completed. The exterior of the transporter was camouflaged to suit the rest of the exterior design.

Alcyn busied himself with programming the computer system, checking the flight data against more sophisticated co-ordinates between the two planets. He checked and rechecked. There was no room for error. At this time, he wondered if Hammond and crew had completed the transporter to match in size and he hoped the co-ordinates at the Earth end were accurate. An error at either end would be disastrous. At the end of his work, Alcyn stood back and looked at the completed transporter. He was ready to try it out.

Nervously, Zantha and Patrum looked on as Alcyn stepped inside. Zantha had her fingers crossed and whispered to herself, "Please no mistakes. Come back safely." Partum drew her in closer and whispered back, "He is going to be okay. I have never seen him work so hard and so carefully before. He was like that before. I wonder if he recalls all the battle tactics?"

Zantha snuggled into Patrum. "They will come back. I bet he didn't use all the gained previous knowledge to down the motherships."

Patrum commented, "This war will be different. A new and meaner enemy coming from an unknown place. If people find the location of the rip, that will be the turning point."

CHAPTER 9

Earth. Daraxon Technologies Inc. Australia.

Hammond heard the sound of the transporter operating in the room now dedicated to the transporter system and the attached viewer. He ran to the room. He gasped when he saw Alcyn slumped on the floor. Hammond dragged Aclyn out and checked his pulse. It was weak. Hammond pushed the medical emergency button. Two minutes later, medical staff entered and carried Alcyn to the medical room on the floor below.

Minutes later, Alcyn showed signs of recovery and groaned. He saw Hammond's concerned face looking at him. Alcyn rubbed his head. "That was a rough trip. It needs fine tuning for a greater distance."

Hammond nodded. "Don't get up yet. Rest. The staff here will check your vital signs more thoroughly than just pulse alone." Alcyn gave a weak smile and nodded. He rolled over on the bed and went to sleep. Around him, staff took blood for testing and linked up a drip.

The next day, Alcyn was sitting up in bed and looking at the drip inserted into his arm. He pushed the call button. A doctor accompanying Hammond walked in. "Nice to see you up," said Hammond. "I'm feeling much better."

The doctor started to detach Alcyn from the equipment. "Everything has checked out. You're free to go. But take it easy for the next two days. Then you should be okay to run around and do what you have to do."

Alcyn nodded. The doctor left the room.

Alcyn spoke to Hammond, "The transporter is set up. It is about fifty metres up the street opposite the administration building. To go in and out, you go through the motel. The agreement is anyone who comes via the transporter from the planet stays there. But we did install an emergency exit just in case something unforeseeable occurs."

"How many rooms are in the motel?" asked Hammond smiling at the idea of a motel stay.

"Three hundred. They increased the bed numbers by fifty. That fifty is solely for VIPs from anywhere on Genesis. But if war comes, that may be taken over by the military."

"How much does it cost per night?"

Alcyn shrugged. "Since there is no currency comparison, it is a box of wine and a box of food supplies or items of clothing or even some gadgets per person from this planet. I told them of the fabulous items you have here, food, clothing, wine and, so on. These are in high demand in Genesis. The place is resource poor but very safe to live."

Hammond chuckled. "Does it work out that the more you take or the better quality the item is, the better the room?"

"No. All the rooms are the same standard. All with a king bed. Much the same as here. Earth people will feel very comfortable. Now let's improve that ride for long distance."

For two days Alcyn and Hammond worked on the transporter. They double checked the systems and the microchips. Alcyn knew he was missing something and started the process all over again. Hammond had left in frustration and returned to his office leaving Alcyn to work alone.

Alcyn sat back trying to recall from his previous life what he had done to make the ride less straining on the body. He sat in an office chair and swivelled it around like some theme park ride. He stood up and looked into the control panel again. Nothing stood out. Then he dismantled one chair and examined each component. He left the room to get something to eat. He was halfway to the lift when the lightbulb flashed on. He ran back to the dismantled chair and looked at each component. Then he examined each microchip. "Ah-ha! There you are." He pulled out one chip and studied it in detail.

The crystal coating layer was too thin. Then he examined each microchip in turn. Alcyn pressed the intercom to get Hammond's attention.

Hammond walked in. "What have you found?"

"Chips five to ten need a thicker layer of crystal. We need to check all the chairs. The annoying thing is, we need to pull apart every chair to get to the chips."

Hammond nodded. "Who do you want to help you?"

Alcyn thought for a second before answering. His mind flipped through the people on the planet other than Hammond. "You, Titus, and maybe Lenax and Egan. It wouldn't hurt them to learn about the transporter. We can skill them up for maintenance work. Actually, some earth people can be trained as well. If this transporter gets heavily used which I think it may be in the future, then the selected earth people will have to know what to do. Which physicists and astronomers do you know?"

Hammond drummed his fingers on the only workbench. "The best brains work on the Hadron Collider scope. Maybe we can headhunt from there for starters and then we raid some space agencies and universities."

One week later, two physics professors, Robert Goldsmith, William Atkins, and an astronomer, Regina Appleton, were looking at the array of components across the workbench and a series of chairs in different stages of a rebuild. Titus, Lenaxs and Egan were introduced to the newcomers after a short orientation in a conference room. The six trainees wandered towards the demonstration seats before them. They whispered between themselves. When their curiosity was satisfied, they returned to the workbench to look at the components neatly displayed. All six men followed Alcyn's instruction while Hammond moved around the group offering assistance.

At the end of two weeks, Alcyn, Robert, William, and Regina entered the transporter. Close to an hour later, they landed on Genesis. They were ushered to the reception desk where they handed over bottles of wine and trays of fruit and vegetables. Then it was up to their designated rooms.

In the morning, Alcyn introduced the trio who were wearing translators to his parents and to the rest of the administrators. Zantha noticed the earth people looked shellshocked. "Come," she said warmly, "I have arranged for a twelve-seater pod to fly you around our planet." The group was driven by a hovercraft to a spaceport. Zantha pointed out the various features of the planet: the goods and its deficiencies. On their return, they were given a banquet held in their honour.

The next day, the group was back in the rooms of Daraxon Technologies. Buoyed by the experience, they looked at the transporter in a different light. Space travel by ship was now almost a thing of their past. Ships still served a purpose. In their eyes, earth crafts were now primitive.

Alcyn then repeated the same journey but took Titus, Lenax and Egan. Zantha recalled Titus as a child and gasped. Seeing Lenax and Egan had aged, she suddenly realized she too was older. Her initial feeling of suddenly feeling old gave way to delight. The smile couldn't be wiped off her face the whole time they were there. Partum looked at her and grinned. "I haven't seen you so animated."

She winked as she told how she met Titus as a frightened child who survived massive quakes on Octophoria. The first and genuine quake had killed his brothers and father. New huge crevasses formed. The Lacertians placed bombs deep into the cracks and detonated them when aftershocks occurred. The cycle of natural aftershocks and explosions deep inside the planet ensured the destruction kept occurring. It was in one of these quakes when Titus's mother died but not before she gave Titus instructions to get a microchip of the recordings to Prince Alcyn. To do that, Titus smuggled himself on board a ship going to Daraxon. Then from the spaceport, he hitched a ride on the back of a delivery truck going to the palace.

Then Zantha recounted how she met Tayee's children, Lenax, Egan and Salina. "What a shame Salina isn't here. I would have loved to have seen her. Lenax, you look so much like your father at the same age when we all split up. I wonder if we can all make the trip to Earth now?"

Partum gulped at the suggestion. "You go. I have a mountain of work. The existing jets are being converted into military fighters, just in case our peace is disrupted again. Also, there's been trouble on Affen Welt. The apes have cottoned on we have been mining their planet."

"Aren't the mines well away from any of their settlements?" asked Alcyn.

"They are. The closest mine is over three thousand kilometres away. Some may have seen the crafts flying overhead and then some bright spark decided to follow the flight path from the ground. They found mine number two. They have attacked the workers."

"Be careful. I don't want to find out when I come back from Earth that I am a widow," warned Zantha.

Partum planted a kiss on Zantha's cheek. "Have fun. And I promise I will be careful. I will be taking one of my guns I bought from Earth years ago. The laser gun only kills the chimpanzee. The rest get mild to severe burns. Then

they get very agitated and become more aggressive. I hope the earth gun...
err rifle works."

"Yes. You did buy up a few styles and a load of ammunition. Do you need
more ammunition?"

"It won't hurt to have extra. I will give you the models. Is that going to be
my earth gift?"

"Now. Let me think," teased Zantaha. "What else does my husband require
besides me coming back?" Zantha pursed her lips. "I will surprise you.
Something...just for you and something we can share."

"Put some wine on the list. Red, white or any other colour they have. I saw
some odd colours on that planet the last time we were there. "

When Alcyn returned to Earth, the group now included Zantha. Zantha
looked around at the small welcoming committee. She gave a broad smile.
"Hello everyone." Surprised faces gave way to embraces. As the others
walked out of the room which housed the transporter, Alcyn immediately
made a check on the controls.

Robert, William, and Regina were examining the rest of the transporter.
They turned to face Alcyn when they heard him come in. Robert asked as
he waved his hand in the direction of the transporter. "Just how far did we
travel?"

Alcyn knew he was going to be questioned. *These sharp enquiring minds
needed to be satisfied.*

"We went close to 800,000 light years one way. More questions?"

Regina asked, "Exactly what technology is being used here? We have never
seen anything like it."

"The reason Daraxon Technologies wanted people with a minimum of a
doctorate, is the ability to understand neutrinos and their behaviour. We
know about high energy and general neutrinos. We also have neutrinos in
our body."

Alcyn stopped to rethink his explanation attempt. "In your body, everywhere
in your body are

fast moving crystals-like matter. If don't have these crystals, you are dead.
Doctors know if the heart stops, the person is dead, but the heart helps
to pump the crystals around before being stored in every body part. Every
plant and every animal have these bio-crystals." Alcyn looked at his mini-

audience to see non-belief written across their faces. Alcyn sighed. "The crystals have already been found by a couple of earth scientists. You need an adapted electron microscope to see moving things." Alcyn went over to a computer and typed in crystal energy. The information flashed up. He allowed the trio to read some of the contents. "The companion to the discovery is negative hydrogen. Regina, you know the sun emits negative hydrogen." She nodded. "The negative hydrogen is absorbed by plants and the sunlight hitting the body. Now if we take the crystals and break them down, we get neutrinos. The neutrinos in the body break down in the transporter through flight and as you near your destination, the body reassembles. The seat you helped to repair and reconstruct, is a stabilizer. That took some work to get it right; about twenty years. The mesons, the sub-atomic particles, didn't want to keep up with the rest of the body. It was like they had their own agenda or time frame. Neutrinos and mesons need to be together for the reconstruction of any life form or object when they reach their destination. No reconstruction, you get scattered matter."

William nodded. "This makes the Hadron Collider Accelerator look like child's play. Any more wonderful advancements?"

Alcyn sat at a console. "Please sit down. This will take a minute or two to fire up. What do you want to see on this planet?"

"How about our old workplace? The Collider Accelerator," suggested Robert.

"What part?"

"Let's be bold," said Robert. "The canteen first and then the engine room."

"Give me some coordinates," requested Alcyn.

William pulled out his phone and tapped into Google to search for the coordinates. He read out the numbers.

The viewer part of the machine turned on. All four could see a handful of staff sitting around tables with discussions going on. The words were clear. "We are like flies on a wall," said William as he leaned closer. Alcyn quickly pulled the height level back when he saw a gust of wind forming and people suddenly looking around wondering where the gush of air was coming from. "Sorry, I forgot the five-metre height rule. We nearly had a person sucked up. Where is the engine room?"

As Alcyn repositioned the viewer, Robert asked, "What do you mean sucked up?"

"The viewer creates a vortex. That is a problem I never had a chance to sort out before when in a past life I was using this machine."

Regina asked, "Past life?"

Alcyn wasn't sure how to answer it. "When we die our souls leave our bodies. Then we review our lives in the Hall of Records. If we didn't achieve what we set out to do, then we are jettisoned back to complete the job. Apparently, we plan our own destinies before we are born."

"What happens when we achieve our destiny?"

"I really don't know. I can speculate. We move on to do something else. Who knows? Our memories are wiped, well that is what I am told. But whoever wiped mine didn't do it right. I get flashes of the past. Sometimes it is helpful as in this situation to repair the transporter. I really don't want to talk about those matters."

William changed the subject and gave a small cough. "Can we see other planets using this thing?"

"Yes. That is how Jed came to be on my planet. I was observing him and got too close. He was sucked up. We kept him on the planet as we learned from the past, animals and people died on the way back. It took some doing to make the adjustments. The adjustments were not complete. When the war broke out, we had to build a transporter here by carrying one transporter inside another. The two were separated for more efficient travel. That was an experiment in itself and lucky enough, it worked."

"Can you show us another planet?" repeated William.

Alcyn nodded. "My father said there was trouble on Affen-Welt. That is a resource rich planet owned by apes of many sizes and breeds. Genesis is short on mineral resources, so we mine that Affen-Welt on the sly and keep well away from any ape colony. But some apes must have seen our crafts and followed the general direction and stumbled across mine number two. Affen-Welt is, in galactic terms, close to Genesis.

I know the coordinates of Affen-Welt and mine two. Shall we try?"

It took Alcyn a few minutes to enter the data. The screen before him came to life. It first showed the planet. Then he quickly zoomed in on mine two. While William, Regina, and Robert were trance-fixed on the screen and trying to absorb what they saw, Alcyn's eyes were scanning the surroundings looking for any apes.

He spotted four medium-sized ones in their battered vehicle. "Uh-oh. Trouble. He lowered the viewer over the vehicle. As the vehicle started to be lifted off the ground, Alcyn suddenly pulled back. The apes and the vehicle crashed to the ground. The vehicle caught fire to send a plume of black smoke into the air. Other gorillas hiding in the trees clamoured down and screeched and hoot their shock and anger. Although no sound travelled through the viewer due to its distance, all could see the agitation. Alcyn zoomed down again and lifted gorillas into the air and dumped them onto the fire. He repeated the process with five more apes. With another group, he let them rain down from the sky. The other gorillas stopped their screeching and hooting to look up at the sky. They saw nothing. Again, Alcyn lowered the viewer and scooped up more. Again, he dropped them from a height. As the second group of gorillas came crashing down, the others gathered their weapons ready to attack an invisible enemy.

They ran to their concealed vehicles and drove away. Alcyn lifted the first vehicle and dumped it on the second leaving the site. The cars following swerved to miss the disaster before them. Many crashed their vehicles into each other or struck close by trees. Alcyn swooped down again and lifted

those running away and dumping them on the now burning vehicles. A few survived the onslaught.

Alcyn was about to lift them up when he noticed three of the small group were on their knees and bowing to the ground. Alcyn smirked. "One problem solved. And maybe another has started. I hope it doesn't become holy ground. The last thing we need is a place of pilgrimage. Pass me that photo over there. The one with Mark in his space suit."

Alcyn fed the photo into a slot. When the photo came out, Alcyn converted it into a holographic image. Then he sent it down to the bowing apes. Alcyn manipulated the image to make an arm point back to where they came from. When the apes didn't move, another swirl of wind made the apes stand up and run. The image chased the apes a few metres. Then the image of Mark pointing appeared again showing them the way out. One ape picked up a stone to strike the image. The stone travelled through the image. The apes screeched again. Alcyn lowered the viewer again to create a wind gust. The apes ran away. Alcyn smirked. "Mark you just became a god of terror in the eyes of these apes. Don't ever go there in case one of these gorillas tries to toss a stone at you. It won't travel through."

Alcyn closed down the machine. He swivelled it around to stunned professors. "If this machine was on a ship and had a tube coming out of the bottom of a ship or jet, it can become a weapon." Seeing the look of horror on the trio's faces he added, "The gorillas are cannibals and are partial to most forms of meat. We are fighting one lot of meat-eating lizards and sure as hell, we don't want to know if these creatures have an appetite for humans."

"Excuse me. Did I miss something?" asked Robert. "War with whom and are we in danger?"

"Not yet. The lizards haven't found this planet. It is my job and with the help of Daraxon Technologies, I was recently informed of a race of humans from what you call Lyria have been battling these creatures for twenty-five years. My planet of Genesis is suspected to be on the radar of these lizards. If not, we won't be far behind. I was informed that all the human races in the universe are trying to protect Earth. We have all taken major casualties." Alcyn said softly to himself but was not expecting Robert who was standing closest to hear him. "Earth must be saved at all costs?"

Robert asked as he glanced at Regina and William. "What is so important about Earth that it must be protected at all costs?"

Alcyn closed his eyes. "I wish I knew all the details. I was told by Zindel, Earth must be saved. Let's say, Earth is very important to all human races in the universe. It started as an experiment. Then things changed after that. Every human race in the universe wants to protect its babies and their future. The planet is important and the people in this mixed-up world are important. That is all I am prepared to say. Humans are all brothers and sisters, no matter where they live. Family helps family and the universal human family is pulling together to do just that. Please no more questions. "

Alcyn closed down the transporter and the viewer. He doubled checked the transporter and the viewer were closed down and removed the starter switch. He went into a trance just for a few seconds. "I have to go. Zindel is calling me again." Alcyn left the room and disappeared into the lift.

CHAPTER 10

Daraxon Technologies Inc., Australia.

Attack one.

Zindel was in the room, now dubbed the 'mind-control room,' with a stranger. Zindel looked at Alcyn as he entered. "Alcyn, this is Ustin."

"Nice to meet you," said Alcyn.

Ustin gave nodded. "Likewise. I have heard much about you. All good, I can assure you."

"I saw you were operating the viewer. Did you see anything?" asked Zindel.

Alcyn nodded. "There was trouble on Affen Welt. The apes are rising up against my people. I just gave them a reminder to keep away as we have kept away from them. I think they got the message."

"Did any apes die?" asked Zindel.

"About forty, fifty at the most. I just hope they don't make that area a ceremonial place."

Zindel gave a slight bow. "Only time will tell. Now the good news. I have managed to recruit another emissary." Zinndel gestured towards Ustin and added, "Ustin is in charge of sectors twenty-one. That is the next zone. I will let Ustin say what he has seen."

"In sector twenty-one which borders the edge of Zindel's sector twenty, we have spotted a number of crafts. They don't belong in my zone. They don't respond to any identification requests. They are huge crafts." He showed a holographic picture of the craft. Alcyn gulped when he saw the picture. He whispered, "It must be Draconian."

Ustin confirmed. "You are right. It is. Over ten have been spotted and traced going to Normaria and Lacerta. They come in at the edge of sector nineteen." Ustin displayed a holographic map above their heads. He pointed as he spoke. "Zindel has informed me they have taken over the galaxies of Oberon and Amada and are in this galaxy plus penetrating Normaria. My sector twenty-one sits beside Normaria. Zindel has informed me of the long, drawn-out attacks and what has happened to the human race in these galaxies. I fear the same will be happening in my sector. I am here to help. I will be bringing my team of five to assist. But first, we must pool our current minds and search the universe for that rip. Since we do not know what the rip or hole looks like, we will be starting systematically searching bit by bit. For this, we need to use the cranial neurotransmitter. We start in fifteen minutes."

Ashton who was quietly sitting to the side and listening in followed Alcyn out of the room. "I don't think I am ready to do this. That headwear looks daunting."

Alcyn placed a friendly hand on Ashton's shoulder. "I used to use one before. It speeds things up, allows you to extend to distances far greater than the brain by itself, and the clarity is superb. It is exhausting. As they were just about to turn into the bathroom, they looked around at the rattling sound echoing up the hallway. "Food has arrived. Make sure you eat it. The brain needs fuel. You may just want to sleep as soon as the session is finished. That is normal. See you back in the room."

Zindel assisted Ashton to place the cranial neurotransmitter on Ashton's head. He ran a few quick tests. "It's working. Let's have a test run on the moon. Focus." Ashton felt his mind travel through space. He came to the moon and then panicked. He was back in the room again.

"One more try. No one can see you, but you can see them. Focus and hold that focus," explained Zindel. Ashton tried again. He felt himself going through space. He was back on the moon. He saw the small moon base and went to look at the facilities. Then he came back. "I think I got the hang of this now."

"Good," said Zindel. "As you have had such limited experience, I want you to hold my hand. You will need a bit of reassurance." Ashton nodded.

Ustin drew in a breath. "Follow me to Julos in sector nineteen." When he felt everyone was keeping pace, he went a bit faster until they all hovered over the void between Julos and Oberon. In thought transmission he said,

"We go right. We will skirt around the edge until halfway around. That is as much we can do on this trip.

They were close to the quarter mark of the galaxy's rim when Alcyn said, *Stop. I think I saw something over to my right. I think there is a ship near that pulsar. There it goes.* The group turned their attention to the fast-moving object. Alcyn swore, *A Draconian mothership. Is anyone for a bit of mayhem?*

Ashton replied, "It is totally my style." Ashton and Alcyn left Zindel and Ustin behind.

Wait for us, called Ustin, *we don't want to miss out!*

When they approached the ship, Ashton asked, "*What do we do now? We don't have any weapons.*

Ustin replied *We do. Our brains. We get inside the brains of the Draconians on the flight deck and the engine room. Then we take over their arms, legs, thoughts, and any other bodily function.*

Zindel leaned over to Ashton, *copy me. The two of us can suddenly make the commander have a medical episode. I take the brain, and you do anything else you wish. Be a puppeteer.* Ashton smirked. *I've done that before. That's my specialty.*

Ustin went for the navigator. The navigator began to follow Ustin's instructions. *Turn the ship around and delete all maps from all systems.* Ustin watched as the Draconian did as instructed. *Now enter the following coordinates.* Ustin watched the Draconian punch in a set of coordinates that redirected the ship towards the nearest star. The commander turned around when he noticed the ship going off course. He was about to roar his anger when he suddenly broke out into song and started wriggling in his seat in time with his own singing. He lively tapped his fingers over the control panel to assist the turning of the ship in response to the new coordinates appearing on the screen in front of him.

The staff on the deck looked stunned until one had the mental capacity to snap out of the shock and scream orders. "The commander has become unhinged! I am taking over!" He ran to the controls to slow down the ship. The commander gave him a powerful backhanded slap which knocked the Draconian to the floor.

Another tried to subdue the commander by taking the fire extinguisher to spray the commander. The commander went suddenly silent and looked at the Draconian with rage. The Draconian holding the extinguisher, then yelled, "Fire! Fire!" and started spraying his people and the controls with foam. The commander tried to walk over to the Draconian but slipped on the moist foamy floor. The ship's control panel started to malfunction as the foam seeped through the edges of the control buttons and levers. Eventually, the control panel short circuited. The ship came to a halt. It was drifting helplessly in space. Zindel and Ashton looked at the mess. *We better find the other two and see what was done in the engine room.*

As they left the flight deck, they noted some of the crew members were being controlled by Ustin's team. Some were dancing while others were engaged in fights. Drunken brawls and assaults on the females slowly spread like cancer through the ship.

 The commander of the ship slowly came back to normal and roared, "Who did this mess?" All pointed to the Draconian who was now nursing the extinguisher as if it were a baby. He was gently rocking and singing to it. The commander's anger was further enraged when the attack alarm sounded.

Zindel asked Ashton, *Did you push that attack alarm button?*

Yeah, It will keep them occupied trying to find an invisible enemy. I always wanted to push one of those buttons.

The commander wiped the foam off the controls and the screen leaving a thick smear which blurred the limited data. He turned on all the controls the best he could knowing some were completely jammed. He ordered those on the flight deck to give readings as to which way the threat was coming. Everything was negative. The commander slammed his fist down on his chair when the ship began to rock. There was a thud followed by a hiss. The commander yelled through the communication system to the engine room. There was no answer. Then he looked up to see all the fighter jets hovering outside the mothership. The commander screamed for them to return. No reply. The ship rocked more and began to burn.

Alcyn grinned. *Okay everyone follow me to the fireworks display. I am in this jet over here. Ustin take the one on the far right. Zindel, you take the far left and Ashton, take the one way over there, the big red one. Shoot on all the others. The rest of you fly as many jets as you can into the mother ship.*

The commander saw from his window his pilots ramming the mother ship. Others were shooting each other until there were four left. The group of four turned their attention to the observational deck. *Direct all the jets into the deck's window and get out of here before the ship explodes.* The commander was speechless when he saw the four jets fly directly into the large observational window. A small hole was formed. The window began to crack. The decompression sucked all those on the flight deck out of the window. The ship spun out of control and exploded.

Let's go back, said Ustin. *That is enough for the day.*

How many Draconians went down? Asked Ashton not quite believing the experience.

Not enough, said Zindel. *But it will give them something to think about when the ship fails to reach its destination. Back to Earth and slowly come back to reality when we reach Daraxon Technologies.*

Zindel, Ashton, Alcyn, and Ustin, and his crew slowly removed their helmets. Although exhausted, they smiled and cheered. "We smashed them!" said Alcyn. He stopped suddenly when he saw Hammond with Robert, Regina, and William looking at them.

"Smashed who or what?" asked Hammond when he saw the cranial neurotransmitters which he hadn't seen for over twenty-five years. "I didn't know they still worked." He nodded towards the helmets.

Ustin said, "Of course, they work. And brilliantly so. We just knocked out a mothership in Julos. It was a combined effort. We were scouting for a rip or tear in the universe and sharp eyed Alcyn saw a ship. Well, the ship is history now."

Regina asked, "What does the rip in the universe look like?"

Zindel blinked and said in a matter-of-fact way. "We have absolutely no idea. Do you have any ideas as to what can cause a rip or tear or hole, whatever you like to call it?"

William looked firmly. "It is all theoretical, theoretical quantum physics. Not my strong area but I may know someone who has an idea on the subject. Do you want me to contact that person?"

Zindel nodded. "Please. The more ideas, the better. No rush. Tomorrow will do."

Hammond asked, "How big was the mothership?"

Ashton answered before the others could, "About the size of this entire complex including the surrounding grounds. Just massive. Much bigger than anything we could ever build."

Ustin added, "We may have to rethink any attack plans or defence plans."

Hammond asked, "I don't believe we have been introduced. Hammond. One of the Bosses of this facility."

"Ustin. I am one of the emissaries like Zindel. Here are five of my crew. Now we know just what we are up against, we may have to impose on you. We have our work cut out. The more we can get to help, the better."

Robert picked up one of the cranial neurotransmitters to examine it closely. "What does this do?"

Zindel took the helmet off him. "More advanced technology. It expands the brain and makes it more efficient."

Robert realized he wasn't going to get any technical answers. He didn't quiz the helmet and how it worked anymore.

"Where is Julos?" asked William.

"Five galaxies away. You don't want to go there. It's the main hub for the Draconians," replied Ashton.

CHAPTER 11

The Draconian Command.

The Reptilian Universe.

General Sanyana read the report. He looked at the other general and the colonel and leaned back in his chair. "One mothership never made it to Indulos. Debris has been found in the area and is currently being analysed. The demise of the ship does not look natural. One body was retrieved and is being examined. A mother ship that was two days behind the first found the beacon with flight data and voice recordings from the deck and data from the engine room. Something made the commander and some of his staff go crazy."

"How so?" asked Colonel Yuma.

"Listen to the recording. Make your own assessment," replied General Sanyana. He pushed the button. Assorted noises and singing were heard, the yell of fire and the sound of the extinguisher. Then the voice of the commander screaming orders and cursing the crying person with the distinguisher followed by yelling about the crew shooting each other in space. More yelling and cursing when four fighter jets flew at the ship's observational window. "That is certainly not natural," said Colonel Yuma. "Was it a burst of powerful magnetism? There is a pulsar not far from that area."

Sanyana shrugged. "It's impossible to know. If it was an outburst, the second ship would have also been affected. It wasn't."

General Blaze was deep in thought. "In the early days of this invasion, it was said Prince Alcyn was able to get inside Lacertian brains and make them do acts of sabotage. This has a similar pattern.

Wasn't Alcyn killed in the palace on Daraxon?"

"Yes. The coward blew himself up with the palace. There was a crater which over time has filled up with water to be a lake, a toxic water lake full of radiated water. Either he escaped or someone has developed the same skills and employed the same tactics."

Sanyana cringed. "That is a powerful weapon. Invisible. Unstoppable. Unpredictable. Worst of all untraceable. The only skilled humans are on Lyria. Someone there must have developed the technique or Alcyn was hiding there all these years. We step up attacks on Lyria and we make sure that Alcyn is dead. And if he is dead, find the bastard who can do this mind control. We will need to capture all Lyrians and interrogate them before consuming them. Do you all agree to change the order? Capture, interrogate before consuming Lyrians?"

Sanyana looked around the room to see the others nodding.

Blaze added, "We interrogate the upper ranks. They would be the only ones privy to such information. Let us move on with the rebels. They are causing more havoc. A small group attacked our jets flying over Segmar. They downed ten fighters before departing."

"Are they hiding in another part of Segmar?" asked Yuma.

"I doubt it. The distant planet of Beta Cancari has reported rebel fighters attacking our and Lacertian crafts. The attacks are frequent and always occur close to the human settlements. It looks like they are trying to protect the native humans on the planet. These humans are small in stature. Word has it, they are not nice to eat; sinewy and somewhat flavourless." said Colonel Yuma.

"Then we shall step up our presence in Beta Cancari. When the rebels are captured, we make a big example of them. Hopefully, it may deter more Lacertians from rising up to defend humans or demand greater rights," said General Blaze.

Yuma said, "The Lacertians will only stop causing trouble if we restore their previous work status."

"Umh. Tell the politicians that," replied Genera Blaze who was now looking at some photos coming in on his personal communication system. "He transferred the photos to form holographic images. The images filled the room.

The others looked up at the information. There were more pictures of the downed mothership.

"The visual recording is starting to come through," he said. All were silent. The commander was seen singing, dancing and tapping multiple controls. Then there was a moment of normality of the commander before the fire extinguisher was spayed. The most horrifying to them all were the images of four fighters suddenly firing on the escaping crew. Then at the end, the rebel crew flew straight into the fight deck to smash the observational window. Then there was an autopsy report on the dead body pulled from space. Burns and more burns. Nothing else. "It starts off like Alcyn's tactics. Then again, it may not be. The rebel could have been disguised as deck staff. The rebels and Alcyn must be working together. That is the last thing we need, Draconian rebels. We have enough issues with Lacertian rebels" said General Sanyana.

"Or Lacertian rebels have penetrated our motherships. Tighten security," said Blaze who was fuming at the visual information.

"Now we have evidence to show those stupid politicians that rebels have escalated and infiltrated our ships. Now they might listen and give the Lacertians some responsibilities which they had before. Just a bit of give to calm things down. They were very capable and thanks to our politicians, made them next to useless. But they will pick up again to their previous level. We better put a proposal to the politicians and evidence of what happens when you break a good working system," said Yuma.

"Unfortunately, some will see it as a sign of weakness to give that bit of occupational promotion. I suggest we aim for the twenty-year-old age group. The rebels are mostly in the age bracket. Those thinking to join the rebels may change their minds and supply information to us. In the meantime, we give Beta Cancari a hammering," said Sanyana.

CHAPTER 12

Beta Cancari.

The Mammalian tribe rushed to the main cave for protection. As they entered, Brondie made a head count. All were inside. A hessian like cover was strung across the entrance to make it look more like the surrounding boulders. The filtered sunlight didn't penetrate more than a metre from the entrance. All members were quiet and motionless with fear.

Brondie laid on the ground on his stomach and put his head out under the hessian cover. He watched as the Lacertians investigated each of the lower caves. He could tell from their gestures; they knew people were around. Personal effects which were left in each cave were examined by the Lacertians. The search ended abruptly. Their eyes were directed upwards by a loud noise.

A Draconian fighter swooped low. The Lacertians fired their laser guns but to no avail. The jet was going too fast. More jets came. Two styles of jets fought in the sky. The search party made use of a cave that they investigated before. They remained until the above dogfight had stopped.

Nage who was leading the search party called the home base. "Draconian crafts have trapped us in a canyon. We are safe."

Kyrina responded, "Stay where you are. I will be sending whatever jets we have to divert their attention. Did you find where the humans go?"

"Affirmative. We are not far from them. They are hiding in some caves. We are using one of their temporary abandoned caves for shelter."

When the aerial battle was over, the search team managed to get back to their small carrier craft. They flew zigzag at low level but did not land anywhere near the base. They landed in a small clearing surrounded by towering trees some eight kilometres away. They quickly covered the craft with nets and camouflage material. They climbed a small hill where they could see the base and give a warning if any Draconian crafts neared them.

From the south and still at a distance, Nage saw a dark cloud. Nage took out a set of binoculars to examine the ominous shadow. He called to base. "We have a visual of a swarm of Draconians heading this way. Evacuate now. Evacuate Now!"

Kryrina, who was the only Lacertian rebel in the base, picked up the transmitter and hobbled as fast as her legs could carry her. She went to a set of shelves at the back of the room and pushed a button. The shelves slid open. She went inside, and quickly closed that door before going down a set of steps. She approached a second door which automatically opened. The smaller door led her to a small passageway. The passage was a natural forming drop in the cave system. A ladder was fixed firmly in place. She climbed down to a small room. She turned on the surveillance cameras in the main headquarters. She could see every detail of the room she just vacated.

She felt the ground shake. A bomb had exploded close by. She waited for a few more minutes before trying to decide to move further down her escape route or stay where she was. She looked again at the screens. Draconians were in her base. She whispered to herself, "Welcome to my den." She pushed a button on a console where the screens were. The bomb in the base exploded killing all six Draconians inside.

Kyrina ran to the next exit which took her through to a volcanic-formed lava tunnel. She sighed with relief when she saw glimmers of daylight. When she reached the exit, she cursed at what she saw. She radioed Nage. "I am safe, but I may not be for long. The Daconians have made a new base right outside the escape exit. I will call when I can."

Nage felt helpless. His best friend was trapped, and he couldn't rescue her. He cursed.

Kyrina settled herself slightly further back in the tunnel. She afforded herself time to rest, if not sleep. She had already formulated plans to escape through the night.

Only using the dim light of the moon, she crept out of her hiding place and down a small slope.

She climbed into the nearest jet and removed the starter switch. She repeated this action five more times. As she removed the switches, she hastily shoved them into a plastic bag. She wanted to disarm more jets but didn't want to push her luck. She edged her way to an area not guarded by any Draconians. She crept out of the area where the jets were stored. As she escaped, she looked back to check the Draconian camp to make sure no one was following.

When she was close to a kilometre away, she dug a small hole and placed the starter switches in it before covering them with dirt. She looked at the rock and its surrounds to memorize the location. She moved on.

She crept quietly away before breaking out into a fast hobble. When she was halfway to the cave where Nage and the others were hiding, she turned on her communication system. "I'm halfway. Not far from the base of the hill."

A voice of one of the team responded, "I see you. Be careful coming up."

"Thanks. See you soon."

Kryina reached the cave where the others were hiding. She sighed with relief. "Hello," she nodded to each. "Nice to see you. There is a small landing base right outside the escape route. I disabled six of the eight fighters by removing the starter switches. I hid the switches in the dirt beside a rock. I didn't want to get caught with them. I didn't want to push my luck by taking more switches."

She sat down. Nage said, "They are coming here in force. I am not sure if they are going to use this place as a base for attacks on Segmar and Xion or trying to wipe us out. What something eat?"

Kyrina held out her hand. "Thanks. I had to blow up the base. Six down. Just a dint in their numbers."

"We saw and heard the explosion. You were very thorough," said Milo who was one of the other group members.

"No real choice. Too much valuable information inside, but most of the important stuff is still lining the walls of the tunnel. I just hope those camping near the exit, don't wander in. We'll be screwed then. Tell me, where did the small humans go?"

"They found a u-shape area in the canyon. It is quite good. There is some evidence of farming starting up. They have a great water supply. It trickles out into a pool and then disappears underground. The nicest water I have tasted for a long time. There were more caves to explore. Most are no more than a metre or two deep, just enough to offer some shelter for a family. They hid elsewhere as personal effects were left behind. I think I know where they are hiding. The Draconians ended our search."

Kyrina considered the information. "Let them be. Draconians are the problem. Now we should all rest. We are going to have a busy day."

The group was woken up by the sound of Draconian jets flying over the area. Nage counted five.

He watched which direction they were flying. The sky seemed to be full of jets all heading in the same direction. "They're flying towards the abandoned Pleiadean city. The radiation must not bother them."

Milo snarled. "Of course not. They send in Lacertians to clean the place up. It does not matter to them if Lacertians die from radiation poisoning. Lacertians are disposable."

"If they have cleared that rubble away, and have decontaminated everything as best they can, they have homes for their growing numbers. We need to get one of their radios to find out what they are up to," said Kyrina feeling angry that more Lacertians could be used in such a manner. She had thoughts to liberate as many as she could but what would be the cost? They were walking dead.

More of Kyrina's group found their way to the cave. They brought news.

"We didn't want to use the communication systems to tell you, the Draconians have been given orders. One is to wipe us out. We are supposed to be captured alive and made an example to all other Lacertians thinking of rebelling. That was the good news. The other bite of not-so-good news is they attacked Xion and Segmar is on the list. When? We don't know. We didn't get that bit. Now the bad news is a reversal of some of the laws governing what jobs the Lacerians can do. Some genius has decided to give Lacertians some of their so-called higher-performing jobs back. I bet that was to create an incentive to break up the growing rebel membership. The new jobs are going to the twenty to forty age group."

Kyrina groaned. "That is our main membership. No more recruiting and let's hope that the recent converts don't give their local groups up to the Draconians. As soon as they think we have been wiped out, they will reverse the decision for Lacertians to have some of their old jobs back. It will be back to slavery and menial tasks. Thanks for the news. Exactly, how did you come by all this?"

"Some small foot patrol was sleeping on the job. We saw a bag with an aerial and guessed it had a radio. They must be awake by now and accusing each other about the disappearance of the radio," Roni held up the radio.

Kyrina clapped her hands. "We were discussing how to get one. Well done."

Nage ventured to the cave entrance to look at the sky. "We are basically trapped here. We can't fly. There are far too many Draconians. We can't go by foot, as there are far too many ground patrols."

He walked back to the group. Milo suggested, "We never explored the true depths of these caves. It is a good opportunity to do so. There could be a way out. Anyone want to come?"

Kyrina agreed with the idea. "Take two others with you. Let's see what is in here."

The first exploratory team returned three hours later. They returned with satchels of native berries. "Look what we found! One of the turns in the cave system goes to a clearing which has filtered light most of the day. Some water and heaps of bushes with these berries. There were other berries which we had never seen before." The berries were placed in the centre of the group. One of the younger females, Cerella, sighed with relief and smiled. "A last something a bit different from rations. No offense Kyrina and Nage, but they do get a bit boring." Nage chuckled. "I have often thought that too. Would you like to divide out the berries?"

The group packed up their camp and moved to the place where the berries were found. "We set up camp here for a couple of days while the other part of the cave system is explored," ordered Kyrina. An hour after sunrise two teams of three set out in different directions."

Late in the afternoon, the parties returned to report. Group one reported, "More caves and more caves. Some had stalactites and stalagmites. One of these caves with stalagmites and stalactites had some water disappearing underground. Otherwise, nothing."

The second team leader reported, "Maybe we have a chance to upset some Draconians. In one of the longest lava tunnels, is a hot mud pool. The place stinks of sulphur. The sulphur is so thick on the ground, you can scrape it off with a shovel. We couldn't see how far the mud pool was due to the sulphur. Too dangerous. We went back a few hundred metres and down another tunnel. It went quite deep before giving a turn to be above another Draconian base. We saw humans were in a cage, obviously, stock. Lacertians were there as well. The Lacertians are chained by one leg and doing the hard labour of clearing the ground. We saw some Draconians with a chart and pointing to locations which we couldn't be sure was north. It looks like they are building a big base. The interesting thing is their water supply is right up against a cliff wall from a waterfall which is about twenty metres high. We can drop a few shovels of sulphur into the water from the top of the waterfall to give them stomach pain if not kill them. We can also make sulphur bombs or grenades to create a bit of havoc. Ideally, making an explosion to create a muddy landslide would do the best job. Unfortunately, we don't have that capacity."

From another of the group, Arika suggested, "Maybe we can make bombs. The walls in another cave close by are lined with graphite. We mix the graphite with the sulphur. At least it will make some fireworks. A distraction."

Kyrina thought about the information. "Old fashioned, but it could work. Let's plan this attack and let the Draconians build their base. We can infiltrate at night to plant explosives for maximum destruction. No one takes this planet from us. The Pleiadeans gave it to us. The Draconians have no right to steal it. Let's do some small experiments in bomb-making."

The radio crackled. All went silent. It was a news report:

This is Draconian Command. This is General Sanayansa. Congratulations to the battalions in Normaria. The planet of Xion has been taken. Segmar is under heavy attack and is expected to fall shortly. Beta Cancari is also under our control. Congratulations to that battalion. Unfortunately, the leader of the rebels, Kyrina has escaped. There is a million credits bounty on her head and half a million for each other member of the rebel group.

Milo said sarcastically, "Only half a million credits. We have to do something about that."

Arika gave him a jab in the ribs. "Now, now. Don't be upset. After the bombings, you will get your wish." Milo blew her a kiss. Arika pretended to catch it.

"Let's get started on making bomb," said Kyrina.

Throughout the day, the small rebel group made their bombs. They rested until the early hours of the morning. Bombs were placed around strategic rock overhangs and on the upper ends of a cliff face. Three nights later, most of the bombs were in place. Now it was time to place bombs around the Draconian camp. Then it was waiting for the best opportunity for maximum damage.

A large Draconian ship circled the sky just over a week after the last of the bombs in the camp were set. Kyrina spoke softly, "There is the prize hovering above us. Just wait and see who or what comes out of that ship."

Fifty fighter jets poured out of six exits. Then from an upper level, a personnel craft flew out.

Nage used his binoculars. "I see some V.I.Ps in that craft. From this angle, I just can't see who is inside." He waited until the craft came closer and was descending. He grinned. "Let's give them a welcoming surprise."

He looked at Kyrina for confirmation. "Let it land first. Only that craft goes and all the bastards inside. Make it look like some careless base work. They have been removing trees all week with mini explosives. Get ready just on touch down." Nage nodded. He counted down and then pushed the remote control for explosives ten and eleven.

The craft went up. The fireball pierced the sky before extending itself horizontally. The heat caused the other primitive bombs they made to explode in the camp, a chain reaction. Many Draconians were instantly killed. Many more laid injured. The hovering mothership disappeared instantly. "Did you get a look at the faces inside the V.I.P. craft before it went up?" asked Milo.

Nage replied. "I am not sure. Some colonels and a couple of politicians. I only recognized one politician. That was Hashim. Maybe it was an aide with him. I didn't recognize the colonel."

Below the cave where the rebels held out, a fire raged through the camp. It was uncontrolled. The smoke billowed into the sky. The group watched the fire burn. Late in the afternoon, the small amount of rain put out some of the smouldering material. Kyrina cautioned the group.

"Don't go exploring the mess. There could be survivors ready to shoot." Using the binoculars, she looked to where the bedraggled humans were corralled. A few survivors were writhing from their burns. The group could not see any of the enslaved Lacrtians. Nage lamented, "We don't have much of a choice. We will have to shoot the humans to put them out of their misery. Our medical supplies are just about non-existent since our own base blew up."

The next night when the rebels were sure no other Draconians would arrive to rescue the survivors, Kyrina's group ventured into the destroyed camp. The devastation was complete.

Cerella went to the enclosure where the humans were stowed. A tear crept out of one eye as she pointed her laser gun at a man. The man looked at her with accepting empty eyes. "Sorry," she said to the man. "I don't have medicine to help you." The man nodded and pointed. "You are a rebel I have heard about. There is a baby buried under the collapsed shelter. Take the baby. Put me out of my agony." Cerella shot the man and then walked to the mangled mess which was once a crude shelter. Inside she found a baby sleeping in a reinforced section. The reinforcement was enough to keep debris away from the baby. Around the dirty naked baby was an empty cup and an empty bottle of water. No food. Nothing else. Cerella picked up the baby to take it to Milo and Kyrina.

"Look what I found," said Cerella. "Just over there in that pile. I would have missed it except for the injured man telling me where he was. How old do you think it is?"

Kyrina laughed. "You are asking me that? I have absolutely no idea. I never had children. I have no idea what to do with her or is it a him?"

Milo looked at the child. "It's a him. We take him to the Mammalians and leave the baby with them.

It is better it grows up with them."

Kyrian nodded. "Yes. We can take him there. A good idea. What do we call him?"

Cerella looked at the boy. "I call you Foundling."

"What kind of name is that?" asked Arika who was now just steps away from the group.

"Have you a better suggestion?" asked Cerella.

"Nah. Just don't get attached."

They were soon joined by more members of the group. Roni placed a bag down. "Okay break up the dotting. I got a nice bag of goodies. He tipped his findings on the ground. Kyrina gave a sigh of relief.

"A few medical supplies and canned food from Lacerta. What a luxury! Well done."

Two days later, Kyrina's group was at the u-shaped area in the canyon. They surveyed the area before approaching. Akira volunteered to take the baby to the Mammalians.

Carefully she left the cave. She was shadowed by Milo. She walked to the edge of their settlement and waited.

A Mammalian child screamed and ran for cover. The scream alerted the adults in the group. Armed with bows and arrows, they approached Cerella. Cerella placed the baby on the ground and stepped back. She pointed and then gestured for them to take the baby. She turned and left.

Milo, who was watching Cerella coming up the hill facing towards him all the time, noticed the Mammalians examining the baby. He was different. Fair hair, green eyes, and pale skin. They too looked confused and wondered where such an odd baby came from and why did the creature give the baby to them. There was a heated debate. An outcast was now in their midst.

Brondie considered the situation. "Leave this ghost baby with me. Maybe he is an omen. Maybe he is an orphan, and the creature gave it to us to raise."

Brondie's wife, Netis, looked at the baby. "He looks cute, but he could be evil. I will raise the child, but I will kill the child if I see any evil coming from him. I will call him Gannon." She looked at Brondie. "No one in this tribe will look after such a baby. Where did that creature find such a child? If it turns into a lizard creature, I kill it. It looks healthy but is it evil?"

Brondie could only think of one possible answer. "The mother maybe dead. Do you remember we heard rumours of a tribe of people? They were tall and had fair skin."

Netis nodded. "Is he one of them?"

Brondie shrugged. "Who knows? They all disappeared. I was told many were taken away by those creatures. They are the same creatures which make war in our sky and destroyed our land. That creature who gave us Gannon was not scared of us."

Netis grunted at the comment. She whispered, "Stupid men."

The rebel group watched the baby being carried to a cave. The adopting mother placed the baby on the ground outside the cave. The boy cried. She picked him up and carried him inside. "One mission accomplished," said Kyrina. "Let's get back to this never-ending war. Her thoughts drifted back to the Pleiadean president she briefly met a few years ago, *He's dead along with the rest of the settlement. I wonder if there are any other survivors out there. I hope so. I am getting very tired of battle, day in and day out.*

CHAPTER 13

Genesis.

Same Time period.

The first lot of the earth military advisors arrived via the transporter. They were met at the special entrance in the motel. Each carried a box of mixed products; ten arrivals with ten boxes. More boxes of equipment were in the transporter. Those boxes would be unloaded later. The military advisors checked in. Then they were led to the administration building across the road.

Partum and Zanthe acted as the main host and introduced them to the gathered crowd which was a mix of politicians and military personnel. Tayee and Alcyn PZ who arrived earlier acted as diplomats and interpreters.

Tayee introduced the earth people to the Gensesians in the conference room. Then he briefly explained the information given to him by Zindel. There were spreading attacks by the Draconian race who fancied humans as food. "We have confirmation, they are in this galaxy. Okay, it may seem for our earth counterparts a bit farfetched or in the realm of science fiction, but it is true." Tayee looked around the room and noticed the earth delegation looking overwhelmed. He decided to go back in history, a short exposé to ease their minds. Then Alcyn PZ took over.

"There is a group of advanced humans who have helped us and will continue to help us in this battle.

Zindel who made a fleeting visit to the U.N. a few months ago has been seeking assistance from other ambassadors-cum-warriors. He realizes he alone cannot fight these creatures. His help is co-dependent on us, we lesser developed humans. Recently, I have had the privilege of working with him to destroy one mothership." Alcyn stopped speaking for a moment as flashes of the destruction crossed his mind. He looked up and continued. "That mother ship had about one hundred fighter jets and as a guess over 2,000 Draconians. It was heart-warming to know, that that monster of a ship and its passengers will not cause further harm to the scattered human races in this universe." Alcyn saw an earth general ask, "Exactly how did you do it?"

Alcyn looked at the others in the room before answering. "I hope I can make this as simple as I can.

On Earth, in the cold war era, certain countries had spies trained in remote viewing. They were given coordinates for their minds to travel and explore such locations. The spies physically stayed in their country, but their minds travelled abroad. Some groups of people call this astral travelling; the military called it remote viewing. The small group of people I was with did the same thing. But due to the vast distances, we had to use a machine on our heads to boost both range and power. Using the cranial neuro-transmitter, as the head-set machine is called, we were physically on Earth but our minds were in the galaxy of Julos. We were looking for a tear in the universe. We have no idea where the tear is or even what it looks like. All we know, when we find that tear, rip, or hole, we can attack the incoming Draconian ships.

"On this exploration, we spotted a ship. As an experiment, we entered the brains of some of the Draconian staff, namely the flight deck staff and the engineers. We made the navigator wipe the data of all flight paths to anywhere. This was a decoy. Then we added the data to fly into a pulsar. The commander's mind was taken over, and let's say, he wasn't himself, singing and dancing and he changed the controls to suit the new navigational path to the pulsar. Then another Draconian lost his mind and used the fire extinguisher to spray all over the control panels and other staff. He wasn't exactly popular as the foam seeped into the controls and locked them in place. The engineers were made to add foreign substances into the nuclear reactor which powered the ship. It takes a while for the foreign matter to go through the system.

"Ashton who is a member of our team pushed the fire alarm button. The jets sped out of the mother ship. That didn't save them. We crawled into the minds of four pilots and opened fire on the escaping fighters. Then we made the four-renegades fly into the flight deck of the mothership. Bang. Everything shattered into thousands of pieces. We know we cannot do this technique of remote viewing and attack all the time. It is both physically and mentally draining. It is also random, too random to be the only form of attack.

"Zindel has given us plans of an attack craft. He is supplying Daraxon Technologies. He also gave a race of people called, Lyrians, the blueprints for manufacturing sophisticated jets. When the crafts are built, he will supply a new weapon which he calls a cannon. The cannon shoots out a mix of radiation rays, artificial gravity, anti-matter, dark matter and an electromagnetic field which is similar to black holes shooting out star matter. His problem is he needs pilots. He said the controls are simple to master. The issue is for a pilot to think well ahead of the craft's travel speed. The pilot has to know what will be ahead of him before he gets there. It is not as easy as you may think. These crafts are designed for deep space attacks. These need to be coupled with jets that are defending their home planets. Of course, it is better to fight in space away from planets, but the reality is, we need home defence. Now we need to combine our resources to defend ourselves."

There was a knock on the door. There was a hush. Partum said loudly, "Enter." A young lady walked in holding a note. She gave the note to Patrum. He accepted the note and excused himself as he read the short note in front of others. As he read the note, colour drained from his face. Zantha looked concerned and whispered, "What is the matter?"

Partum stood up and excused himself for interrupting the flow of the meeting. "We just got word of two events. The first is the planet of Xion. It is already under Draconian control. Segmar could fall any day. The second is much worse for us. At the same time, a distress message has come from one of the mining camps on Affen Welt. A Draconian mother ship was spotted flying over the planet. It hasn't yet attacked the camps but is currently exploring the planet. It will be a matter of hours before the camps will be attacked. The supervisors are closing all camps and leaving some of the heaviest mining equipment behind in the haste to get out. Affen-Welt is not far from here. We will be next under attack." Partum sat down in his chair as other Genesians murmured their concern.

The earth people looked confused and worried. One earth advisor asked, "How much time do you people have before you are attacked?"

Partum replied while his face remained pale. "We simply don't know. It could be a week. It could be months. Regardless, it is now urgent we unite and battle this enemy." He looked to Alcyn. "Can you get in touch with this Zindel person and tell him what has happened?" Alcyn nodded and moved away from the conference table. He moved out of the room but returned minutes later. "I have sent a message. Zindel is in sector nineteen. That is where the galaxy of Julos is. He will communicate by hologram. He'll respond in a few minutes."

There was a whoosh sound. A one-metre-tall hologram image of Zindel appeared on the table. He looked grim when he introduced himself. "I am Zindel. Alcyn PZ has informed me of the nearby attack on Affen-Welt and the two on Xion and Segmar. I am aware of the fall of Xion and now Segmar has fallen. Umm messages via telepathy travel faster, safer, and more reliable than hardwired communication systems. I will advise my superiors about Affen-Welt. I will also inform my research team to step up the production of my war jets, but I require pilots. I will be coming to your planet tomorrow at the earliest to scout for pilots. Have any details of any attack plans ready for me to review." With that Zindel disappeared.

Zindel cursed and contacted Ustin of the news. Then he refocused his attention on the Draconian mother ship heading for Lacerta. He fired his new cannon on the craft. The ball of mixed star matter hit the base of the ship. It instantly blew up causing a fiery ball. Extreme heat. Extreme light. Only a few remnants escaped the vaporization zone.

When Zindel arrived at Genesis, he went directly to the administration building. Zantha, Partum and a group of other administrators met him at the entrance. He was ushered to the room where he saw ten earth people and Alycn PZ. He greeted them before placing himself on the nearest seat.

One of the head engineers, Ortzi explained. "All the camps have shut down. Most of the equipment has been brought back. We had to leave behind all the large pieces of heavy machinery. We did move that equipment underground into the existing tunnels. The equipment was covered with sheeting to keep most of the dirt out. The tunnels were initially sealed with doors. The doors were covered with different sized boulders and dirt on top to resemble a dead-end. We feel the equipment is secured as much as it could be under such short notice. The above ground tell-tale signs of mining have been hidden as much as possible with a mix of transplanted trees, rocks, dirt, and holographic images of the surrounding landscape.

That cover will not last long, about a month at best. It will require a team to recharge the holographic images to keep the mining activities hidden.

"The craft we saw was the mothership. It was absolutely enormous, much bigger than any Lacertian ship we had ever seen in the past. That is going by the information in our joint short history. By comparison, our crafts look like toys. We don't have hope of defeating such large crafts. We didn't hang around on Affen-Welt to see what the fighter jets looked like.

"The mother ship circled the planet more than once. No doubt it was scanning for life forms. We are not sure if it detected us. It would have detected the apes and with luck assumed our mining operations were also part of the ape population. The apes also mine and manufacture but to a limited degree. We know they can make cars; not fancy ones but they do serve their purpose of moving around quickly."

Zindel added, "The mother ships I have seen carry about fifty to two hundred plus fighter jets and a lot of foot soldiers. As an estimate, each craft has about 2,000 to 5,000 personnel on board. Half of that population are Lacertians. Most are modified ones with that drug. These are disposable soldiers in the eyes of Draconians. The rest are Lacertian slaves or assigned breeders. The Draconians have reduced Lacertians to slaves for all dirty and hard labour. They are also disposable." Zindel heard a series of gasps. He continued, "I do know for certain; we have Lacertian rebels helping us on other planets. Some just want to help Lacertians and others want to help both Lacertians and humans. The apes have no friends. So, it will be interesting to see what they do with the apes; eat them or enslave them."

"As for the defences here, what do we have available in the way of fighter jets and pilots?" asked Zindel.

Patrum squirmed in his seat. "Very little. The population which migrated here barely reached a million. We were focused on building everything from scratch and exploring this planet for resources. Water, edible and medicinal plants are its strong points. Minerals are its weakest. There are pockets of rare minerals but that is about all. That is why we mine Affen-Welt. The population has expanded another 20,000 since settlement. Most are in their teens or young adults who are all learning different occupational skills. Flying a craft is compulsory but none have experienced defensive flying. We don't have people to teach them for starters and in the past, it wasn't necessary. Although we did try to make a small team of defence personnel, it has kind of fizzled out as not many saw any career advantage. A few hell-raisers stayed on as they saw the idea as a legitimate way to express their desire for speed and danger." Patrum coughed. "We have ten such youths."

An earth advisor spoke, "We have pilots, but we don't have them trained in the equipment that is required. I doubt we have any who could operate in space. I think they could defend our planet at the best."

Zindel looked at the advisor. "I have crafts being built but no pilots. But my crafts are for deep space. Zindel gave a deep sigh and muttered to himself, "Nothing matches. Start thinking laterally besides mind reading skills. The Lyrians need help as well."

Zindel went into a trance; he communicated with Ustin. *Can you get other emissaries? We need to stop the spreading invasion.* Ustin dropped what he was doing. He replied. *If we can get ten of us together with their trainees, we may have a chance. I have been looking at Sector Nineteen and studying it for anomalies. I can't identify anything yet. It would help if I know what I am* looking *for.*

Zindel closed his eyes. *A rip, a hole, just something that is unusual. Sorry. I can't be more helpful.*

Try looking down from above rather than being in the sector. Something may show up that way.

Ustin nodded. *I've done that. The only thing that is worth checking out is a large black mass surrounded by a massive thick dust and gas cloud at the edge of the galaxy. It is so dense I found it difficult to penetrate by myself. I'll go back there now and will report back.* Zindel snapped out of the trances and focused on the meeting.

He made a hologram of sector nineteen. The image floated above everyone's head. He pointed with a laser beam when he noticed the dense cloud Ustin may have been referring to. "My friend Ustin is examining in detail this area here. It is a super dense cloud of gas and dust. Normally, the clouds have a white hole or star manufacturing new stars. Powerful gravitational forces with assorted sound waves, light waves, microwaves, gamma rays, and so on. I will know in a day or two if this cloud is a possible gateway to the other universe. I give it a fifty percent chance."

Partum asked, "If it is?"

"Then we can do some decent planning for the attack but being in a cloud will be problematic. It will be a new set of obstacles. Let's find out what is in that cloud before panic buttons are pushed."

Alcyn PZ was more focused on Affen-Werlt than what was going on around him. His mind slipped in and out of trances. He spoke while in one of the trances. "*A mother ship has landed on Affen Welt. It is on one of the ape-created clearings. The underground apes came out to defend the area. They were killed. The Draconians are using the modified Lacertians as food tasters. Many Lacertians are seriously ill with food poisoning. I think many will die.*"

Patrum asked, "Are they using Lacertians as lab rats?"

 Alcyn put his hand up to stop him from talking. He gave a description of what he was seeing. "*The large jungle gorillas are coming out of hiding. They are attacking the Draconians and Lacertians outside the mother ship. Guess what? The gorillas are winning. They have killed all Lacertians and Draconians who didn't make it to the ship.*" Alcyn shook his head and was back in the room again. "Okay, the apes aren't exactly welcoming the Draconians or Lacertians. Do we use them as pawns?"

Patrum recalled the first big skirmish when Prince Alcyn told him when he visited Earth. "When you were Prince Alcyn, you transported the apes to three Lacertian ships. Two were destroyed. One was hijacked by the giant ape who directed the craft into a super nova. We need a transporter with a viewer to do that trick again. But I doubt it would work. The Draconians now know, the apes are not worth pursuing. However, if they wake up to the fact the planet is rich in mineral resources, they may exterminate the apes by whatever means they think suitable and mine the planet. We can't afford that to happen. We must wait and see which direction the Draconians will take on that planet.

We are not that far away from that planet. If they find us, we are in trouble. Now let's get back to organizing tactics and resources."

When the meeting was over and a rough plan was in place, the earth-based people entered the transporter.

Back on Earth, they went to the conference room in Daraxon Technologies. The room was full of delegates from fifty nations. All were eager for the report.

CHAPTER 14

Lyria.

Same Time Period.

The president of the planet Lyria, Folami, inspected the first batch of crafts. She looked at the blueprints and then back at the crafts. Her eyes were going back and forth. She rolled up the blueprints, and handed them to the head of manufacturing, Kerron. She walked around the nearest craft and climbed in. She studied the controls. Just a few controls. She thought, *Minimalist in design. The complexity is obviously in the electronics.* She climbed out of the cockpit and asked, "Show me the electronics and the motor system." Kerron took her to an assembly room where two more crafts were being built. He pointed. "Before I show you the electronics, I need to show you the fuselage. The two are integrated." Kerron held up what appeared, at first sight, a sheet of metal. "This is the outer skin." He held up another sheet that had a slight blueish tinge. "The inner skin. Now watch what I do." He placed the two sheets together. They fused instantly leaving no evidence they were two separate pieces.

Then he took the sheet over to the test room where a chamber for controlled tests was set up. He placed the sheet inside. He handed Folami a set of protective glasses before lowering the protective shield. "I am going to run every light beam, every sound beam, every chemical we know onto that sheet. I will run all items simultaneously to speed up the demonstration." After ten minutes in the chamber, Kerron said, "We wait ten more minutes for decontamination and for the temperature to drop."

He opened the door and held up the sheet. "You saw the impacts. You saw some dints and some damage. The sheets self-mend. Not a sign of damage can be seen even under high-powered microscopes. Absolutely nothing."

He carried the sheet back to the workbench. He added what appeared to be a fine piece of fabric. In fact, it was the electronics of the craft. Kerron carefully placed the fabric on the blue side of the sheet which was previously fused. The same again occurred. The electronics fused into the sheet. It self-welded to be totally seamless. "Now follow me back to the test room and to that chamber."

Again, Kerron flooded the chamber with assorted technological assaults. The sheet at one stage appeared to start to liquify. Then seconds later it repaired itself. When the tests were over, and the required wait time was finished, he opened the chamber and pulled out the sheet. It appeared as if nothing had happened. Perfect. The electronics were tested after several barrages. Nothing damages the electronic. It self-repairs. It is virtually indestructible."

Folami took the sheet and inspected it. She tossed it on the ground and stomped on it. A dent appeared then it disappeared. "Give it a test now. Just see how well that kind of treatment does to the electronics."

Kerron ordered a test on the sheet. There was a minor glitch at first which seemed to repair seconds later. He reported back. "The glitch repaired itself. It took a shade longer than normal."

Folami took the sheet again and placed it in another chamber. "Let's see what happens now."

She turned on the chamber. Multiple hammers came out slamming the sheet at different strengths and speeds. After three minutes, she stopped the machine and waited for the chamber to cool down before opening it. "Test it now," she ordered as she handed over a very dinted sheet.

After a battery of tests, Kerron reported, "A near total system failure. It took a long time for the self-repairs to complete. Two have not self-repaired."

Folami smirked. "Never tell me something is indestructible. Add an impact shield to all assembled crafts and to others coming off the assembly line. Now pilots. Who and how many do we have?'

Kerron ran his hand through his hair. "The academy is training all pilots. The pilots who use our crafts are being retrained for this style of craft. All new intakes are learning this advanced jet craft first and then they will be learning our style of crafts. That makes about two hundred pilots being retained for this new craft and five hundred more going directly for the new craft."

Folami was surprised. "We need more pilots. That is not enough. I will make it compulsory for our teenagers to learn to fly our two main war vehicles. It will not be popular, but our choices are limited. Each teenager will have to sign in for one of three time slots on the weekend. That is as much flexibility as we can afford at the moment. Each class will be two hours in length. By the time most finish the final year, they will be qualified pilots. It will be a bonus for their career paths. I will leave it to your staff and the academy to organize pilot training to teenagers." She gave Kerron a nod before walking away to her craft.

Kerron cursed. He could already hear in his mind the head of the academy, Boazal, screaming through the communication system. He looked at the sheet of metal which had undergone a physical pounding. It looked normal. He ran another test. Two repairs had not been completed. He isolated the area and examined them in detail. He cursed again. They related to the air filter in the craft. He made notes. He would try to contact Zindel with the discovery and get advice as to how to repair the fault.

CHAPTER 15

Lords of the Universe.

Same Time Period.

Xetron turned on the holographic communication system. He began the meeting with Thuma, Jose and Azna. He had already spoken with Sigma before and had recorded his thoughts on the situation.

Sigma was away to personally examine the effects of the invasions in sectors twenty, twenty-one, and now threatening eighteen. Sector Nineteen would take longer as he wanted to see just where and how the rip or hole occurred. Like everyone else, he wasn't sure what he was looking for. He told Xetron, he would report back as soon as possible. He hoped the inspections of sectors twenty and twenty-one would be complete before the conference was over.

Sigma came online. He reported. "Sector twenty-one has had invasions. The people who are still there have been displaced from their homes and living in squalid conditions in what best can be called stys. The smell of death is everywhere. Xion and Segmar have fallen. Beta Cancari is a bit unusual. I have seen Lacertians attacking Draconians. It looks like a rebel force going against the Draconians. Nothing more to report there.

"I am in sector twenty now. All of Amada and Oberon are under Draconian control. There is some resistance to the Draconians but that is slowly dying down. The Draconians have withdrawn a directive that restricted Lacertians to menial tasks. The humans are still in a bad way. They are being farmed only. Very few are used as servants or slaves. When they reach a certain age, they are used or sold off for food. That is all I can say about these two dismal galaxies. As for the White Galaxy as it is referred to, The Milky Way, the planet of Lyria is still holding out against attacks. The Draconians have discovered the planet full of apes, Affen-Welt as the Genesians call it. It is too early to tell if they will settle on the planet. They have discovered the apes are toxic.

"As for sector nineteen, I only see Draconians taking over all Lacertian planets. I am about to start searching for the rip or gap to the other universe. I will report back if I see anything which could be a possibility." He closed down the communication system.

Xetron looked at his colleagues. With a slight disappointment in his tone, "He has basically confirmed what Zindel had mentioned before." He looked to the other three. "We have been here before the dawn of time. Surely, one of us must know how this rip could have occurred or even what it looks like. What about the research teams? Have you asked them to give us guidelines as to what it could look like?"

Thuma nodded. "I have. Simply it could be anything anywhere. They did some experiments. The results show one consistency. It depends on the surroundings and available material as to what a hole or rip looks like. Change something by ten per cent, you get a different appearance, naturally a different result. There are too many variables in the galaxies. Even colliding galaxies or black holes can disguise a rip or be a rip itself."

Jose looked perplexed. "My research team has had similar results. Anything and everything could be a hole or rip. I am going to be hypothetical now. Suppose there is no rip. Suppose there was a malfunction or random event which occurred; it went unnoticed. Suppose the evolution of these creatures are of our own doing? An accident. Something pushed under the carpet so to speak."

Azna closed her eyes and scoffed at the hypothetical. "Really? How could any of us be so negligent?

Audits on everything are so thorough. I very much doubt it. I do believe sector nineteen is the source. We should focus on that area and assemble all emissaries to assist in searching. Zindel has already asked Ustin for assistance. He needs more support. I think the best thing we can do is make battle crafts and wipe out as many Draconians and Lacertians on the existing planets. When we find the rip or source, then we attack it. Does everyone agree to call in all emissaries?" There were a series of nods and yeses. "I will contact the emissaries and reassign them to help Zindel." The communication system closed.

Xetron sat back in his chair and swivelled it to face the large glass wall separating him from space. He drummed his fingers on the armrest. He contemplated the idea Jose mentioned; an accident within sector nineteen. Precious time would be lost searching for a rip which no one knows what it looked like. He swung his chair around and pressed a button. He spoke directly to his audit team. "Find me the creation records of sector nineteen. Bring all the input and results data. Be on standby for retrieval of more ancient history."

Two hours later a hefty file appeared on his large screen. Xetron read the information carefully. Nothing was out of order. He read it again to be sure he hadn't missed any detail. The chemical mix was right. No abnormalities. With confidence, he closed the file but kept it just in case he needed to refer to it again. He requested the next file containing the plans for the creation of the stars and planets.

The base page was blank, a blank canvas. That was normal.

He read the next file twice. Speeds, light, sound, time, matter, gravity, and location were in order. Something in location nagged at the back of his mind. He read that part again. He still drew a blank. Xetron asked for a planning file, a file which existed well before sector nineteen was created. He studied the map.

He drew a green line around the boundary of sector nineteen. He looked at the perimeter and the immediate surroundings. There could be something. He enlarged each sub-section looking for anything that was out of order. Nothing. Then he focused his attention on the internal section. Again nothing. Going slightly further inwards, he scanned each section. Nothing again. He continued this method of examination until he reached the centre where the largest blackhole spun around engulfing all types of matter approaching its boundaries, the event horizon. The event horizon was designed as a cosmic vacuum cleaner sucking up traces of anything that ventured too close to its borders. He studied the black hole more. At a critical time and when the mix was right, it would shoot out star matter, the regeneration of stars, or other trace matter to keep the engine rooms of the galaxy in motion. Again nothing. Xetron called for the latest observational data.

When the new data and current positioning of planets and stars arrived, he overlaid the new information over the original. He punched in information regarding the precession of the stars and planets during the time of creation and compared each unit to the current day. There was nothing until he reached two million years ago. A smudge showed up. He highlighted the spot and enlarged the picture. He examined it carefully. He tapped his finger on the spot before saving it to a different file. He continued his examination in 100,000-year increments. The spot was there. Over thousands of years, it changed ever so slightly, growing bigger and rounder. It never moved even when everything around it moved in the ordained natural procession. He smiled to himself. "Got you."

Xetron then went back to the original preplanning files. He examined the exact same spot. Nothing.

He enlarged the area over one hundred times. A smudge mark finally showed its presence. A flaw in the fabric of space. He re-contacted the other lords with his findings.

Xetron immediately examined the area. He groaned at what he saw. He spoke to Sigma. "It is buried in a cloud of dense dust and gas. It was the one Zindel and Ustin reported earlier. It is so dense; it is impossible to penetrate with a single mind. I am taking a guess, a black hole and a white hole working in unison or joined one behind the other. The typical funnel feature will be non-existent. How can that happen?"

Xetron replied, "I have absolutely no idea. Can you go in and collect the sample?"

"I will give it a go," said Sigma.

A minute later, Sigma reported, "I have a sample for analysis. I could only get to the outer rim so it could give a false reading."

"Something is better than nothing," replied Xetron.

When Sigma returned to his laboratory, the samples were given to his researchers. "I want the results like yesterday," he informed his workers. He saw them drop their current tasks and immediately start on the analysis of the sample placed on the bench.

Two days later Sigma received a report:

'Chemical Analysis of All Samples of Dust and Gas.'

He passed the report to Xetron. Xetron read the report in detail. He compared it with the original chemicals used in creation. Nothing was out of order. He knew the sample was from the edges of the sector. The flaw, he thought, was much further into the system. The only thing he could see was a smudge, but that could be anything like a new system self-forming. He was annoyed. He sent the research work he had done and coupled it with the most current analysis to all the Lords. He highlighted the smudge for further examination.

Xetron swivelled his chair to look at space. He closed his eyes to allow all the data to run through his mind. *A smudge? A flaw? But nothing appeared out of place. That smudge was now rounder and larger.* Something wasn't right and he wondered just how he or anyone else could physically examine the exact spot. It was gnawing at his mind.

Jose contacted Xetron the next day. He praised Xetron for the work he had done. Jose said,

"I think I may have a way to penetrate that smudge or cloud."

"How?" asked Xetron.

"It is an experiment. It is risky. It could be a waste of time as well. We call all the emissaries plus all their final-year recruits to assist. That would make about fifty minds all wearing cranial neuro-transmitters going in at the same time. It is worth a try. If we do succeed, then we can work out a strategy to close the hole or rip and then wipe out all the Draconians. I am willing to call everyone in. Would two days be enough time?"

Xetron considered the idea. Make it three days. Make all of them fly into our base on Aryn-Adon 2.

I will notify the staff of the incoming emissaries and recruits."

Three days later, Xetron and the other Lords of the Universe addressed the group before them.

Xetron gave details of the mission and the location of the target.

There was a series of clicks around the room as the cranial neuro-transmitters were placed on heads. Everyone adjusted their seats to their most comfortable position. On the countdown of three the collective minds focused on the location of the flaw or smudge and its surroundings. A few hours passed before each returned. Each was given time to write their report. They were collected by Azna. The group was dismissed but told they had to stay at the base.

Azna and the rest of the Lords read through and collated the results. Two stood out; they had different information from the rest. Where others had reported the chocking mass of gas and dust similar to the laboratory chemical analysis, and general physical structure of the location, these two had seen something different. A near perfect circle with the edges glowing in red, blue, and yellow. The glow of the colours was like flames of a fire. The centre of the circle was black but at regular intervals, electromagnetic waves, microwaves, gamma waves, and radio waves shot across the lower half. It was followed by an intense white light that glowed for ten seconds before disappearing. The top half showed no activity. The location on both reports were the same. Xetron held up the reports. "I think we have found the source. We will bring back the group for a more detailed examination.

The next day the group was back. Xetron gave more precise details. He added, "If by any chance we see a mother ship coming through, blow it up immediately. Do not ask for permission. He pointed to the left side of the room. "This group heads for the engine room. Stop the engines. Get them to mix fuels or clog up the workings of fuel lines. Anything to make a mal function. To do that you need to crawl into their brains and take control of either Lacertians or Draconians. Make them wreck their own ship." To the middle group, he stated, "Go for the ship's decks on all levels. Crawl into their minds and create havoc with behaviour and anything else to make chaos. Make them your puppets. The sillier the actions, the better." To the group on the right, he smiled. "Attack the flight deck. Get them to break their observational glass and wreck their controls. Again, crawl into their brains."

The group focused on the narrowed search area. They examined it in greater detail. Then one emissary brought the attention of the others. "Look up. Near the top of the circle. A mother ship is coming. Fun time starts now."

As pre-planned, the groups went into attack formation. Within minutes, the ship exploded sending its debris not only through the cloud but also to the unknown space behind it. Before the group could get back to the initial task, two more mother ships appeared. Again, the groups split up for the different areas of the ships. Two explosions. More debris. Sigma called the group to stop. "Head back to base. Nice work."

When all returned, Azna commented, "Excellent work. Write your reports about what you observed in that ring. No need to mention the destruction of the three ships. We all know what each of you did and the results. We will see you all tomorrow. Get some rest and don't forget to hydrate and eat well."

Thuma and Azna read through the reports. Many were the same. Although they were told no need to say what they did to the Draconian ships, some felt the need to share their experiences. Thuma and Azna chuckled at what each did on the ships. Thuma laughed as he stopped reading further and read the report aloud. "On board the ship, I managed to get the Draconians dancing. Some were in pairs doing something akin to a waltz while others doing something which resembled rap. Some were in a congo line. The Draconian music was turned up to full volume. The alcohol came directly out in bottles; not a glass to be seen. The Draconians who slipped stayed down on the ground laughing and cuddling whoever fell on top. On another floor, the males became very amorous towards any female they saw. Age and rank didn't matter. It was an all-in affair. Again, work was abandoned. In the mess hall, food fights broke out. Aggression was at its peak. They attacked each other with weapons. Within minutes, there was only one survivor standing and he was covered in a mix of Draconian blood and food. The survivor walked out of the mess hall and joined in the growing orgy."

Thuma put the report down. "I did say create havoc, but I wasn't expecting this level."

Azna smirked. "We didn't clarify what we meant by havoc. They achieved it. If the Draconian command saw what was going on, they would have shot their own staff. That in itself would have been highly distracting. Let's see what happens tomorrow."

Jose's eyes surveyed the room filled with recruits wearing their head gear. I heard that you guys were very creative and downed three mother ships. Now, the same applies. Down any mother ship. But this time we aim to go through that circle. The top half seems to be the main entrance. Please avoid the lower half as it is full of nasties. We are going to see what exactly is on the other side of this flaw and take any attack to their home universe. Get ready. Start the cranial neurotransmitters. Get comfortable. Go."

The group focused on the top half of the circle. They entered the top half and paused. They looked around. The back of the ring was a completely white glowing circle. In front of them was total blackness. Azna commanded, "I see where the white light emanates. The hole is either adjusting itself from all the forces in the lower half or is making incremental expansions. It is a black hole joined to a white hole with no connecting tail or accretion and a very small event horizon. That is an anomaly. The dense cloud of gas and matter is totally separate from the hole. Unique. Let's go a bit deeper."

One voice from her left side said, "Trouble coming to the far left." Azna looked at the ship. "Retreat to the entrance and just on our side for an attack."

They waited for the ship to pass through. Again, the groups attacked the ship. Like the ships the day before, it blew up. When the debris settled, they were surprised another ship appeared. It was attacked and exploded just outside the circle. Another ship following retreated when it saw the one in front explode.

Back at the base, Ayrn-Adon Two, the Lords thanked the group. "Reports in tonight. Tomorrow is a rest day. Then we will advise what will happen."

The Lords looked at all the reports. "We must close that hole. But I am so tempted to explore more of that universe," said Thuma.

"Me too," said Jose as he sipped on a glass of wine. We must consider the consequences. If we close the hole too early, what happens to sector nineteen and does it impact other sectors? If we show our hand too early, we could place ourselves at a disadvantage. We need to strategize."

"I hear earth people are best at strategizing for war," said Jose. "Do we call them in?"

Azna frowned. "No way. They are still primitive."

Jose threw two fists in the air. "Exactly. The civilizations are all geared to so-called modern techniques. Going back to basics with an untapped line of ideas will confuse the enemy. A confused enemy is at a disadvantage. They wouldn't know what hit them or what will come next. Let's just say when mud flies in all directions, it can penetrate the most difficult locations."

Sigma considered the options. "Okay, for now, we just have a look at what is in that universe. Gather information. I think the final-year recruits can go home now. We go in with the emissaries, a small reconnaissance group."

"Agreed" chorused the others.

CHAPTER 16

Earth.

United Nations Head Quarters.

The delegation which had visited Genesis was now accompanied by Hammond, Tayee, Ashton, Alcyn PZ, Wilbut and Tanke. The delegation reported on what they saw on the planet of Genesis and what the threats the humans on the planet were about to face. Then it switched to the oncoming threat which could appear at any time in the near future.

Hammond suggested what he recalled Prince Alcyn mentioned before his death the tactics he used successfully against the Lacertians. He looked at Alcyn PZ as he spoke. "Do you recall any of the tactics you used in that life?"

"It is very hazy. Mind control of the Lacertians is about all. The fuzzy bit has something to do with chemicals."

Hammond coughed. "Yes, chemicals. This planet is full of useful and dangerous chemicals. Useful when they serve man, but dangerous when they are abused. You used household paint and fashioned them into balls. The idea was from a game where people wore protective clothing and ran around shooting balls of paint at each other. Paint ball. You took the concept of the balls but added household paint weighted a bit with a metal or a dense plastic ball inside. They were used for hand-held sling shots. The normal balls of paint, that is not having any solid barbs, tasted like some sweets manufactured on Elkondite. The Lacertian bought them by the thousands. They were addicted to them like drugs. The red and black balls were banned as they were toxic and highly addictive. White, green, yellows and blues were the most popular and created the greatest highs without actually killing the Lacertians. When we evacuated, the Lacertian government at the time manufactured the paint balls. They became disgustingly wealthy. The modified Lacertians were the biggest users. This caused a bigger rift between the vegetarian and meat-eating Lacertians. The Draconians took over control. We know the red and black still exists somewhere. As a guess, buried in some underground chamber. Toxic materials were always buried underground but the locations were never revealed to the public. We guess that the Lacertians copied the manufacture of the paint and the creation of the pain balls. When you used the balls on the dinner table on one ship, you had the batch injected with some toxin to cause mass illness, if not death to the consuming Lacertians.

"Then you use mineral turpentine and clear varnish over one ship. It caused mayhem. Varnish sent the Lacertian males into a sexual rampage, raping the females or fighting over the females close by.

The mineral turps smelt like their urine and was pumped through a ship's water system. Naturally, many became ill and even died. Do you recall any of that?"

Alcyn PZ shook his head. "No. But it must have been fun climbing into their brains and plastering the ship with such toxins."

"The chaos caused one ship to self-destruct. Actually, you did cause about eight ships to self-destruct, one other to go into the waste galaxy and one to be overtaken by the massive gorilla from Affen-Welt."

"I don't recall. Maybe later I will recall some vague image. What has all that got to do with any of this?"

"Paint and many chemicals here are harmless to most humans or can make them seriously ill. They recover with appropriate treatment or people can self-recover to a certain degree. People learn and never go back for seconds."

Hammond saw everyone in the room nod. "While the delegation has been away, I have my teams researching toxins and other ideas which would make humans very unpalatable or even poisonous to both Lacertians and Draconians. Some of it is just household items which would give these creatures something to think about. The air force on this planet cannot defend us in the sky. Draconian crafts are so much superior. Sending pilots to their death is not on. The armies around the world would never be able to cope. The soldiers would be obliterated in minutes. That is a wasteful use of soldiers. Sailors would be another group of sacrificial lambs. Not an option."

One of the delegates asked, "What are our options? No air, no land, and no sea defence."

Tayee replied, "Use them to assist the manufacture and distribution of household chemicals. Get them to train civilians in their use and safety. Encourage people to eat certain foods which will make humans here revolting to Draconian taste buds. We can make them very sick and without proper medical techniques, many will die."

The same man asked, "Exactly what do you encourage people to eat and do?"

Tayee smirked. "You're going to love the answer. Get them to eat a lot of eggs, garlic, onions and chilies and have lots of coffee. Pepper sprays will upset their system. From what I understand is, Draconians and Lacertians don't like what we call nice smells. Perfumes, deodorants, insect repellents, and sunscreen are just too much for them to handle. Many are in the households now. Just everyday things. We need to teach the population how to weaponize them. That is where the armed forces will be of most use; distribute the materials and teach how it is a weapon."

"There will be panic buying and shops will be overrun," warned another delegate.

"At this point in time we just run television ads stating how these chemicals and food items can be used when and if the event occurs. Ask people to grow a few vegetables but include onions, chilies, and garlic in the mix. Only when the time comes closer and an attack is imminent, the armed forces just buy a case of an item every month and stockpile them around the cities for easy distribution,' said Tayee.

Wilbut added, "I get the idea now. On this planet there are shops that make replica guns to shoot gel bullets and some toys which shoot water. Water can be switched to other chemicals like bleach, insecticide, disinfectant, and so on."

Tanke said, "Some chemicals will be better than others. But if they act as repellents and cause stomach and skin issues with the Draconians and Lacertians, they just may back off. A no-go zone.

I will compile a list of foods and ordinary household chemicals which may assist. They may need mixing to be effective."

Milway walked in eating ice-cream from a tub. "This nitrogen ice-cream is delicious. I was watching how they do it. The guys were in protective clothing from the cold. Shhh and presto, instant ice-cream. Earth people are so creative."

One delegate spun around. "Of course. Lizards are cold blooded. They can't handle the cold. Nitrogen blaster guns or guns need to be developed." He beamed with excitement before blowing a kiss to MIlway. She caught the kiss and placed it on her forehead. She grinned and nodded her acceptance. "Frozen nitrogen needs to be added to the arsenal. I bet they won't try to land near the poles but will head for the sub-tropics and tropical areas. The seasonal snowfalls will also be our weapon. They hide in the buildings and turn up the heat. We turn the power off so they can't heat themselves. We can sew the sky with silver oxide to create rain and hopefully it will convert to snow in the winter months. Alternatively, we put nitrogen through the air conditioning system. Mustard gas, DDT, methane gas and carbon monoxide, and nasty agent orange will work as well. Now, we have some kind of plan for a possible attack. We can now help the people on Genesis as well."

Zindel made his presence known by hologram. "I was eavesdropping. I like the nitrogen and mustard gas ideas and snow dumps. The people from Lyria have been fighting this war for so many years and protecting Earth. Now Earth can help out in a practical way."

Tayee asked, "Can they make frozen nitrogen or make other gases?"

"I am sure they could make frozen nitrogen, but it has never occurred to them to weaponize the gas. Other gases? No. The planet of Lyria does not have assorted plants like this planet has and their crops are limited in range. I do not know which. But I will put it to them. Chemical warfare using plants. Thanks."

He switched off but returned minutes later. "I just spoke with the president. They can make frozen nitrogen. That is all but she asks how do you apply it?"

Tayee replied, "If there is an occupied building, then through the air ducts. If in the sky, then I am not sure. Maybe they have to get close to a craft spinning out of control and give it a blast to ensure it doesn't come back. Have pilots carry some in mini cans on their uniforms. If they are captured, they give the enemy a dose. We can also make pepper spray and mustard gas spray as well. See if pilots are willing to carry such cans. Draconians will be looking for guns not stuff disguised as food." Zindel disappeared again. He was back again, "Okay, they want 100,000 recyclable personalized sized frozen nitrogen spray cans for a trail. The Lyrians can top them up as required. How long will that take to get together?"

A delegate swallowed hard. "A month. Maybe less. It is a matter of cost."

Zindel placed his hands on his hips and was showing signs of anger. "Give it to them free. They have been defending Earth at their expense. It is payback time. I will deliver the cans to them. Just organize the shipment. I will be back in three days for the collection or the first 10,000 cans. Other gases will be accepted." He disappeared.

CHAPTER 17

Lyria

The Lyrian president, Folami greeted Zindel at the main administration office. After the usual pleasantries, Zindel asked, "How much frozen nitrogen can you manufacture?"

"Unlimited. Why?"

"This idea has come from Earth. The lizard races die very quickly when exposed to cold. Knowing the size of these creatures, they will need a big dose of frozen nitrogen." Folami drummed her fingers on her armrest. She was deep in thought. "How do we administer it?"

"Method one which was suggested by earth people is to douse any building they are in with the gas. Feed it through their air-conditioning system and then turn off their power supply. They are happy to supply other types of gases and chemicals. They call it pest extermination. Method two. The pilots carry a cylinder in the form of missiles. They drop the missiles to release the nitrogen. Alternatively, they do aerial spraying using silver oxide at a designated location. Method three. Make it a part of every person's uniform to have a hand-held can. If someone is captured, they spray the Draconian or Lacertian with the gas. This may allow one person to get away. The first 100,000 cans are being made now. I said for the can to be recyclable. You can fill them up whenever you need to without having to rely on earth people. "

"Most pilots generally die before they get home. I was told two or three Draconians carry them off."

"Okay, what if the pilots did this new technique? For a short while, it will make the other two surrounding the pilot let go in surprise."

"Hmm. Not really convinced. There are no Draconian bases on Lyria. We don't know where their other bases are. But the idea of dousing the building or using missiles is very appealing. I will keep them in mind."

"I know exactly where some of the bases are. They are the planets in other galaxies."

"Give me the places and I will try to work out if our crafts can go to those locations.'

"I bought another gift from Earth."

"Oh?"

"Earth is covered with a myriad of plants. Many are edible, some are not. Some edible plants can be altered into a toxin which can temporarily immobilize a Draconian. But to their own much smaller and generally harmless lizards, it can be deadly. I bought 1,000 pepper spray cans for a trial run. The pilots can also carry this as standard equipment in their uniform. Earth people do not know if one puff or emptying out a can will kill or immobilize a Draconian. Here is a demo."

Zindel stood beside Folami and held the can as high as he could before giving it a squirt into the air away from their faces. Both coughed. Folami's eyes started to swell up. "That should kill a few." She gasped for air. She reached for a buzzer. "I need a doctor. An allergy reaction. Hurry." She turned to Zindel. "That is utterly disgusting. I like it. It won't be fool proof. What happens if the pilot in his rush squirts himself?" She coughed more to clear her throat from the particles of gas.

"Drop. Temporarily blinded and very uneatable for a while. The spray may repel the Draconian or Lacertian at best."

Zindel apologized through his own coughing. "That was far more pungent than expected." The pepper spray seemed to fill the room. Folami was now breathing closer to normal. She said in a hoarse voice, "You did not spray that near my face, yet I reacted."

"It is supposed to be sprayed into the face of Draconian. Law enforcement agencies use it to subdue some out-of-control people on Earth. It stops their shenanigans immediately. The victim receives medical attention."

"What kind of people would use such a weapon on their own?"

"You have not seen what happens when an earth person goes berserk. Any attempt at reasoning is useless. By accident, they found the same gas immediately kills their local lizards. Their lizards are very small and some humans have them as pets."

"And we have been defending these people?"

"Don't get me wrong. They are very creative and have a massive arsenal of equipment and ideas.

They are somewhat primitive in many ways." Folami held up her hand. The doctor walked in.

When the doctor left, Folami asked, "Just how creative?"

"The more creative ones will turn any object into a weapon for self-defence. Sometimes, it is a just spur of the moment, an adrenaline rush for survival. Those who fail to be creative either die or be left with some disability; mental or physical or social. It depends on the situation."

Folami looked at Zindel firmly. "Okay. They are aggressive."

"They can be very loving as well."

"We used to do spot checks on the progress of humans. Just observations from afar.

"We just saw environmental destruction and regional wars. Nothing like you say."

"You didn't mingle with the population. That is why you missed it."

" I would like to test this err…pepper spray. Come with me. We have a teenager Lacertian in captivity. He gives the jailers a rough time. His report is as long as a jet landing strip."

Zindel went in the president's craft to an island in the ocean. When they arrived, they were met by the supervisor, Lech. He led them to the only captive Lacertian. Lech asked, "This experiment you are conducting, is it lethal or are you going to give me and the staff more work to do in medical research?"

Folami shrugged. "All of us will find out soon. Gas masks will be advisable."

Lech was surprised at the request and was about to question the need. "Both of us had a smell of this when it was directed away from us. I had a sever reaction. I do not want to experience that ever again. Masks."

The Lacertian was brought close to the bars. He was standing about a metre back. Suddenly, Folami squirted the pepper spray directly at the Lacertian's face. The Lacertian screamed and gasped for air. He dropped to the ground. Lech opened the door. He took the Lacertian pulse. "

" I think he's dead. If not, his pulse is extremely low. What is that stuff?"

"A spray from another planet. How much is still left in the can?" asked Zindel.

"About half," replied Folami.

There was a groan and a slight movement. Zindel took the can and sprayed the Lacertian again.

Zindel said, "Not quite dead." He emptied out the can. "It looks like one can kill one teenage Lacertian. Two would be needed or a larger can for a Draconian or an adult Lacertian." The supervisor nudged the Lacertian with his foot. He was expecting some movement. There was none.

"I will get this body examined." He pressed a button on his hand-held communication system and gave the order for the body to be examined.

Two hours later, the examiner wrote a report and sent it to Folami and to Lech.

The External Examination of the Lacertian:

The body appears to have been burned by an unknown chemical. Blisters were evident between the scales around the face and shoulder area. The nostrils were severely burned making it very difficult or impossible for the Lacertian to breath. Cells in the nose broke down and basically, liquified. The rest of the exterior was blistered like the rest of the face.

The Internal of the Lacertians:

From the nose to the stomach, the area was burned. It was riddled with blisters and puss. The lungs showed early stages of liquification. Death would have been painful.

Chemical Analysis of the Toxin:

It appears to be plant-based. Plant unknown. Whatever the plant is, it should not be consumed in any way.

Zindel received a copy of the report and forwarded copies to Earth and Genesis.

He added a note with the Genesis report:

I will try to secure cans of this spray for you.

Hammond will send a few cartons via the transporter.

CHAPTER 18

Genesis.

The city's attack alarms filled the air. People ran to either their allocated places for defence or into the nearest hiding place. Patrum and Zantha ran to the transporter and waited for the cartons of spray to arrive. There was a swoosh sound indicating the transporter had arrived. They needed to wait a minute or two. Alcyn PZ stepped out to see his anxious parents. He heard the alarm screaming in the background.

"Have they landed?" he yelled dismissing any form of greeting protocol.

Patrum yelled back, "We don't know yet. How do these cans work?"

"It is advisable for the user to wear a mask. If there is no time for a mask, then the user must make sure they don't accidentally spray themselves. The stuff stinks worse than a sewer plant." He opened one box and held it up well above their heads. He gave a short blast. They all coughed.

Zantha spluttered, "That is disgusting."

"I was told one can kill one Draconian or Lacertian. Aim for their face. It drops them dead like insects. Help me carry the rest of the boxes to wherever they are needed."

Partrum, Alcyn, and Zantha entered the motel foyer carrying a box of pepper spray cans. Zantha led them to a cellar where staff and a handful of guests of the motel were hiding. They gave one box to the staff with a few directions on how to use the cans.

Through the network of tunnels, Patrum led Zantha and Alcyn went to another basement in the administration building. In this basement, was a second control centre assisting the above-ground control centre. Another box of pepper spray was dropped off with brief instructions. Ten more boxes were delivered to bunkers via the underground system of tunnels.

The last box was more dangerous to deliver. Alcyn volunteered to do the delivery.

"I will stay there until I deem it safe to return. Now go back to the admin building basement and wait for me."

Alcyn ran with the precious delivery across the open ground, dodging rays as he moved closer to the control tower. He opened the door and slammed it firmly behind at the same time reaching for the lift button. For some unknown reason, he opened the box and pulled a can out just in case it was needed. The lift was on the way down. He spun around to the door he slammed shut. It was now open and Draconian filed its space. Alcyn sprayed the can into the Draconian's face. The Draconian instantly grasped his neck, stumbled back, and collapsed. Alcyn sprayed the rest of the contents down the Draconian's mouth before shoving it into the Draconian's mouth. "Eat the dessert too, asshole" Alcyn closed the door again. He left the body outside as a warning to any more Draconians thinking of using the door. The lift doors opened. Alcyn rushed in and pushed the button to the top several times.

As soon as he reached the control room, he gave each person a can, with some instructions. "It works," he assured them. "I just used one downstairs. They drop dead in a matter of seconds."

One of the controllers asked while still watching the sky, "What is it?"

"It is from Earth. It is called pepper spray. It is derived from an edible plant. They worked out that the gas from the plant can kill lizards. Smart people. Just don't spray it on your own face. It hurts like hell."

Just then the building shook. A downed Draconian jet wing had clipped the tower. The craft spun out of control below. Alcyn saw the Draconian crawl out and look directly at the tower. "Get ready, the first incoming is going to climb this tower," yelled Alcyn. Alcyn watched the Draconian scale the tower. When the Draconian was two metres away, Alcyn sprayed the Draconian's face with a long squirt. Immediately the Draconian lost his grip and fell to the ground.

Another Draconian who landed close by saw his comrade fall. He shook his head and wondered what had caused him to fall so clumsily. He started to scale the building. He reached the top and smashed the glass. A controller sprayed the Draconian in the face. The second Draconian fell to his death.

From above, the Draconian commander on the mother ship noted the control tower had caused two deaths. He zeroed into the control tower. "Take that tower. Capture the people inside," went the order to three more crafts.

The jets circled the tower. With each circle, they came a little closer. One Draconian reported back, "There is nothing. No weapons we can see. Not even a shield."

"Be careful. Go closer. They must have a weapon inside. Some short-range weapon," said the commander.

As the crafts edged closer, Alcyn went to one of the smashed windows, assembled an AR15 short barrel rifle with a silencer he smuggled under his jacket. He pointed the rifle at the craft's fuel tank area. He shot several times before it hit the target. The craft dropped like a lead balloon. On impact with the ground, it exploded into a ball of fire. A controller standing beside Alcyn asked,

"What the hell is that thing?"

"This is a baby rifle. Earth people have hundreds of designs for different purposes. It is really confusing what to pick out. I got this one because it can hide in my clothes. It is awkward to carry in its concealed state. Alcyn refilled the rifle. "This is my last lot of bullets."

Alcyn fired again. Another craft went down. His attention was drawn to the other side of the room.

A Draconian had scaled the tower and smashed another window. The nearest controller sprayed the Draconian with pepper spray. The Draconian fell to his death. The head controller yelled, "Evacuate. Use the pole to go down quickly!"

From the commanding mother ship, the commander grew annoyed. He ordered, "Blast the tower. All of it!" More Draconian crafts came. They bombarded the tower. It crumbled to the ground.

Deep in the basement of the tower, Alcyn and the control tower group huddled in the now overcrowded space. One man said in a nervous voice, "We have to leave this place. It will be a tomb."

Another voiced his concern. "The Draconians will dig us out. We are dinner for sure." There was an explosion. The rubble was blasted away. Alcyn looked anxious. "Bad company is coming. Get ready with the spray cans. I think I am out of bullets."

Daylight filtered through. A Draconian was lifting the last of the rubble. His face was close to the slither of light. Alcyn whispered, "Lift me on your shoulders."

To another and held out his hand, "Can." Alcyn could see the Draconian's face. It was just inches away. Alcyn covered his nose and mouth before squirting the pepper spray through the gap. The Draconian fell backwards while holding his neck. He tried to scream but the sound was a mere garbled noise. Alcyn held out his hand again. Another can was placed in it. The tactic was repeated three times more. Draconians lay dead outside.

An order from the commander from the mother ship filtered through to the nearest craft.

"Get one of those dead bodies. These people have a weapon that kills us instantly. That place maybe the storage area and the toxins are leaking out. Don't place your face near the rubble.

Cautiously, one craft landed. The Draconian pilot walked slowly towards the closest dead Draconian.

Alcyn peered through the hole. "Can." He waited. The Draconian didn't approach but began to lift a deceased companion. Alcyn gave back the can and looked at his gun. He added a silencer. He checked the gun for bullets; just two. Two more than what he had thought. He aimed carefully knowing a miss would be fatal for the group. Pfff, Pfff. The two bullets hit their mark, both in the Draconian's back. Alcyn wasn't sure of the sounds he heard after the shots. He was sure one bullet hit the spine and the other further up. A trickle of Draconian blood poured down the Draconian's back. He was now sure he had shot the Draconian in the neck.

The commander from above sent two more Draconian pilots to retrieve both bodies. The bodies were taken to the medical bay for examination. The commander went to see the damage himself. He slammed his hand down on the examination table when the doctor pulled out two mangled bullets from one Draconian. "What are these pieces of metal?" he demanded. The doctor looked up from the dead Draconian. "I have never seen such penetration of foreign matter in any body. It is not a laser. There are residual chemicals around the area. I will get that analysed with the metal."

His attention turned to the other dead Draconian. The doctor jumped back in horror. "They have mastered a chemical that instantly kills us. It appears to be airborne. This male suffered a dreadful death. We must find the source and dispose of it as soon as possible if we are going to conquer this planet. In all my years, I have never seen such a chemical that could kill so effectively. It must be reported to the main command in Draconia immediately."

The commander kept staring at the second dead Draconian. His fury was mounting every second. "Every planet with humans did offer some challenges. That was to be expected. But this chemical is innovative. I just hope it is confined to this planet. How did they make such a toxin?"

The doctor shook his head. "Absolutely no idea. The tissue scaping may give us some of the chemistry and hopefully a clue. No matter what we learn from the composition, it will never be accurate as the chemical is totally mixed with the tissue cells. It's ingenious. It is frightening. It could also be toxic to their own species. I am guessing, the humans here may spray their own bodies with this chemical. If they do and it is safe for the humans, a Draconian ingesting it, will die or become seriously ill." The doctor took numerous tissue samples before placing the Draconian pilot in the freezer. "I will let you know of the analysis as soon as possible."

The commander stormed out of the room. He would send mission control the updates when the analysis was complete. Now all he could do was contemplate new tactics. Two planets. One was overrun with toxic creatures which looked like primitive hairy humans. The second made him wonder if these humans were edible or not. No matter what, they had to be exterminated. The planet was appealing. The humans on it were not. He recalled the crafts attacking the planet.

The commander called the pilots to the mess hall for a mass meeting. "Do not attack these people. They have created a toxic spray which is guaranteed to kill or make you seriously ill. Go in groups of three. Land on the planet in groups of three. Two are to act as guards while the other collects samples of plants. Bring the plants back. The plants are to be brought back for analysis. We need to discover the plant which this new toxin is made of. If we fail to find the plant, we will just burn the foliage and starve these humans. We will starve these humans off the planet and those who survive will be cleansed before being converted for food. At this stage, shoot to kill any approaching human but do not consume. We shall also do the same for the first planet with those hairy deformed human-like creatures." The commander answered a handful of questions before leaving.

It was a few days before the commander received the results of the chemical which killed his soldiers. He studied the report.

Chemical Analysis Report on the Chemically Downed Soldier.

This is a fast-acting agent which can kill a Draconian in a matter of seconds.

From what we can assess from the limited laboratory equipment and no witnesses, humans used a spray can for delivery.

There is minor evidence that hydrocarbons were involved. It is unclear at this stage if the hydrocarbons when activated are purely a delivery system or react with the chemical formula to make it a potent mix. We have determined, there is a mix of chemicals that attack the skin, eyes, and the metabolic system of the Draconian. The chemical/s integrate into the cells resulting in instant blindness if the eyes are sprayed, the lungs become dysfunctional, and the nose tissue dissolves. The heart goes into cardiac arrest. The body just shuts down in a matter of minutes.

One chemical we found in minute traces is called Choralenzylindenemalononitrile, also known as C.S. for short. There is evidence of other chemical/s. They are of unknown origin and makeup. The unknowns appear to breakdown on exposure to air. We could not determine if they break down as soon as they hit bodily tissues or when it is absorbed into the body. The other possible chemical carriers is to assist C.S. to help chemicals to disperse through the body.

Recommendations:

1. Goggles and masks become standard issues for all soldiers.

2. Samples of tissue but preferably a container be sent back to Draconia for more detailed analysis with more sophisticated laboratory equipment.

Report Two: The Pieces of Metal and Chemical in the "shot" Draconian Soldier.

The mangled pieces of metal were heated and stretched to their original format. See pictures of before and after the restructuring. The chemical composition is steel, coal and lead. The object can only enter the body by using an instrument giving a high-velocity force. It is safe to hold at any time even with the chemicals it discharges are still inside. The metal casing, as I prefer to call it, is a delivery system for the chemicals. The hole it makes in the body causes the most damage. The chemicals are delivered directly into the blood stream and tissues. Very effective in immediate or partial immobility. A skilled operator can kill a draconian with one shot.

Chemical Analysis.

This has a mix of chemicals that immediately cause extra pain after the 'missile' is fired.

The main part of the mixture is carbon, potassium nitrate, and sulphur. Other chemicals are in trace form and their composition is unclear.

Recommendations:

1. Soldiers should avoid being struck down by the 'missiles' at all costs.

2. The soldiers should take cover if these are fired at them. Soldiers need to carry a large metal shield, or a shield made from double poly-carbonate.

The commander drummed his fingers on the armrests of his chair. Goggles? Masks? Shields?

He looked up the inventory for stock. He slammed his hand on the desk. There were only masks for pilots for emergencies. Goggles and shields were not available. He swore. "Those humans must have had inside information on our inventory. Who would have leaked that information? A friendly Lacertian?

He had already sent the reports to mission control in Draconia concerning the initial attack on this new planet. Now this report concerning new chemical attacks and their delivery systems wasn't going to look good. The search for chemical-producing plants were also a failure. The failures would reflect on his record. He thought to himself, *Those higher up are going to be furious. Humans are not supposed to be advanced in the sciences, but here they are.* He added that part to the report. He was going to minimalize the impact on his record.

On Genesis, people moved about but were on high alert. More preparations were made for both the hiding and storage of supplies. Goods from Earth kept arriving: more pepper spray, mustard gas, and guns with ammunition. All people over seventeen were trained in their usage. Then came loads of disinfectants, bleach and garden poisons with spray containers. parents and children were armed with these and taught how to use them. Sling shots with poisoned paintballs arrived next. They came with instructions; aim at the face, preferably the eyes and mouth and the genitalia. If supplies run out, use stones and small pieces of rubble. A warning came with the slingshots: they do not kill but can offer seconds of escape time. Practice with stones.

Alcyn with a small group of soldiers from Earth were now training the Genesians on weaponry and self-defence. Alcyn became exhausted after a week; multiple trips to and from Earth, acting as interpreter, and helping with lessons began to take their toll. When he fell asleep, it was not the best rest. Flashes of his past life began mixing with his dreams. He would wake up with a scream, yell, or covered in sweat, his heart rate racing and heart pumping much too fast. He ached all over. He took a couple of days off to rest but that period was interrupted.

Alarms of fires breaking out in the countryside where their crops were grown, signalled a new form of attack. Knowing what he learned about Earth's bush fires, he rushed to the administration building.

"We can put these fires out quickly. We dump water from the air on top." He showed film clips of fires on Earth and their techniques of putting them out. One administrator pointed to the fire trucks. "We don't have those vehicles. We don't have trained men. Our major source of crops is already destroyed."

One advisor from Earth who was attending the meeting said, "You are right. Aerial water bombing is the only option. The Draconians have decided to starve people, rather than use brute force as I was told was always done in the past." The advisor thought for a few seconds before adding.

"Fire retardant spray will be needed. Do you have any?"

There was a chorus of "No."

"Then we shall get some. When it arrives spray all the buildings in the city and all the crops. You will be painting the city red. The crops will be red as well. The retardant will wash off, but the vegetables may change in flavour. Run food checks for safety. While I am away organizing the retardant, get all you citizens to start making mini gardens everywhere. It will preserve the pants you use for food and keep the genetics of the plant pure. I am not sure if the retardant will alter the plants. On Earth, it doesn't but I cannot say for this planet. Begin water bombing immediately. Convert some of your larger crafts to carry water. Water pumps will be needed to get the later into the crafts. You do have water pumps, do you?"

"Yes," said Patrum. "All sizes."

"Then get stated," said the advisor. "I will see what I can do on Earth. Activate your shields again. At least protect the city."

CHAPTER 19

Earth.

Alcyn and the advisor parted ways at Draxon Technologies. Alcyn immediately went to Hammond and Tayee to give a report on Genesis.

"They are under attack. The Draconians are burning their crops as a new tactic."

Hammond and Tayee looked surprised. "They are trying to starve people. That is new," said Tayee.

"Very new. While on Genesis, I started to have flashbacks of my previous life. I did some nasty things to nasty Lacertians. I have to contact Zindel immediately. I must let him know of these flashbacks and new war techniques. He will tell the Lyrians for sure. At least they can be prepared.

I am going into the mind training room. No disturbances. I will put a sign up. I don't know how long I will be in there." Hammond gave a nod. Alcyn grabbed two bottles of water from a machine and food items including chocolates from another.

In the room, he consumed his food and drinks. Then placed a note on the door and locked it from the inside. He placed his cranial neuro-transmitter on, got comfortable and then focused.

Zindel was further away than he expected. He was in Cancari B. Zindel felt a tug in his brain.

Alcyn PZ sent him the messages. Then briefly disappeared. The new tactic Draconians disturbed Zindel.

He relayed the messages to the Lords of the Universe and later to the Lyrians. Both times he heard their alarmed expressions. With Folami, he sensed rage. He knew immediately, she would make new decisive defence decisions.

He recontacted Alcyn for information regarding how Earth was helping Genesians. Alcyn sent him the details of cargo and training techniques.

Alcyn removed the helmet and consumed more water and nibbled on the last sandwich before trying to contact Tanke.

Tanke stopped reading the document she had in her hands. She smiled. *Hi stranger,* she replied to the telepathic message.

Sorry I have been a bit busy. The Draconians are using new tactics. My planet is the testing ground.

What are the bastards doing? asked Tanke.

Burning food crops to starve my people. They didn't like us using Earth's pepper spray. They are burning crops hoping we can never produce the chemical again, said Alcyn. *Can I pop over?*

Yes. Just give me a few minutes to be presentable, replied Tanke.

Alcyn focused more on her. *You look presentable enough for me. I'll be there in five.*

Alcyn went immediately to the mini transporter. In five minutes, he was in Paris and in less than a minute later was at Tanke's door.

Tanke listened to what Alcyn said about what had happened on Genesis. She was concerned. "I will advise the various diplomats as I see them. All they see is a young female doing a job of a person who should be in their forties. They discriminate. So, I just plant the information in their brains. Then there is no excuse for them to say I didn't get the message. Sometimes I hear their thoughts which have conflicts between what they have to do or say as directed by their governments and their personal beliefs. It can be amusing when they curse their own bosses. When it comes to lured thoughts and discrimination, I like that because they suddenly trip over their own feet, or I get them to do something embarrassing. It makes them pay attention. I told Patron what I was doing. All he did was laugh. He told me he did the same thing at times to make sure he was heard."

"What kind of embarrassing things have you done?" asked Alcyn.

"Tripping over their own feet is the most common one. If the same jerk does it again, their trousers suddenly drop if it is a male. If it is a female, that depends on if her hair suddenly loses its style or has one or two of her blouse buttons pop. It depends on who and my experience at the time as to what I do. I get the messages across. It is surprising how attitudes change. I am slowly getting there with the diplomats. They are starting to realize I am not a joke. Anyway, is there something I can help you with?"

"Tomorrow I will go back to Daraxon Technologies. I need some help with understanding toxins produced on this planet."

Tanke turned on the television and flipped to a streaming channel offering documentaries. She sorted through the long list until she found a program on poisonous animals in Australia, and the Americas. Then there was a documentary about illegal drugs and the damage they cause. "Watch these. You will get an idea or two."

Alcyn wrote down the names of the creatures and their toxins. Then there was a list of illegal drugs At the end of the programme he said, "I think it is enough. We can get the drugs and toxins and inject them into paintballs and other substances which appeal to Lacertians and Draconians. We just might have a chance. The Lacertians really love the taste of paintballs. Apparently, they remind them of some sweets that were produced on Elkondite, a planet which disappeared in an explosion. Earth is producing these paintballs with some substances which makes them ill but does not kill them. I want to up the anti."

Tanke just listened but noticed Alcyn nodding off. "Bedtime," she whispered.

When Alcyn returned to Daraxon Technologies he asked Hammond and Tayee to increase the poison dosage in the paintballs. Tayee considered the idea. "How about we leave the paintballs as they are? We produce new products which have red, black and clear gel balls. I vaguely recall the red and black balls were banned from the Lacertian market as they were considered toxic or highly addictive. I can't recall which. Anyway, we get the Lacertian sympathizers to sell these on a black market. Finding the sympathizers will be difficult. We get them to just place these new balls on dinner tables for the elite and hand them out as advertising samples to their teenagers. Let's get them addicted or dead."

Alcyn considered the three colours. "Let's up the ante in every way. Red balls have a cocktail of spider venom, Black have a cocktail of snake venom and the clear gel, the slightly more rarer ones in the packets, have conch and sea snake venom. The more regular colours could have assorted other chemicals and poisonous foods. For example, green could have garden chemicals, yellow loaded with eggshells ground to a powder, tan spiked with coffee and shallots, and white and pink with a mix of illegal drugs. All should also be flavoured with meat. Meat-flavoured balls will disguise the toxins and create a novelty effect. They like sweets and meat. If both are in the one package, it will be a hit…more ways than one. "

"How about we dust the paintballs with a drug called ice?"

Hammond smirked. "Frosted balls for the existing colours will add to the range. It will be very appealing and novel. But does ice work to kill them?"

Alcyn shrugged. "There is only one way to find out."

Hammond asked, "Just who is going to deliver the paintballs?"

"Ashton, me and anyone else who wants to come," replied Alcyn.

"Have you asked Ashton?" asked Tayee.

"Not yet. But he has worked with the various resistance groups on different planets."

"Ashton may resist because he has a family and is considering adopting two more embryos. He won't leave Kora to raise the children by herself. I believe she was also one of the resistance fighters skilled in computer hacking and reprogramming. I believe on Nubia; the Lacertians were never able to fully remove her program on water supply distribution. The other people on the security team on the Explorer BCXS did the same type of work; raids to rescue humans from slavery and from being farmed for food, bomb attacks and so on."

Alcyn clapped his hands. "Just who were on the team. They sound ideal."

Hammond walked over to Alcyn. "Ashton, Kora, Eldon, Nodin, Ichiro, Garyth, Frode, Eraton, and the boss and teacher, Neo. But I doubt if they would do more raids. Kora, Ashton, Garyth and Eraton are on the most wanted list. There is a high bounty on their heads. If they get caught, they will have a most horrific death."

 "At least we can put the idea to them. They haven't been on an active mission for over a year. The Lacertians and the Draconians must think they have gone into hiding or retired or dead. Going back will give the enemy something to think about," said Alcyn.

Two days later, Neo and his former students assembled at Daraxon Technologies. They listened to Alcyn's plans. Kora just refused to participate. Ashton put forward a tweaking of the plan. A debate followed. Issues were sorted out. Planning was in its advanced stages. The only issue was getting to the planets; Isobola, Nubia, Centari and Daraxon. Getting to Genesis which was about one-third of the way was easy. The Explorer was just too large and would attract attention. More planning was needed.

A week later the select group was loaded with cartons of supplies at the transporter. Thirty trips spread over five days saw everything disappear from Daraxon Technologies and land in Genesis.

Pepper spray, doctored paintballs, doctored gel balls, guns with ammunition, food, and alcohol from Earth filled two storerooms in the basement at the motel where the transporter was attached. Zindel was contacted.

Zindel looked at the supplies and nodded his approval. "The Lyrians are willing to loan you one ship staffed by their people. They will also use my new fighter crafts to deliver you to any destination.

Exactly, how are you getting in touch with contacts to let them know you are coming?" asked Zindel.

Ashton pointed to his head. "Telepathy. They will let us know where and when."

Zindel was uncomfortable about the method. "Just be careful. You have been out of action for a while. The people you were in contact with could be dead and the replacement people may not know you."

Ashton replied, "Point taken. I will not send anyone down unless I am two hundred per cent sure."

CHAPTER 20

Nubia

Zindel led a small fleet of ten converted fighter jets to the planet of Nubia. When Nubia was occupied by humans, it was the leading planet for all types of medical research and the manufacture of medication. Other planets did make their own supplies, but the breakthroughs always came via Nubia. When the war with Lacertians started over twenty-five years ago, the research stopped. Only medications which benefited the Lacertians and later the Draconians were manufactured. Humans became the test rats for research projects. Many redundant factories over the last ten years were re-purposed to make novelty-shaped food products and some sweets. To Zindel and the rest of the Pleiadeans on this mission, it was the ideal launch pad for the new products.

Under the cover of darkness, and in the mountain tops semi-circling one of the cities, Garyth and Earaton landed. They were met by a small group of human resistance fighters. Garyth and Eraton greeted them. "I am Rayanna, Larton's daughter. My father is in poor health and couldn't meet you."

Garyth introduced Eraton. "Kora is unable to come. Eraton is replacing her." Rayanna looked a little disappointed. "I was hoping to see her again. It has been a couple of years. She is a legend. Is her health, okay?"

"Yes. She was the first Pleiadean in eight hundred years to give natural birth to a boy. Between motherhood and caring for about 400 Pleiadeans in cribs, she has her hands full. They are the last of the Pleiadean Embryos. She may drop a message via telepathy. She has been practising that skill."

Rayanna nodded. "She sounds busy. On what planet is she on?"

Garyth wanted to avoid the answer. "Sorry, I am not permitted to tell. The new colony of Pleiades, Cancari B was attacked. Just a handful have survived along with just 400 cribs from a stock of 5,000."

"So the Draconians have expanded?" she enquired.

"Unfortunately yes. Just recently they attacked the colony Price Alcyn found. Prince Alcyn died two years after the first wave of the war. Anyway, let's get to your camp. There is much to catch up with and explain what to do."

 Larton hobbled with the aid of a walking stick from the mini communication area of the hideout to the small dining table which doubled as a conference table. "Our numbers have depleted. Some were captured and killed. Some were just killed and some just disappeared, most probably killed. Now tell us what is your plan? We are so overdue for an attack on the facilities."

Eraton explained what was going to happen. "We will expect the first cargo to arrive within a few days. Until then we plan our moves here. Which food factories are the easiest targets?"

Rayanna spoke, "Since there hasn't been any real attack on any plant anywhere, some places have relaxed their security. The food plants have reduced their guards by half, but we don't know what CCT is still operating. The control system for manufacturing is about the same. Instead of medication, it is packaged dried food for Lacertians and Draconias on spaceships."

"Are there any Lacertian sympathizers?" asked Garyth.

"Not on Nubia. Well, I don't know of any on Nubia. I have heard there are a few on Isobola."

On the night of the raid, Rayanna led the group of ten to the food factory to make dehydrated snacks. Each put their large cartons of poisoned paintballs down while they examined the perimeter. Rayanna pointed to a loan guard. Garyth signalled for them to stay put. He aimed a pistol with a silencer at the Lacertain. Pfft. Pfft. The Lacertain dropped like a stone. "Follow me," whispered Garyth.

He used his modified sunglasses. "Blue." A blue beam shone out of the middle of the glasses. The beam cut the wire mesh of the fence. Garyth whispered to himself, "I am out of practice with this contraption. Focus." Three sides were cut. He hit the ground when he heard the noise of a patrol vehicle. When it passed, he pushed the mesh in. He signalled the others to follow.

Rayanna with the group ran to the nearest building. Eraton tested the door. "Stand back." Then he ordered blue again. As the blue beam shot out, he moved his head around the edges of the door snapping any metal keeping it closed. He grabbed the handle and pulled it out. The door was placed to one side. "Come," he whispered to the others.

They walked down a passageway. Garyth held his hand up to signal stop. He wasn't sure if the camera spotted them or not. "Red," he commanded. The camera melted. Rayanna led them to the production control room. "The nerve centre," she said. She stopped the production process. She opened a computer and found the packaging labels. She altered the label to add 'Try our brand-new sample product enclosed with this product. Tell us if you like the new sweet. Contact the manufacturers.' She looked at the diagrammatic scheme of the factory where the others were focused. "Where do we go now?" asked Rayanna. Kayla, one of the females on her team, pointed to a location on the diagram. Rayanna looked at Kayler. "Continue the programming."

Eraton pointed his finger at the diagram on the large display showing the movement of food through the processing. "We go to building two. We drop the balls into this unit."

Kayler said, "I am finished reprogramming it for the sweet drop. Let's move."

In building two, they looked at the massive machinery. It was initially disorientating. Kayler pointed to the machine. "It's here. We load the balls into the top. The machine will just automatically drop one ball per packet. We need to turn this machine off first before loading up the paintballs. How many balls do we have?"

Garyth said, "About twenty thousand. Twenty thousand potential deaths or seriously ill lizards."

Each box of balls was added to the feeding machine. Using the packaging program she downloaded on her tablet; she added the count of 20,000 into the system. She turned the machine on. They left the building. Eraton went with Kayler to restart the manufacturing. The rest went to the hole in the fence.

When Kayler and Earton joined them outside the perimeter, they hit the ground. Another patrol car slowly drove past. Garyth swore as he saw the car stop and the two Draconians got out to walk in their direction. He waited until they were closer. His pistol came out. Four shots. Pfft. Pfft. Pfft. Pfft.

Both Draconians dropped to the ground. Garyth ran to the car and drove it to the dead bodies. With Earton's help, the two Draconians were placed in the car. The car was driven further down the road and into some bushes. "Do you have a knife on you?" asked Garyth.

Eraton handed him a paring knife. "That is all I have."

Garyth stabbed each Draconian where the bullets had entered. He left the knife in one Draconian and wiped his prints off. "Now they look like they had a heated argument," said Garyth. "Let's get out of here." Garyth and the Eraton turned on the special sandshoes and ran at superspeed towards the others. The group left the factory and went to the next one just kilometers down the road.

They scouted the grounds for guards. No CCT was installed. A new factory built the last year was complacent with its security. It was a clear run.

This time, with the assistance of the other rebels, Garyth and Earton poured cans of cleaning fluid they found in a cleaner's cupboard into the food mixture. The food mixture was in a huge vat with paddles stirring the contents. Every can was emptied. For good measure, Garyth and Eraton threw in thirty kilograms of chilli and garlic pulp mixed with twenty kilograms of ice. They returned all the cleaning cans to the cupboard and made sure they took the empty packets of mixed chilli and garlic pulp and ice with them. Mission completed. They hurried out. They went back to the hideout as fast as they could. They quickly said their goodbyes to the remaining eight Nubians. "If possible, tell us what happened," said Eraton.

Both waved as they ran to a clearing not far away. Garyth and Eraton disappeared. The pick-up craft beamed them up.

Two days later, Larton, Rayanna and the rest of the small assault group heard via the intergalactic news channel, that over fifteen thousand Draconians and ten thousand Lacertains died from consuming food. Many more were seriously ill. They were taken to hospitals that couldn't cope with the volume of suddenly ill land-based Draconians. And Lacertians. Making their tasks more difficult was not knowing what poison they were dealing with.

There was a community announcement to warn citizens not to consume products coming from two factories. The news reader conveyed to the public not to consume the new free sweet sample supplied in the named packets and return the food from the second factory for chemical analysis. The news reader announced that the food was contaminated with an unknown substance causing instant death and acute food poisoning.

Larton, Rayanna and the rest of the group cheered at the results. It was a massive hit.

Larton couldn't wipe the smile off his face. "That was the best attack ever. Now let's see what they do on Isobola. I can't wait."

CHAPTER 21

Isobola.

Neo and Ichiro were dropped off in a forest near one of the main holiday resorts. The resort was known for its five-star service and entertainment venues. It was the playground for the politicians, the rich and famous and all their families. People of all ages always felt safe and carefree. The children were always professionally entertained. This allowed the adults to socialize without keeping one eye on their precious tribe. The parents occasionally did take their children around to suitable events or participated in family-oriented events. Those venues had signs up, 'Parents must be accompanied by two or more children'. Most laughed at the requirements, but all enjoyed themselves in the family-friendly surroundings.

At one a.m., the resort was at its quietest. Slightly less than a skeleton staff were on duty. Ichiro and Neo with five of the rebels pretended to be slaves delivering food to the kitchen. They each pulled a cart loaded with assorted coloured paintballs and these included the 'new' black, red gel balls. They were directed to the kitchen and restaurant by one night staffer at the reception. Ichiro and Neo were intending to leave the boxes for the staff to sort out with Ashton's and Alcyn's telepathic help. The only kitchen hand looked at the boxes and smiled broadly. "Finally, the shipment has arrived. We have been waiting for months. Don't go. I want some help. See the bowls over there?" He pointed to a table that was loaded with clean crockery ready for the breakfast service. "Load up these overdue treats into bowls and place one bowl per table of four and two on larger tables." Ichiro and Neo with the rest of the group went to work and disappeared as soon as the task was completed.

The next morning, the guests who arrived early were delighted to see the treats on the table. They chattered their praise; delicious, exciting new flavours made their mouths water for more.

The children slipped out of their parent's control and tried to steal more from other tables. The kitchen staff brought out more balls and ate one of each colour themselves. They wanted to find out what the guests were raving about.

Within one hour later, most of the guests along with any staff who tried the new sweets were dead. The children died first. The parents panicked and in doing so accelerated the poison through their system. They died soon after.

The management was shocked. He and other staffers counted over one thousand dead. Not knowing the cause of the mass deaths, the owner walked around while holding four of the new sweets. Without thinking he ate a few while doing his inspection. He delighted with the flavour. He consumed the second ball. Slowly he started to feel ill. Suddenly held his neck and gasped for air. He collapsed. Two uneaten sweets tumbled out of his hand. A staffer accompanying him screamed. She slipped on the balls. The balls exploded releasing the toxic matter. She inhaled the fumes. She convulsed and choked on her own vomit.

Back on Nubia, Larton and his small group of followers were listening to the news. They cheered again. Another mass poisoning and this time the so-called cream of society went down. From experience, Larton knew, the so-called cream of society were the greatest oppressors. Just over one thousand down was good news. Larton slapped his hands on the table. "Just beautiful. Now there will be a mad scramble to the top. Daggers will fly everywhere. Instability will weaken them. " Lartaon stilled himself. He received a message from Ashton. "We are going to Daraxon next and then Centaria. Expect more but different." Larton snapped out of the daze. He whispered to himself, "Thank you."

Larton stood up with the aid of his walking stick. He went a few metres away from the group and stared up at the sky. He smiled as he rotated. *Dropping them by the thousands in raids is a dream come true. We just might win this long-drawn-out battle. Just who came up with the toxic stuff is a genius. A thank you for every dead Lacertian and Draconian.* He was ready to go back to his group when another telepathic thought and a different voice entered his brain. It was Alcyn this time. *I am Alcyn, not the Prince Alcyn you know. A new Alcyn. The poisons are from natural substances which are not available in Oberon or Amada. However, you can use cleaning agents as mini bombs. It worked well in Pleiades before it was blown up. Kyros's daughter is an ally. She heads the resistance group with Lacertians. Trust her.* The message stopped. Larton was confused, a Lacertian helping humans was not in his realm of knowledge. He looked at Kayler and Rayanna as they approached. "I just got word. There will be more attacks but not in Oberon. Amada will be next. Spot attacks like here. Find me information on President Kyros; his coup de tat, family everything. We just may have more local help than expected."

Rayanna frowned. "What is the sudden interest in Kyros?"

"I have my reasons," said Larton. He looked at an out-of-date map and pointed to the galaxy of Amada.

CHAPTER 22

Daraxon

Zindel with a group of Lyrians headed for the planet of Daraxon in the Amada galaxy. They were two light years away when they detected alarms for an attack sounding over the planet. Zindel and the Lyrians knew that they were detected. Zindel and the Lyrians aimed the cannons at the four hovering mother ships suddenly appearing in front of them. Four ships exploded. The space defence was destroyed.

Small fighter jets from the Daraxon scrambled to meet Zindel's mini armada in space. Without guidance from any mother ship and very little guidance from ground control, the pilots were not

co-ordinated in their defence. The cannons which fired from the Zindel's designed crafts built on Lyria were no match. One shot at one craft frequently resulted in nearby crafts exploding. The blast area was so large, and devastating, that few Draconian pilots escaped and returned to Daraxon.

The handful of survivors radioed in their experience and what they witnessed. The Daraxon command contacted the Draconian command in the other universe.

The attack stopped as fast as it started. Zindel's and the Lyrian crafts disappeared. The Draconian command on Daraxon went into panic mode. The four circling mother ships were gone and just over half of the ground crew were destroyed. The planet was open to attack. Not much helpful guidance came from Draconia.

Nodin and Eraton slipped onto Daraxon in two medium cargo ships loaded with gas cylinders. Under the cover of darkness and with the help of the local resistance group, one hundred large containers containing methane gas, tear gas mixed with pepper gas and mustard gas. The cylinders which were on wheels for easy manoeuvring were delivered to their designated locations. A mix of cylinders were placed at each air-conditioning vent at selected buildings.

The first was the four-story administration building for the city of Carnel, the old capital when Prince Alcyn was alive. The cylinders were loaded into the lifts at the end of the workday. Disguised as slaves going in to do menial tasks, no one questioned the movement of cylinders. On the rooftop, the genuine cylinders were redeployed with a timer to shut down at nine-thirty the following morning. Then the new cylinders would then activate. It would take close to twenty minutes for the poison to spread through the building. The upper floors would be the first to be gassed as they were closet to the cylinders and their main vents. Silently the group moved out to the next site.

The next was a major shopping centre that was six stories high and sprawled over two acres. Extra cylinders were laid on their sides and pointed towards a vent which was to draw out the heat for cooling down. This was to expedite the flow of toxins through the system.

In the main food hall, the towing ceilings which normally exposed the daytime sky through the skylight was now almost completely covered. A large adverting blimp filled the space. Under the blimp was a spinning sprinkler system ready to distribute its toxic substance, a blend of liquified chilli, garlic and bacteria from rotting food were added to agent orange. The timer was set. All the emergency exit doors were locked. Nodin used his glasses. A red beam shot out to melt the surrounding metal frame on to the door. The locks were given a similar treatment to ensure to stop Draconians and Lacertians from trying to escape.

The final drop off was at an enclosed auction centre designated for trading humans. The rebel group shot the guards with dart guns loaded with tranquilizers. Again, behind the air conditioning vents, cylinders containing tear gas and frozen nitrogen gas with an assisting propellent gas were installed. Above the stage area, bags of jackets were placed ready for the contents to fall onto the stage. It was just a matter of waiting for the show to being.

At mid-morning, the first stage of the attack began. By remote control, the air-conditioner system to the administration building switched tanks as pre-programed. Then the different gases were released spreading into the eyes, mouths and lungs of both Draconians and Lacertians. Panic set in. There was a rush to all doors within the various office floors. The lifts became useless as fallen bodies fell across open lift doors preventing the lift doors from closing. Some tried to smash windows by using their fists or furniture. The furniture would bounce back off the reinforced glass to hit the thrower or a Draconian or Lacertian close by. Trapped in the building, there was nearly one hundred per cent death rate.

While emergency services were rushing to the administration building, the shopping centre was next to experience an attack. From the safety of the water inspection tunnel just ten metres away from the front door, Eraton and two others emerged wearing Lacertian suits. They placed workman barriers up around the front door before using lasers to melt the architrave metal around the door. The door jammed onto the wall. New patrons to the centre were directed to one of three side doors for access. When completed, they placed an apology sign on the door and directed Draconians and Lacertians to an alternative access. The barrier was left in place. While the group disappeared down the water main access, Eraton activated the gas cylinders and turned on the blimp by remote control.

The blimp directed everyone's attention when Draconian music sounded out across the food hall. A laser light show ensured the Draconians and the Lacertians below were drawn into the entertainment. At first, looking like it was a part of the entertainment, a toxic show poured down directly over the crowd. It burnt eyes and entered mouths when any Draconian or Lacertian screamed. The poison entered their lungs via nostrils and throats swelled killing most in less than two minutes. The gas spreading through the air-conditioning system chocked others in different parts of the shopping centre. Some Draconians and Lacertians convulsed and went into spams before succumbing to the pollution. Bodies laid everywhere. Those trying to open the emergency exits to escape fell dead. The bodies blocked all access. Eraton met up with Nodin. They moved on while most of the rebels dispersed.

Dressed in their Lacertian costumes, the remaining group entered the auction venue. Above the stage, two of the resistance group were ready to tip the jackets over the humans. Eraton and Nodin walked on stage carrying laser wands disguised as electric prodders. The auctioneer and the bidders thought nothing of the Lacertians handing out a bit of discipline. It was normal. This time the prod hit the chains linking the humans by foot. The chain snapped. Just before each jab was supposed to be given, Nodin and Eraton would whisper, "This is a breakout. Act as if you were being struck with the prodder. We are cutting the chains. Put on the jackets on command and follow us out." The bewildered humans complied. They were used to following orders without question. Nodin disappeared off the stage to exit the emergency door.

Nodin used the remote control. Frozen nitrogen leaked out when the air conditioner fans went full speed. The temperature started to drop. The Draconians began to protest about the uncomfortable conditions. Too late. They began to shiver uncontrollably. One by one they began to collapse. On stage, the jackets rained down on the humans below. "Put on the clothes and follow me," said Eraton.

Obediently the humans put the jackets on and followed Eraton off the stage and to the only operational exit door. Eraton spoke to Nodin on the other side. "We're here." Nodin opened the door and assisted ushering the humans into six waiting transport vans. The vans drove away to the countryside. They pulled into a semi-collapsed barn. One barn door was fixed firmly. The other which swung previously back and forth on one buckled hinge was repaired. The van drove inside. They humans were ordered out.

The drivers opened the doors and ushered everyone out. Nodin and Eraton took off their suits and placed them in a large bag. Eraton opened a bag of tools he just previously placed on a makeshift bench. One of the rebels spoke. "We are going to cut off the rest of the chains. Lay down on the bench. Keep still." He demonstrated just in case some of the younger humans didn't understand. Nodin noted the smiles creeping across the faces of the escapee. He nodded. One by one the final leg chains were removed. Then each were directed to another table where food and water were set.

When the last chain was removed, Eraton packed up the tools and suits into a neat bundle. He radioed in for pick up. An hour later, one Lyrian cargo transporter which disguised its signals to penetrate the field of new crafts circling the planet, landed. Everyone bordered the craft and headed back to Lyria. Seventy-six humans were saved. They were going to be settled in Lyria.

Draconians on the mother ships circling another planet, heard the distress signal coming from three locations on Daraxon. The commander cursed. He turned on the scanners to see if there was any enemy aircraft.

Nothing showed up on the screen. He turned on all communication channels to Daraxon hoping to learn what had happened. He received sketchy details. It was enough for his anger and stress levels to jump about twenty points. He swore. He tried to communicate with anyone in the administration building and flight control. There was no response from the administration building. The flight controller was ignorant of the attack. Then he tried all the emergency services. Eventually, a female voice came through.

"Identify yourself," demanded the commander.

"Taufa. I am a reporter. I heard your signal."

"What is happening down there?"

"Three attacks. Thousands have died from chemicals," she spluttered between gasps of air.

"What chemicals?"

"How the fuck should I know? I am a reporter, not a chemist."

"Where did the attacks take place?"

"All were in the capital city of Carnel. The administration building, the largest shopping centre and the auction house. At the auction house, all humans were seen getting into military transporter vans which headed north. No one took much notice of the vans as they were all Draconian vehicles."

The commander sighed but the rage was at explosive point.

He ordered to his crew via the intercom system, "Get me security. I want them to go down and get first-hand information." To his staff on the deck. "Land on Daraxon."

When the crew landed, the commander drove in a hovercraft with a few of his staff to Carnel. He was directed to the administration building. He noted the organized chaos. Lacertians in less than effective protective suits working in pairs carrying out the dead. The dead were tossed into waiting vans. When the vans had six corpses, they drove off to the nearest cremation centre. Then the vans returned to collect more. The cycle continued almost non-stop.

At the shopping centre, it was much the same. Lacertians were do all the dirty work with minimal protection. Bodies close to the newly carved-out openings were removed first. As the Lacertians worked their way towards the main food hall, they stopped working and retreated.

The stench of the chemical absorbing the bodies presented a new level of toxicity. A few only agreed to remove the dead when given oxygen tanks and masks. When the commander saw these bodies coming out of the building, he was horrified. Like hundreds around him, the commander covered his nose. The chemicals had eaten their way into the bodies of the Draconians and the handful of Lacertians. The van driver refused to place the growing pile of bodies into their vehicles without the protection of masks and any other protective clothing. These bodies were driven to a different crematorium for immediate disposal.

The commander walked over to one decease child and then to an adult. The child 's chest had exploded from the toxin. The adult's body displayed chemical burns and the chemicals were still active; chewing away at the victim's body as he watched. He stepped away just in time. The adult's chest exploded from the building-up chemical reaction. The splatter sprayed over the Lacertians holding the body. A few by-standers received a few drops. They all screamed their horror. Panic. Where the infected body touched a Lacertians or an onlooker, their skin received a mild burn. More screams. More panic. The commander examined himself for spray. A scorch mark had formed on his shirt. He ripped it off. He examined himself. No burns. He gave a sigh of relief. He moved on to the auction centre on the edge of the city.

When he arrived, he saw Lacertians wearing warm clothing. The commander, still shirtless wandered over to examine the bodies. Some were frozen dead. Other Draconians were being treated for hyperthermia before being sent to the local hospital. He asked for the person in charge of the retrieval. He was directed to a military doctor. The commander introduced himself and explained his shirtless state. He held his ID up for the doctor. "What happened here?" asked the commander.

"I have never seen anything like it. We are not exactly sure. It was an attack to save humans. No one knows at this point in time, exactly how many humans escaped. It is an estimate between sixty and one hundred. It was extremely well organized. Our own military could learn a few tips from this attack. Sealed doors. Draconians squealed when they couldn't escape and froze slowly to death. A chemical of unknown origin was released through the air conditioning system. Well, it is unknown until we do a few autopsies." The doctor held up a packet. "These were dropped from above the stage. Humans put them on to keep them warm through the freezing process."

The commander examined the package contents and nodded as he absorbed the information. He asked, "How many dead from this attack?"

"Two hundred but many more are expected to die later if we don't get their body temperatures up.

The temperature dropped to minus ten, deep freezer temperatures. If you touch a finger and try to lift it, it snaps off. Disgusting. Effective. I have no idea yet how the event occurred."

One week later and on his circling ship, the commander read the reports from the three attack sites.

He wanted to supress the number of deaths but knew very well, the media would soon find the truth. He cursed at the unknown attacker or attackers but at the same time admired their skill. He had to let the Draconian command know of the attack. He was very concerned it would reflect on his competency and his career. He braced himself for the consequences and considered his options: voluntary retirement, forced retirement, demotion, or trial. Reluctantly, he sent an email and attached the reports. Just over twenty thousand Draconians dead in one hour. Many more seriously ill and expected to die. Others would never fully recover from the chemical effects. *Clever, dangerous bastards,* he thought to himself. *Lyrians? If not, Pleiadeans. There must be a colony of Pleiadeans or even Draconians somewhere on this planet or in this galaxy or in another galaxy. Their absence from attacks over the years was now understood. They were developing chemical weapons.* He added that to the report as a feint bid it would give him some redemption.

On Nubia, Larton and his followers cheered again. The Draconian losses were much higher than they could have imagined. When the others were asleep, he whispered to Rayanna and Kayler, "Centari is next."

"How do you know that?" asked Kayler.

"The stars told me." He winked.

CHAPTER 23

Centari.

Using telepathy boosted by the cranial neuro-transmitters, Ashton, Zindel, and Alcyn scoured the Centarian sky looking for a suitable place to attack. Alcyn lamented, *I can't see anything that will cause maximum damage with minimum effort.*

Ashton replied, *What about just dropping bags of beef jerky from the sky after a few jets do a fly over with advertising flags. What corporation needs discrediting?*

Zindel searched the planet. *How about the processing plant outside the city limits. Humans are converted and sold in jerky packets.*

Ashton said in matter of a fact manner, *Earth can produce all sort of flavoured jerky, including chilli. How about we buy the expired or near expired stuff in bulk and place a nice sauce of standard chilli and scorpion chilli. Another flavour soaked in a blend of Bifen LP and Reclaim with a touch of onion. And another flavour of eggshells and agent orange with a hint of cockroach spray. One sprinkled with assorted illegal drugs. Earth gets rid of the confiscated drug pile and these guys get to taste them. But the big tester will be one with tick venom. In humans it makes people allergic to all forms of meat, eggs and any form of dairy products from any animal. With luck, it may work in reverse with Lacertians and Draconians.*

Zindel asked, *What are those items are you talking about?* Ashton briefly explained. Zindel contacted Folami on Lyria. *Call off all crafts. Retreat. Give the Draconians a false sense of security. We are going back Earth to manufacture some deadly nice snacks for the Draconians.*

What? Do you want to feed those bastards? asked Folami.

Of course. Earth has a story called 'The Last Supper'. The title sounds very appropriate, but I have no idea what the story is about, said Zindel.

One month later Zindel and with the help of Ustin, the delivered sample boxes of poisoned jerky made from assorted dead cattle, dead horses and other animal carcasses to Lyria. Zendel and Ustin proudly presented sample packs to Folami. She looked at the professionally packaged food. Zindel said, "Don't even think about eating this. It would kill you or at least make you seriously and permanently ill."

"Follow me to the jail. We have a few Lacertians and Draconians who would love what they believe is human jerky."

Zindel followed her to the jail cells. Lech met them at the gates. "Folami. It is nice to see you again."

Folami reciprocated and introduced Zindel and Ustin. "We have some product testing to do. Have you fed them yet?"

"Their meal is due in fifteen minutes. They are just about at riot as we don't feed them human or other possible meat."

"Who are the most troublesome?" asked Zindel who was looking around at the facility.

Lech said without second thought, "There is one Lacertian who has always been super mean and a major bully. Then there are six Draconians who are totally demented."

Folami ordered, "Take me the bully and the psychos."

"We don't let these guys out. They are permanently in solitary."

Letch called out to the only Lacertian. "Hey! You. Number 276 it is your lucky day. We got you some human jerky."

The raspy voiced hissed, "About fucking time." He held out his hand through the bars. Zindel gave him the plain beef jerky repackaged in the appropriate Centari manufacturer's packaging. The Larcertian ripped the packet open and smelled the contents. "Hmm. It seems a bit different to the usual stuff." The Lacertian continued eating the product. The Lacertian gave the sign of approval. He bellowed for more.

"There is no more for you. Give the others a turn," said Lech.

Lech, Folami, Ustin and Zindel slowly walked down the aisle. The Lacertian's voice screamed behind them, "I WANT MORE JERK. GIVE ME MORE!"

His ranting drew the attention of all the Draconians in solitary confinement. They had their hands out ready to accept the uncommon, packaged treat. Lech went to the youngest rebel. Zindel handed him a packet. The flavour said, "Basted in blood." The Draconian smiled and ripped the packet open. He didn't smell the contents but guzzled the contents down. He burped, "I want more." His thrusted his hand between the bars hoping to grab another packet Zindel was holding.

Lech walked the group down further. Lech stepped towards at what he considered the king of all troublemakers. Lech handed him a packet. The Draconian hissed his disapproval, "FLAVOURED WITH GARDEN HERBS? WHAT CRAP IS THIS?"

A voice from across the aisle yelled, "If you don't want it, give it to me."

"Fuck you. It's mine."

The Draconian ripped it open. He nodded. "This is actually quite nice. Another packet?"

Lech hissed, "No. You have to behave a lot better before you get another."

Lech stopped outside a cell. "Hey. 391 get off the bed. You scored a jerky treat. Lucky you."

Lazily the old Draconian wandered over and placed his hand through the bars. He just snatched it without a word. He read the flavour, 'Fire'. He mumbled, "Can't they think of better names?"

He slowly ate the first piece. He coughed. "Yep. I can see why they call it Fire. It burns your mouth." He continued eating.

Zindel handed one young rebel Draconian a packet labelled, 'Crunchy'. The Draconian ripped it open and consumed the contents. "Yep. It is crunchy. He picked out the pieces caught in his teeth. "I WANT TO TRY ANOTHER FLAVOUR. GIVE ME ANOTHER PACKET!" he demanded. Zindel nodded. "Don't be greedy." One of your friends hasn't had any yet."

Lech handed the last Draconian one packet called, 'Salty.' The Draconian ripped open the packet and shoved the contents down his throat. He shook his head and held up the packet. "It wasn't salty, but it was delicious. It's more like a good strong alcoholic drink. MORE!"

As Zindel, Ustin, Lech and Folami looked back on the test subjects, they could hear demands for more and Draconians comparing their flavours.

They went through another set of iron gates to watch what would happen. The demands for more slowly changed. Now there were screams of agony. Others were rattling the iron bars to their cell. Then there were sounds of vomiting and verbal abuse. Eventually silence.

The group examined each cell. The Lacertian which had the plain beef jerky was alive but cursing as his other inmates were now obviously dead. He swore and rattled his cell bars. He spat at Folami and Lech. He missed. He ran to the toilet in his cell. Diarrhoea. He cursed, "YOU GAVE ME LAXITIVES! LAXITIVES!"

Lech, Ustin, Zindel, and Folami held their noses as they went back deeper into the cell block.

The smell of dead Draconians made them want to gag. Lech opened an emergency box and pulled out four of eight masks.

They looked at the cell where the Draconian was served 'Baste in Blood'. What was in that packet?" asked Folami. Zindel squinted his eyes to read the name on the packet. 'Basted in Blood'.

"On Earth, there are animals called frogs and toads. Most are harmless but there are species that exude highly toxic poisons. The moist coating which acted like a sauce in that packet contained a blend of frog and toad poisons. We need to get an autopsy done on all of the dead Draconians to see what bodily effects they have besides the obvious vomiting, diarrhoea, and affixation."

They stopped at the cell where the inmate consumed 'Flavoured with Garden Herbs'. The Draconian's stomach was swollen. His hand was around his neck. "Affixation," said Folami. It took an average of five minutes to kick in. What was in that?"

"The Earth people said it was a combination of lawn and garden spray to keep lizards from eating plants. There is supposed to be a touch of onion and garlic as well. Garlic and onions are plants human can consume but is toxic to earth lizards."

"Never heard of onions and garlic," said Lech.

They moved on.

Lech cautiously picked up the packet outside the next cell. He read the label, 'Fire."

Ustin took the packet from Lech and smelled it. He coughed. "What is in that?"

"I was told a huge mix of hottest chillies on earth chili with a touch of eggshell."

The group looked at the body. The Draconian had his head in the toilet and excretion rained down over his legs. Folami looked at the contorted body, "He didn't know which end to put on the toilet. Effective."

They moved to the next cell. Zindel said, "This one had 'salt'. There was salt but only a token amount. The rest was a cocktail of very addictive drugs."

Lech asked, "Why the hell is he wrapped in his bedding and on the floor with his clothes on back to front and looking like he has a smile on his face?"

"I was told some of those drugs cause hallucinations. I was told the drugs can produce paranoia and schizophrenia which could suddenly trigger the inner most deep fears to surface or as in this case, a false feeling of joy and comfort. The responses are erratic," said Zindel.

The next cell had a junior Draconian. He looked pale. He said in a raspy voice, "I feel sick. My stomach hurts. I want to see a doctor."

Lech was surprised to see the Draconian was so placid. "When these guests go." The group looked around as the security cage opened. A Lyrian was coming with a trolley of food. When he saw the others wearing masks, he immediately reached for a spare mask sitting on the floor. He looked curiously at the group and gasped at the deaths of most of the Draconans. He asked, "Are they able to eat food?"

Lech pointed to the Lacertian. "He can and this one at the back."

The Lacertian took his serving but wasn't really up to eating it immediately as he would have done in the past. The Lyrian with the food was surprised that the Lacertian took the food without the usual aggressive action and abuse.

As he wheeled the trolley down the small aisle, he looked at the dead Draconians. He shook his head.

"What happened here? How come so many dead?"

"An experiment. A new weapon" whispered Folami not wanting the surviving Darconian to hear.

The Lyrian offered the usual food to the survivor. The Draconian took the usual serving but asked for the other plate with a small array of vegetables as well. The group watched the Draconian. The Draconian went for the meat, chewed it for a few seconds and spat it out. He tried the vegetables. He consumed all the vegetables. Zindel pulled the others back and walked them to the security gate.

I think the 'Crunchy' worked. He couldn't handle meat. Keep a watch and see if this is short term or an ongoing side effect."

Everyone left the area. The security gates locked firmly behind them.

Lech spoke into his personal communication system, "Get cleaners and take the dead Draconians to the medical centre for autopsies. Decontamination protocols are required."

Days later Zindel received a report from Folami. The Lacertian has recovered from his bout of diarrhoea. The Draconian who ate the 'crunchy' jerky has improved a tiny bit. He has lost weight as he insists on eating meat and then suffers severe stomach pains. He is a skeleton of himself. If he continues to eat a vegetarian diet, he would be healthy. He doesn't want to listen."

"What about the others?"

"Their insides are a total mess," said Folami. "Internal bleeding in most organs, internal burns in most organs, mass ulceration to the face and chest areas, internal swelling to the point of near explosion, and clotting in different parts of the brain. All are effective."

Zindel replied, "I will report the results to Earth. "I think we can go ahead with the 'promotion' as earth people call it. We need to hack into the company's internet system and advertise the aerial drops of free samples. This will prepare the Draconians and the Lacertians to go outside at the designated time to see the display. The Draconians and Lacertians will see a jet flying at a slow speed with an advertising banner. The following jets flying behind will drop the samples all over the targeted cities. No exclusion zones."

When Zindel and Folami were alone in her office, Zindel said, "The earth people have faked the packaging of a genuine manufacturer on Centari. They are organizing a mass production of jerky of what is considered as seconds and any meat from feral animals causing damage to the environment. The Draconians and the Lacertians just pick up the sample off the streets. It will rain jerky. I will inform them of the test results. The one labelled 'Crunchy' has some effect on converting Draconians to consume less meat or cure them of meat eating altogether, at least in the short term. I will be back with more supplies of these products. Give me a couple of weeks to get more stock and I will help with the aerial drops."

Back on Earth, Zindel reported the findings to the U.N. He requested more in the way of donations of any dead animal to be turned into jerky. "We need about two million packets for the advertising promotion." Zindel heard a wave of chuckles in the room. When he gave the results of the experiment, the chuckles died down. He reminded them, "We don't need these bastards here."

Zindel with the help from Ustin, loaded the first of five mixed batches of 'sample products' into their cargo crafts. The journey from Lyria to Earth would take fifteen hours one way. As each delivery arrived, they were immediately loaded onto the first assault fighters. The fighters were almost devoid of the usual combat weapons. Other defence crafts would accompany them and hover at a distance to monitor any possible attacks of the jets delivering the sample products. Each sample was 75g in size, the minimum size for effective Draconian culling.

A week later the final delivery, the armada of Lyrian crafts guided by Zindel and Ustin reached five light years away from Centari. With the help of Ashton and Alcyn on Earth using their neuro-transmitter boosters, they located six mother ships circling the planet. Each commander of the ship contacted Cemtari stating they were leaving their positions in orbit to investigate oddities forming in space like a sudden rush of anti-matter or the formation of what appears to be embryonic white holes. Alcyn and Ashton had planted such material in the crew's mind via telepathy. Whatever the excuse Alcyn and Ashton dreamed up, the mother ships were lured away. When each mother ship was lured away from their planet, they were demolished by their own crew under the influence of Ashton and Alcyn or the escort ships from Lyria blasted them with Zindel's new cannon design. Now the armada of Lyrian ships were free to enter Centai. Ashton and Alcyn scanned the nearest control towers and entered the minds of the controller. They reported nothing despite the fact the localized internal alarms were ringing. They would announce to the crew, it was a false alarm or testing of the equipment. All was safe and clear. No need for the jets to go into defence mode.

The defence Lyrian crafts shot down any stray Draconian craft that either ignored the control tower's statements or didn't receive it. The jets were so far away' no warning of debris falling back to their planet could alert any authority.

The Lyrian crafts carrying the cargoes of toxic jerky continued to Centari. The craft carrying the large banner and the only one with near full capacity of armoury unfurled the massive banner. As it flew over the two main cities at the advertised time, citizens below rushed out of buildings to see the spectacle of a giant flag. Shortly after, as advertised it rained free samples.

The growing crowds in the street rushed to pick as many samples as they could. When it was obvious that all the samples were collected, some Draconians and Lacertians who had multiples of the same flavour, began bargaining and selling to those who were without or deficient in a flavours. Others were happy to have one or two packets and then squirreled away to consume the enticing morsels.

No area in the two cities was exempted from the bombardment of samples. The Lyrian crafts disappeared as fast as they had arrived. They flew to the defence team's protection before heading back to Lyria.

Zindel and Ustin held their positions to observe the mayhem below. Through their observational scopes and communication channels, they observed both Draconians and Lacertians. The trading and at times fighting slowly died down. Then things slowly changed for the worse.

There was mass vomiting, diarrhoea, Draconians and Lacertians dropping to the ground while having fits and going into anaphylactic shock. Those who took the 'salt' jerky, went into rampages. They attacked and often murdered any Draconian or Lacertian they saw in a bid to get more of the jerky. The effects of the addictions lingered longer, and the withdrawal symptoms raged for hours later.

Two hours later the poisoned jerky had done its work. The Draconian and Lacertian bodies, many contorted and defecated or suffocated on their own vomit littered the streets and inside buildings.

There was an urgent public broadcast and warning not to consume the samples of jerky. The company would be prosecuted. Any Draconian or Lacertian who had not consumed any sample or found samples lying around were to hand them into the nearest police station. Zindel smiled. Job complete.

On Nubia, Larton and his followers cheered. They held a modest party. Larton said, "These attacks explain the huge absence of agents over the last couple of years. They were developing poisons and new tactics."

Like the rest of the group, Rayanna kept smiling and was in awe of the death count on Centari.

"We all saw the so-called promotion before the food drop. It was brilliant. Over one million dead or dying in one swoop. I bet the Draconian Administration from wherever they came from is fuming."

Kayler reviewed the attack that was recorded by some clever Draconian. "They must have lured and wiped out the circling mother ships before the drop off. Those fighters are not from Centari. They are from another planet we haven't heard about, or they are a new model jet secretly developed. Whatever the case, they did a brilliant job. Centari was open to attack with no defence. The previous attacks were mere attacks just appetizers compared to what happened now."

Larton said, "I didn't mind the appetizers, but the main event was a feast. I just hope any resistance groups on Centari take advantage of the attack and start more localized targeted events to free more of their people."

CHAPTER 24

Draconian Command Centre.

News of the mass attack on Centari reached the Command centre in the Draconian Universe.

General Blaze and General Sanyana cursed when they read the reports of the Nubia, Daraxon, and Isobola. Nothing prepared them for the death toll on Centari. Secretly they conferred with each other. "Our heads will roll if the president gets wind of this major assault on Centari. Centari was one of the biggest bases for expansion in, through, and around the wasteland to that spiral galaxy where the Lyrians are. Just how did the Lyrians come up with these plans at a stage when we were almost ready for a takeover?" asked General Blaze

"Look at the footage from the sky and various street CCTs. again. Definitely, Lyrian crafts did this. They must have some secret underground research facility making these products. They faked the company making human jerky. Have the lab reports on the samples collected come back?" asked General Sanyana.

There was a knock on the door. Both men quickly closed their files and looked up at Colonel Yuma.

"I have a preliminary report. It is not good." He opened a screen which showed the initial findings.

Item 1. "The base ingredient in all packets appears to be of animal base. The animal or animals are unknown. To Draconians and Lacertians they have very addictive properties. This is why it was so effective. As soon as someone tasted the food, they couldn't stop consuming the pack.

Item 2. The names on the packets were an indication of the different poisons used. It is not clear at this stage if the names relate to the level of toxicity. Numerous toxins were used, and none are available on any known planet.

The Lyrians must know of a planet that has these toxins or has them in abundance. Alternatively, they have their scientists in a well-hidden facility creating these poisons. We cannot determine which is the correct answer at this stage.

Item 3. None of these compounds existed in the first attacks.

Recommendations.

A. Collect all samples not consumed for further testing and analysis.

B. Collect as many bodies as possible for a post-mortem.

C. Give samples to farmed humans to see what effects it has on them. This will allow for comparisons between the two species. It is suspected some humans will die while others will survive with or without long-term side effects.

The two generals grunted their dismay at the preliminary report. "They have been busy creating new toxins and what have we been doing besides building mother ships and fighter crafts?" asked General Blaze.

"We learned we have to diversify. It took us a while to learn to farm humans and optimize their taste. Now the Lyrians want chemical warfare. They will get it. What do we have to work with?"

Colonel Yuma flipped through his files. "Nothing that much. Let's see. AH HA! Copper dust, ground bird feathers, and ground eggshells. That is it."

General Sanyana became sarcastic. "I bet the humans will eat those items and ask for more. Mobile garbage boxes, that is what they are. We have to reproduce the gases they created and used on us. We can spray the humans with their own toxins."

"Problem. They were plant based. Until we find the plant or plants, then we have no hope of recreating the gases," retorted Colonel Yuma.

"Fuck. We are back to square one," said General Blaze.

There was a knock on the door. Commander Landryk entered. "Sorry for interrupting. We have just received word that eight mother ships exploded at the entrance to the human universe. The only ship to escape said there were no visible Lyrian ships of any order in the area. No other human-made ships or crafts. There was a small armada of crafts from a planet of unknown origin firing balls of mixed matter from an estimated distance of half a light year."

General Blaze slammed his hand on the desk. "Fuck those humans. They have united and they are coming from an unknown planet, most likely in that spiral galaxy. How many mother ships are stationed at Lacerta, Sufus, Marnef, Turbia, and Indulos?"

Commander Landryk referred to his electronic files. "The Lacertian colonies have a collective number of forty mother ships and all undergoing major maintenance. They should be ready in three days."

General Blaze nodded. "That gives us three days to plan a major hunt and attack in that galaxy. We give the Lyrians hell and then move on. Those two new planets that were discovered recently, what's the story on them?"

The one which has the hairy creatures which look a bit human-like, can be settled. The creatures are a temporary problem. The smaller ones are brainless, mischievous, and just annoying. They can be exterminated quickly. The middle-sized ones are by comparison, technologically advanced and are capable of building things. They may be converted into slaves. They are cannibalistic; they eat their dead. The extremely large ones lord over the other two groups. These large ones are non-edible, dangerous, and not trainable. They will have to be exterminated completely. The other planet is occupied by a small group of humans, all edible but smart with their tactics. They are the source of the weapons which deliver deadly metal pallets into Draconian and Lacertian bodies."

Commander Landrk's communication system beeped. He answered but put the system on speaker.

The others in the room sat in stunned silence. The frantic voice at the other end yelled, "Turbia and Indulos are being attacked. Heavy fire at all major cities. The cities are burning out of control. The attackers are going to the countryside and shooting with what is best called fire cannons." There was a crackling sound and then silence.

The people in the room swallowed hard. Anger filled their being. Eventually, General Sanyana spoke, "Tell the politicians what has happened to Turbia. Get the mother ships airborne in double haste. Fuck these humans. Send two motherships to locate other human races in that spiral galaxy. I am going on one of those mother ships to search for those bastards." The group stormed out of the room and dispersed to various parts of the Draconian city.

CHAPTER 25

Earth.

Zindel and Ustin returned to Earth. In a motel room, they briefed Jed, Hammond, and Tayee on what had happened and what could happen in the near future. Then Zindel went to the U.N. headquarters and demanded a meeting with all of the heads of state or diplomats who could assemble at the site at very short notice. Hours later, about fifty diplomats or representatives from different countries assembled. He quickly told them the news and the success of the attacks with laced jerky. He told them of attacks on mother ships galaxies far away. Then he broke the main news.

"It is imperative to stop all space exploration of any kind. Shut down all research into inner and out space, but most important not to send rhythmic radio signals to announce our whereabouts. This has to be replaced with searching the skies for any form of rhythmic or motor signals of electronic or radio or mechanical base. We have a recording of the sounds and will distribute them to all locations. It just search and listen. I want all space researchers including those working at the Haydron kaleidoscope meeting here within two days. This has to be across the planet not just one country adhering to the directive. Ignore this warning at your own peril." Zindel then faced a barrage of questions from the audience.

At the sudden forum, Hammond walked in with Alcyn PZ and a handful of people. Hammanod reintroduced himself and introduced Alcyn for the first time. He reintroduced what he termed as the unofficial 'guardians' who had been living on Earth undetected. Hammond gave a quick history of the escape of refugees to Earth and the role they had been doing since their arrival. Alcyn PZ gave a short introduction to his people. He explained the recent attack on his planet and the likelihood of more severe attacks.

Zindel then introduced himself but before he started speaking, displayed pictures of the Lacertians and Draconians with their combined history. He displayed the recent attacks on the Draconians and Lacertians using earth-made items. He finished with a recording of his crafts and small raiding crew attacking the Lacertrian colonies of Turbia and Indulos. Finally, Zindel showed the star map of the Milkyway. He drew lines linking Lyria, Earth, and Genesis. It was a near-perfect triangle. He added as a final statement, "I suspect there is a corridor in the middle of the triangle, or you may call it a wormhole. Where it goes at the other end is unknown, but I am absolutely certain, the Draconians have found it and are using it. This corridor makes travel in space faster by slicing off days or weeks between planets and galaxies."

"We must shut down any outgoing signals and monitor the sky for this sound." Zindel played the sound of a mother ship and sounds of different crafts which could emanate from the mother ship.

"Please take a recording of this enemy craft to your astronomy base be it just a telescope, research base, or space station. I will be sending a copy as well. The people in the space station must come home now and if possible, bring the space station back down. If you need help with that, my team will assist."

When Zindel stopped talking he was barraged with questions for over an hour. When he had enough, he held up a hand. "No more questions. Start shutting down all research projects and start scouring the sky for those sounds. Zindel spun around and disappeared leaving all gasping. Hammond and his small assembly of people answered more questions, but more were aimed at Alcyn. After a further thirty minutes, Hammond and Alcyn thanked the large crowd and left the podium.

Off stage, Alcyn placed himself on the ground of a hallway. He started to go into a trance. He listened only. He stood up and said, "Ustin has discovered the corridor and as Zindel guessed, it is smack in the middle of the triangle. Ustin and his team are exploring the corridor to learn where the exit is on the other side."

Tayee asked, "Is it possible to disrupt or close down the corridor?"

Alcyn went into a trance again and asked Ustin that same question. Alcyn came back with a reply, "He is not sure at this stage. He needs time to assess."

Hammond closed his eyes and sighed. "We have to get moving and start visiting each telescope sight and space base on this planet. We have to make sure the exploration shutdown is complete and only monitoring is in place."

Tayee was back at Daraxon Technologies looking through the telescope with his sons, Lenax and Egan. "Have all communication channels with every telescope and base open at all times. We have to work around the clock in eight-hour shifts. I will do the late afternoon to evening, Egan take the graveyard shift and Lenax take the early morning. In two weeks, we shuffle around the rosters. I expect the afternoon shift and the night ones to be the busiest with international chatter and so on. I will organize Appleton, Goldsmith, and Atkins to help out. It should be familiar territory for them, and it would be a break from their current routine work."

Regina Appleton walked into the telescope building. She smiled at the equipment before her. She spotted Lenax observing the stars. The radio noise from the monitoring stations was abuzz with voices. Without turning he said, "Hello, and settle in. Try to make sense of all that chatter."

Ten minutes later he turned to Regina, "Your turn to star gaze." Lenax played the recording of what to listen for and then added, "Anything that looks a bit different needs reporting. Anything of any size at any speed." They swapped workstations. Lenax listened to the radio chatter switching his attention at lightning speed from one radio to another. He was so focused he barely heard Regina asking questions. He merely grunted or asked for a repeat. Eventually, Regina gave up trying any conversation and watched through the telescope. Every two hours, Regina and Lenax swapped positions and tasks to avoid fatigue. Tayee and Robert Goldsmith came to do the second shift. The process was repeated with Egan and William Atkins.

The radio chatter between telescope bases and space bases died down. Questions and answers that were evident hours before were now almost non-existent. Everyone was listing for the sounds. When Ustin sent word to Hammond and Tayee of the confirmed corridor coordinates in the triangle. Eyes on the ground directed their focus to that location and the surrounding area.

From the European Space Agency, an alarm went out. "We hear a mother ship sound in that exact spot. Then the Chinese space base confirmed the reading and added, "There are four mother ships coming through. They hastily gave locations of the four ships." Hammond sent a pre-determined alarm sound to all telescopes and space bases. It was followed by, "Shut down as soon as possible.

Total silence." Within two hours, all the telescopes were shut down. Only the space bases were operating and then at half capacity.

In the room especially set up for remote viewing in Daraxon Technologies, Ashton, Alycn, Kora and Zindel donned the cranial neuro-transmitter and focused their attention on the four mother ships which were now splitting up. Two turned towards the direction of Genesis and two to Lyria. Zindel ordered, "Alcyn and I will do the two going to Genesis and you two take the pair going to Lyria. Focus and then attack."

Zindel and Alcyn entered the minds of the Draconians on both ships. Alcyn went to the engine room and made the head engineer go to the computerized controls. The Draconian started to switch the power off around the ship. The power to the automatic doors went down. It was quickly followed by lights and the power to the nuclear plant driving the mother ship. The emergency power generator switched the nuclear plant on and limited the lighting around the ship.

The Draconians knew they were under attack but couldn't escape the rooms. They were locked up.t The flight deck commander was furious and screaming orders. Then the mother ship stalled as the generators stopped functioning. The mother ship began to spin out of control and blew up.

The accompanying mother ship stalled. Zindel held the craft in a stable position by making the navigator change route. It was now at its designated location; stationary and ready for staff to disembark. A broadcast went out to disembark at the new planet. Obediently, the Daconians armed themselves and filed out to the mother ship. The first set to leave didn't continue. It hovered and shot every other Draconian jet leaving the mother ship. Then the jet followed jets that had exited via other doors. From behind the Zindel controlled pilot shot down the other jets. Every so often Zindel would leave the trailing pilot and enter the head of another to make the new pilot fire on those around him. The pilots who witnessed the self-destruction would fire on the out of control-pilot. Zindel then retreat to another pilot. Jumping from one pilot to another, the confused Draconian pilots began shooting at each other. The very few escaping pilots radioed and showed the scene to commander what was happening. Zindel finally took control of each escaping pilot and steered them into the glass-topped observation dome. Two were directed into the opened docking station. Instead of slowing down the pilots continued at full speed to come to an explosive end. Now structurally weakened, the pressure of space took its toll. The mother ship began to implode and then suddenly exploded.

With the job complete, Zindel and Alcyn directed their attention to the crafts still being tracked by Ashton and Kora. Ashton messaged, *They have received distress signals from the other ships. They are in attack mode.*

Zindel nodded. *Okay, we give these guys a bit to think about.* He slipped into the communication officer's mind and sent a new message to the Draconian command:

Apologies. There was a minor skirmish. Four Lyrian ships are downed. All ships going as planned.

When a reply was received, the communication officer deleted it and then replied:

The Lyrians have damaged the communication system of the two mother ships. They only have a small transmission range to us and maybe to other ships in the region.

Draconian command replied:

Notice of damage and communication difficulty is confirmed.

Zindel joined Kora on a ship going to Lyria. Kora was struggling to keep her focus on the commander. He was wrestling her for control of the ship. The ship was wobbling. Zindel gave her a hand and ordered one of the deck crew to go to sleep. *We don't have much time left. I am going to make the other crew go to sleep or slowly jettison them out. While I am away doing that, turn the ship around and head back to the corridor,* said Zindel.

 Kora had a hundred questions to ask but kept quiet. Zindel was going to be much busier than herself. She studied the controls and the navigation system. Jumping back and forth from commander to navigator, the ship turned around and started to head back to the corridor at a very slow speed.

Zindel went from room to room checking for occupants. The mess hall was his first target. About one hundred Draconianas were inside. A Lacertian came into view. He directed the Lacertian to a storeroom. Using some cleaning liquid he found in one storeroom, he rigged it to the air conditioning system. Slowly the droplets spread through the air. Below he could see the Draconians coughing and starting to hold their throats. They tried scrambling for the doors but found themselves locked inside. Slowly, each Draconian dropped to the ground. Some were at their seats with their heads slumped on the table or in their food. Others who tried to head to the doors were scattered at various distances around the room. One door was blocked with dead Draconians who just didn't quite make it out.

The controlled Lacertian opened a door to the dead or near-dead Draconians. He looked around to find a Draconian of a higher ranking. There was a table with four officers. Systematically, he searched for a master swipe card which could open and lock doors. He found a card on the fourth body. The Lacertian left the room. At each door to the mess hall, he placed the card against the control panel. With voice activation, the code was changed. This was repeated for every room or main room to a section of the ship. Zindel went to the engineering control room for air quality control. The controlled Lacertian slowly turned off the air supply in each section. After twenty minutes the effect took place. Mass suffocation began to take effect. Gasps and screaming for non-extent assistance and alarm buttons went unanswered.

Zindel returned to Kora. *How are you going with the ship?*

A bit harder now since the crew is dead. Shifting their arms is really difficult, dead weight.

Sorry. They are all dead now. I can help you. Put the ship into standby mode. It will hover.

On the other ship, Ashton and Alcyn were in control. The engine room was now locked and blocked by a Lacertain. The Lacertian fought initially verbally with the Draconians before going into a full physical brawl. The Lacertian was restrained to a post with cable ties. Then Ashton began working on the Draconians. They fought each other until only one remained standing. The survivor walked over to the Lacertian and cut him loose. Ashton then directed the Draconian to say, "Let's hide their deaths. Toss them in refuse hold." When all three bodies were dumped inside, the Draconian opened the lower hatch without closing off the inner door where he and the Lacertain were standing. All were sucked out into space.

In the control room, Alcyn was toying around with their brains. He made sure all forms of on-deck communications between crew were twisted. The navigator and the commander were the main focus. Jumping back and forth from commander to navigator, the commander yelled at the navigator about his incompetency. Allegations flew back and forth in the moments when Alcyn skipped from one Draconian to another. Eventually, Alcyn made the commander pull out a laser gun and shoot most of the crew. The commander bellowed, "More will die if this keeps up." Then he ordered the remaining skeleton to double up on tasks.

Zindel appeared to Alcyn, *Do you need some help?*

Ashton will need help to get rid of the rest of the crew, said Alcyn.

Zindel slipped away to search the ship. Ashton was moving down the corridor on the second level. The emergency lights were flashing amber. *What are you doing?* asked Zindel.

Mobilizing them into life crafts.

Zindel considered the action. *I have a tip for you. When they get on board, have the driver do two things. Put the craft on automatic to go one light year out and turn off the air supply. Let the crafts drift or blow them up.*

Aston grinned. *Nice.*

I will give you a hand. There are about thirty life rafts. I will take the ones on the left side of the ship.

Ashton and Zindel completed the task and sat back for a short period of time watching craft after craft zoom out to a safe distance from the mother ship. One by one, Ashton and Zindel planted into the minds of the pilots to go deeper into space and then turn off the air supply. Some crafts went out of control as the Draconians and Lacertians died from suffocation. Others just floated aimlessly in space knowing they couldn't return to the ship.

Alcyn who was still mind-controlling the commander ensured the commander and the skeleton crew ignored all communications and signals to and from life crafts escaping mother ship. When the last life raft stopped signalling, the commander looked at his remaining staff, and again yelled about their incompetence.

The commander momentarily came back to his senses when Alcyn left his mind and occupied another crew member. Alcyn commanded the Draconian to pull a laser gun hidden in a deceased crew member's jacket.

The dissenting Draconian turned to the commander and shot him in the face. Then aimed the gun at the others. Still, under Alcyn's control, the Draconian hissed, "Does anyone want to join the commander?"

The few survivors shook their heads. Seeing he had control and the others noticeably fearful of him, he snarled, "Let's go the Lyria."

Obediently, the navigation system was changed. To the horror of the rest of the trembling crew, the dissenter locked in the coordinates and then smashed the controls. Their fate was sealed.

Alcyn hung around a while longer until Zindel, Kora, and Ashton contacted him.

Zindel said, *Keep watch. Alcyn help Kora drive the ship to Genesis. I am going to let both Genesis and Lyria know they each have a captured ship coming in their direction. Kora and Alcyn start taking the ship to Genesis. When I get back, Ashton help me take the other ship to Lyria.*

When they were less than ten lightyears away, Kora and Alcyn notified the administration. Zindel sent a holographic image of himself and the mother ship and asked for orders as to where the ship was to land. A few hours later the captured ship landed on Genesis, not a sole was in sight. Zanthe smiled and whispered to Patrum, "Our gift for self-defence. Zindel must be on Earth and used his cranial neuro-transmitter to get this here. It will be up to us to learn how to operate this toy."

Zindel slipped into Lyria's president's mind. He gained President Folami's attention.

A gift for you. One Draconian abandoned ship is coming your way. Send a crew to take control.

My team will wait until one of your crew arrives.

Folami smiled and nodded. *Impressive. Thank you. We will study the ship head to toe. We might reproduce some for decoys.*

Zindel ordered everyone back to Earth. When all had recovered, he said with pride, "That was fun wasn't it?"

Too mentally exhausted to speak, the others looked at him and gave slow nods. "Fun," whispered Alcyn as he reached for a bottle of water beside his seat. Ashton, Kora, and Alcyn fell asleep in their seats. Zindel watched briefly before going to the small observatory on the Daraxon technology complex.

He knocked before entering. He announced, "The threat has been neutralized. Two ships were captured and taken to Genesis and Lyria. Let the others scanning the sky know but still monitor the sky as more will be on their way." Zindel left the room and looked up at the early evening sky. He sent a message. *Do you like the gift?*

Like it? Love it. It is on the base three for major analysis. When that is done, we will make a couple of smaller-scale replicas and a few decoy shell ones. I have a few ideas in mind. I am sure the committee will approve of the ideas, said Folami.

Zindel said, *Just another update for you. After the delivery of the food samples, Ustin, another emissary, and his team attacked Turbia and Indulos. That has really upset the Draconians.*

Folami laughed. *It gives them something to think about. Have you found the rip in the universe*?

Zindel replied, *Yes, A few of us made some attacks at the mother ships coming through. We passed through the gap to see what was there, but we were not there long enough to see for sure where their* planet *was. Earth people will make more laced jerky if required. But I think the element of surprise won't be as effective.*

Folami agreed. *Once is good, twice will be a failure unless the earth people can dream up something else equally as wicked.*

I am sure they can, replied Zindel.

CHAPTER 26

Lords of the Universe.

Same time period.

Azna examined the crafts at Aryon-Adon2. She looked at the new mother ship being built, the first in ten years. She smiled at both its size and technology. When she completed her inspection, she asked the head engineer, Brandlow, "How much longer before this baby is completed?"

"Just two more days and then three more for all systems check."

Azna nodded approval. "Is the crew being briefed?"

Brandlow looked across to the main building and pointed. "Yes. The second floor, room twenty.'

"Thanks. I just may take a stroll up there and see what the crew are doing."

When Anza reached the room, she knocked and let herself in. The crew in the room spun around from their simulators and stood up. In a chorus, "Greetings Ma'am."

Azna signalled for them to sit. "Continue working." She started circling the room and paused at different simulators where teams of people were being trained.

At one simulator, students were practicing aiming at a circle with zigzagging lines running across the centre. With every direct hit, the circle would explode. One of the trainees asked, "Why are we shooting at magnetic and gravity lines?"

Azna leaned over the simulator. "We have to close up the rip in the universe to keep the Draconians out. Blasting the waves and field is the only way we know how to close it up."

"What exactly is on the other side?"

"I would like to know myself. Draconians occupied the planets for sure. How many planets are unknown, and the size of that universe is unknown. It has to be sealed otherwise our existence will come to an end."

"Wouldn't it be better to fight the Draconians in their universe?"

"Yes it would but it would only be a dream. Logistics, duration, and resources toll are just a few considerations. Drawn-out wars with long logistics have always been the downfall of many great nations. Normally, we avoid war at all costs. This is our final resort, and we must defend ourselves."

Azna received a notice on her communication system. She gave the crew member a pat on the shoulder. "Continue."

When she was well away from any of the training crews, she looked at the text message and gasped as she read the report:

Successful skirmish attacks on Isobola, Nubia, Centari, and Daraxon. Estimated dead combined 2,400,000 and an estimated 2,000,000 injured some of whom are expected to die.

Successful aerial attacks on Indulos and Turbia. Death tally – unknown but all bases and the food supply was wiped out. Unfortunately, humans were also killed.

Azna phoned Jose who had sent the report. "The so-called skirmish attacks, who organized them?"

Jose replied, "Zindel and Ustin using assistance from Earth and Lyrians."

Azna swallowed hard. "How can Earth people help? They are not technologically advanced to assist?"

"They supplied the toxins and Lyrian delivered them. A handful of Pleiadean special forces refugees gave the final touches."

"That sounds highly co-operative. I didn't know there were special forces left anywhere. And…. Earth people can't get off the ground and Lyrians have never travelled to Earth for over 15,000 years. They only monitor Earth's progress."

Zindel and Ustin ferried the equipment to Lyria. Then the Lyrians distributed the items."

"Exactly what did Earth people make?" asked Azna.

"Pepper gas, mustard gas, poisoned paintballs, poisoned jerky, and a few ideas in the distribution of the fake products," said Jose who was now starting to read the detailed list of toxins used. He paused reading the list before him. He tapped his fingers on the desk. "Azna. These technologically backward people are just creative in their warfare ideas." He began to elaborate. "Poisons from assorted frogs, snakes, conch, garden bug control, hallucinogenic drugs, insect toxins...."

"Enough! Earth people have too much time on their hands if they can find these things in assorted animals and plants."

Azna changed the subject. "The new mother ship is beautiful. It is at least double the size of an average Draconian ship. It will give them something to think about."

"Will it withstand the gravitational and magnetic tsunami?" asked Jose.

"It better or we will all be sent back to the stone age."

Thuma joined the conversation. "Ustin and his team have detected a large number of Draconian mother ships coming through the rip. They are heading directly for Lacerta and its colonies; Turbia, Indulos, Sufus, and Marnef. Ustin did an excellent job on Turbia and Indulos."

Jose commented, "It will be a mix of search and rescue, salvage, and war preparations. They are very angry, to put it politely."

Azna scoffed. "Good. We haven't been jumping for joy for twenty-five-plus years. Bullies are always cry-babies when the tables are turned."

Thuma looked through his files. "Zindel and Ustin need to preserve their energy for the big showdown. I will organize other emissaries to give the new arrivals a welcoming party. I suggest Gitana from sector twenty-two and Enver from sector seventeen. They are the closest. They have their sectors under control, no interplanetary invasions and no Lacertian or Draconian issues either. It will give them something to do besides cruising around."

"Exactly what do you want them to do?" asked Thuma.

"Attack Lacerta, Sufus, and Marnef for starters," said Azna who was now starting to second guess the idea. "Zindel and Ustin need rest. They have time off. By my orders, it is do not disturb for a week."

This is the captain speaking.

We will be entering an area of turbulence. Please remove to the provided kitchen any food and drinks. Please stow away all hand luggage in the above lockers. Please put your seatbelts on.

CHAPTER 27

Lord of the Universe.

Attack.

The new mothership slowly rose into the sky. When it was half a light year away, the armada of attack fighters launched. Slowly they positioned themselves in their designated external bay. Now the ship looked like two arches on their sides converging at the control centre. Interspersed along the arches were walkways that went to and from the central control. At every fifty metres, there were living facilities for the crews; sleeping accommodation, mess halls, mini training pods, a lounge with a limited amount of entertainment, medical facilities, and fully equipped pair workshops.

The jets now carried Zindel's cannon with the usual armoury relegated to being back-up and short-range attacks. When jets were deployed, the mother ship dropped her 'babies' like a swarm of bees suddenly emerging from a disturbed hive. The mother ship became a temporary skeleton making itself a smaller target when under attack.

The mothership was nearing the rip in sector nineteen when an armada of twenty Draconian mother ships were detected. Azna and Thuma who were in the central control centre as observers gasp with the rest of the crew. The alarm sounded through the ship. Everyone scrambled to their positions.

Commander Bijan of the Lord's fleet ordered, "Let them through. Attack from the rear. It slows them down if they have to turn the ships around to respond to us. Jets one to forty prepare cannon attack. Two jets per ship. Aim for the underbelly and the exhaust. The emissions will expand the explosion."

Minutes later, the jets were in position. All fired simultaneously and then retreated as fast as they could. Nineteen direct hits saw nineteen mother ships explode simultaneously causing shock waves

of chemicals and radiations disturb the balance of black matter in the area. This effected the gravity waves which cause the remaining damaged mother ship off course. While the Draconian crew were trying to restore their ship's navigational system, the ship belonging to the Lords, fired. The ship was decimated.

Commander Bijan ordered, "Let's continue to the rip. Keep alert for more mother ships."

Azna muttered to Thuma, "I looked at the gravitational shift monitor. Outside is very unstable. We need to do a system's check." She was about to approach Bijan when he ordered, "System check."

Minutes later the navigator called out, "We are off course by one degree. The shock wave was greater than anticipated. Correction is being implemented."

The Lord's mother ship neared the rip. The ship came to a stop some twenty light years away. "Commander, we are too close. We need to be back another five more light years." Before Commander Bijan could respond, the alarm sounded again. Commander Bijan looked at the command screen and swore. "We are surrounded by Draconian jets. All jets attack."

he mumbled to himself, "There has to be one or more Draconian mother ships around."

Bijan ordered, do not disembark your crafts just yet. Just fire your cannons first. After two shots disengage for ariel combat."

The Lords of the Universe squadron used their cannons and backup equipment in a deadly space dogfight. After three hours, the remaining Draconian fighters retreated. Thuma swore and alerted Commander Bijan, "There is another wave of ships. Their jets are retreating to other mother ships."

Bijan ordered, "The large cannon needs to be activated. Crews get ready for shockwaves."

Everyone scrambled to their safety positions. The jets which were out in space, returned home at warp speed, attached themselves to the mother ship and braced for the shockwave. The large cannon on the mother ship fired. The mother ship rocked from the force of the cannons firing. Then a few minutes later there was a rebound wave that was stronger than expected. It was coming directly towards the shaking ship. The mother ship rocked, groaned, and then rolled. When it stabilized, Commander Bijan ordered, "Abort mission."

The Draconians were sent scurrying in all directions. The unfamiliar sensation of the ground moving, and buildings collapsing was psychologically devastating. Numbed by the experience and not knowing the cause, many looked to the sky searching for an invading fleet.

On the planet of Marnef, a Draconian flight controller sent out a distress signal to the Draconian command in the Dranconian universe. Colonel Yuna responded, "Fuck." Then he composed himself, "Just how did the humans develop such technology to wipe out five planets in one go? And this comes on top of the destruction of thirty-two mother ships in two days. There has to be a superior race." He closed off communications and marched to the war room. As he entered, he slammed the door. He gave the bad news to the people inside.

General Blaze slammed his fist on the desk. "Before it was poisons. Now this. We can't lose. We will be executed for incompetence. Send fake reports to the administrators."

"Cover up?" questioned General Sanyana.

General Blaze drew in a long breath. "Damned if we do and damned if we don't. No difference other than we plan our own exile."

"And exactly where do we go into exile?" asked General Sanyana.

"There is a small colony on the planet of Beta Canari."

"That outpost?"

"Better than the other places. No one is making you go. It is your choice."

CHAPTER 28

Beta Cancari.

By Draconian standards, a small Draconian diplomatic service ship landed on the largest base on Beta Cancari. The Draconians at the base scrambled to welcome the unscheduled visitors. The door opened. Stepping out were General Sanyana, General Blaze, and Colonel Yuna. Confidentially they strode towards the assembled Draconians.

"Who is the person in command?" asked Colonel Yuma.

A much older Draconian stepped forward. "I am. Captain Roja. Welcome to the colony. It was called Beta Cancari but we renamed ourselves Pygmius." Roji ushered the arrivals to the main building. Colonel Yuna turned his head towards the diplomatic ship. He stretched his arms sideways just like any normal stretch movement. That was the signal for the commander on board to leave the planet.

Captain Roja asked, "Where is the ship going? Aren't the crew staying?"

General Blaze lied, "They have orders to go to Xion. They will be back in three days."

Captain Roja directed the unexpected arrivals to the main building on the base. He turned to his guests. "This planet is not very big. You may have noticed that in your approach. The humans here are small in stature which is in a way handy as there are no leftovers, a very convenient package. However, they are difficult to catch. They have gone into hiding. We also suspect there is a group of rebel Lacertians assisting them. Just who they are is not known but they have caused significant damage to our crafts and food supply."

General Sanyana looked out of the window to study the immediate terrain. He pointed to the airstrip at a distance from the building.

"Why are there so many jets on the ground?"

"That is a sample of the work of the human sympathizers. We ordered the starter switches almost a month ago only to learn the mother ship carrying valuable parts and other equipment was attacked and blew up with other mother ships carrying other valuable supplies."

General Sanyana gave an order, "Take us to the jets. I want to examine the sabotaged jets."

At the base, Captain Roja escorted the guests around. General Sanyana examined one of the jets missing its starter switch. When he got out of the jet, he looked around at its condition. "The jets are a mess. At least keep them clean and ready for action."

"We did do that for a while. The water supply suddenly became contaminated with high levels of sulphur. It corroded the jets' exterior and anyone who drank the water became seriously ill. We call it a drought. Clean water is scarce now," replied Captain Roja. "The base has been landing attacked by several times. We suspect the renegade Lacertians."

General Sanyan growled, "Have you sent out teams on land to find the bastards?"

Captain Roja nodded. "They are attacked and killed. Those who survive the attack, die from their injuries due to a lack of medical supplies. Now we stick to aerial surveillance and attacks. That was working well until the rebels got themselves our only operational large jet and a six-person land carrier. We lose in the sky, and we lose on the ground."

General Blaze looked furious. "There is no such concept of losing, only winning. Get your act together and start conquering."

Shortly after returning to the main base, a group of Draconians who were on patrol walked into the camp. One was nursing an injured arm. He walked to the medical bay. He was quickly examined. The arm was cleaned and dressed. Colonel Yuna watched the procedure. "Aren't you giving him antibiotics?"

The doctor looked at Colonel Yuna. "We're out of them. Do you have any?"

"He needs proper treatment!"

"If it bothers you so much, recall the mother ship you came on and give us some supplies," retorted the doctor. The colonel walked away knowing that was not going to happen. If the ship returned, they would be arrested and taken back to Draconia to face trial.

CHAPTER 29

Lyria

Folami was in a holographic conference with Zindel and Ustin. They swapped reports of attacks on Draconian mother ships and the outcomes. Jose interrupted the mini conference via hologram. He gave the latest report on the effects of the mother ships being blown up at the same time.

"The mega blast sent gravity and magnetic shockwaves mixed with an array of radiation through space. It caused massive quakes in Lacerta and its colonies. Measurements are being conducted on the effects of dark matter and on the nearest black hole. We will get back with the results as soon as possible. In the meantime, it will be chemical and mind control attacks. Blowing up the hole or rip with its massive gravity, assorted rays, and magnetic fields will be reassessed in the light of the current events."

Folami sighed. "You mean the attacks were a test run to measure the effects of a major explosion that occurred in space?"

Jose nodded. "Yes. We are calculating what could be a tsunami effect of altered gravity, magnetic forces, and all the different radio and sonar waves through space. If we don't then we could wipe out our own races in sectors eighteen to twenty-two. That will leave the Draconians open to all of our planets."

Zindel asked, "Do you want earth people to continue to manufacture chemicals for distribution through the galaxies?"

Jose invited himself into the gathering and grinned. "They will be earning their protection. I believe they have drug lords making some very dangerous drugs. The police have storage and disposal problems. We can fix that issue for Earth. If the toxic drugs can be transported in bulk to Lyria, we will assist in the aerial bombing of Draconian-occupied cities. Other poisons are welcomed. I think they have snake, spider, conch, frog and toad venom to start with. They also have a wealth of poisonous plants. I believe some of those plants a very safe for humans but toxic to Lacertians and Draconians." Jose turned to Ustin who hadn't said a word as he was absorbing new information being presented at the meeting. "Ustin assembled a big team for mind control. Include any Lyians, Ashton, Alcyn PZ, and anyone else for takeover of the main planets in Amada and Oberon. Ustin have your team assemble on Genseis even though there are some Draconian attacks. Zindel, I want you to lead any capable Lyrians. "The holograms switched off.

Folami, Zindel, and Ustin looked at each other. Zindel drummed his fingers on the desk. "Will your people take orders from an outsider?"

Folami responded, "Actually, we don't have much choice. What exactly would happen if the gravity field were massively disturbed?"

Ustin offered scenarios. "Planets might shift. Time may shift but impossible to tell in which direction. Gravity fields on some planets may change resulting in loss of atmosphere. Planets may become dead or as in the Lacertian group, mass quakes killing thousands. Dark energy and dark matter may change due to altered states of fermions in both substances. The universe could collapse in one section of its sphere. That will have a domino effect in other sectors such as other galaxies shifting their positions to fill the void. Alternatively, everything slips into another dimension, namely the fifth dimension. Who knows. If the explosion of about 30 mother ships can upset the closest planets, we must carefully consider the effect of what could happen if the rip in sector nineteen is blasted to smithereens. We close the rip, but we kill ourselves in the process. A pause in this war will be prudent. Now we need to organize teams of mind controllers or remote viewers to keep the pressure up on the Draconians."

"Changes in tactics will keep the Draconians guessing what will happen next. They didn't expect to lose so many ships and Draconians in a short period of time. Nor did they expect chemical attacks on their food or air. Then there were unexplained attacks on their ships from Zindel's small mind control group. Attacks have to be random in time and style. Just enough to frustrate them. Not knowing where or when or what type of attack is damaging psychologically speaking. Many of their citizens just may want to pack up and go back to Draconia. If they pack up, the remote viewers can still attack the ships returning. They have to make sure it is at random locations and random styles.

As earth people say, let's screw them or play with them. Dive them away by creating fear and insecurities," said Zindel.

"Since when did earth people become tacticians in war?" asked Folami.

"They have always been at war with each other. It is like a self-culling process. The best tacticians win. The best-resourced wins. Keeping the supply line as short as possible is crucial. Hit and run at random locations and different techniques of attack is another thing they are good at. Those primitive people aren't too primitive in war tactics. I just wish they could apply that to keep the peace between themselves. But now their mindset could be our saving grace, our weapon," said Zindel.

CHAPTER 30

Genesis

Ustin entered the only motel on Genesis and went directly to the conference room.

As he entered, he looked around the room in a bid to find familiar faces when he was introduced to the administrators by Zindel. He recognized five of the ten faces immediately and offered both a smile and a nod. He placed himself at the nearest seat, just on the right of Patrum. Patrum stood up, greeted him and introduced Ustin to the group.

After the meeting, Ustin assembled a small group of mind-controls or remote viewers as he preferred to call them in an adjoining room. Comfortable recliner chairs were placed in a circle.

Bottles of water and small food platters were placed beside each recliner. The cranial neuro-transmitters were placed on each seat. One by one the people came in. When the group was complete, he introduced the newcomers, Ashton and Alcyn, plus Enver. "Eat and drink up. Make sure you are comfortable before we get started. The sessions will be long and mentally very tiring," said Ustin.

"Let's do a few warmups without the transmitters," said Ustin.

The group placed the transmitters on their laps or on the floor beside them. Ustin rolled ten balls into the centre. "Make them rise and unite as a group," ordered Ustin. The balls began to rise slowly in the air, then they clustered together. "Separate them and make them bounce up and down three times and then fly around the room twice before reforming the cluster." Ustin watched as the warmup instructions were carried out. "Return the balls to the basket. We are finished with the warm-up." He looked around the group and smiled. "Now, I will explain our mission."

In groups of three, the remote viewers searched the area close to the rip. As the mother ships came through, each group nominated which ship there were going to attack.

Ashton was paired with two of the more experienced people from Ustin's group. He sent them a message. *Do you two know anything about these Draconians?*

Not much, they chorused.

Okay. They are greedy, self-absorbed and always in for sex. We can manipulate these traits and cause havoc. Let's find the commander and get him to make a few announcements which will send the crew into a frenzy.

What are you planning to do? asked Higs, one of the new team members.

 Watch, smiled Aston. *Just help me find the commander. He isn't on the flight deck. Resting I suppose.*

After ten minutes of searching, Higs said, *I have the bastard in an orgy on the second deck. I see what you mean about sexual appetite.*

Ashton grinned. *Get one of the females to turn on the monitor and send pictures through the ship.*

Higs went inside the female's head. She withdrew and flipped the communication switch. Then she flipped another for a general broadcast. She adjusted the camera onto the commander and the two other females. Ashton took over her mind as Higs moved out. Through the intercom, she purred seductively, "Guys, I am so hot and so are my room mates. We need more people to join us. There are females in the communal spa desperately needing sexual relief. Help those poor females out.

Please come up to this deck and into the spa. Going through the rip has made us females ever so

hot for attention. It must have something to do with the magnetism boost. Ooh yeah." She blew a seductive kiss and left the system on.

Minutes later, many males left their posts and ran to the deck where most females had their quarters. The males banged heavily on doors until they were nearly knocked down or when the females opened them. The males attacked the females while others fought over a female. With males outnumbering the females one to four, fights for the females became common over the mother ship. The flight deck crew did their best to resist the temptation but gave into the primal urge to mate. The flight deck was abandoned and set on remote. *Damn,* cursed Ja-ne, the other team member. *We need to get someone to move the controls.*

I'll get someone said, Aston. Ashton found a young Draconian and guided him into the flight deck.

The young Draconian was guided to the commander's seat. Ashton filled his head with occupational aspirations. The hand of the Draconian turned off the remote. The young Draconian rubbed his hands with delight. "I can fly this craft. I can do it," he muttered to himself. Ashton directed the craft towards a white dwarf. *Full speed ahead., You can do this. Larceta is just on the other side of the white dwarf.* The Draconian felt a set of achievements. Then he reset the remote control before leaving the flight deck to rejoin the others in the orgies and brawling. Ashton, Higs, and Ja-ne watched as the mother ship was captured by the gravitational force of the white dwarf. *Mission complete. Let's go home,"* said Higs.

On another mother ship, Alcyn with two of Ustin's team, Bolo, and Dice smiled as they entered the navigator's head. All the data was slowly changed making the mother ship turn around and fly back to the rip. Instead of going through the safe top half where the fields were non-existent or widely spaced, the ship flew into the lower half to suddenly compress as if it were going through a black hole. There was a small explosion in galactic terms.

Two more mother ships went back to the rip. Ustin guided one ship to fire on another. The Commander of the ship under attack retaliated. Alcyn's team took control. The two ships fired upon each other until they exploded in space.

Back on Genesis, the team members slowly recovered from their battle. They swapped notes.

When Ashton took the floor he lamented, "If we had the transporter fully operational with the viewer, we could have done more damage."

Alcyn smirked. "Like putting poisonous food on the tables? Or some other stuff to cause a riot?

"Exactly," replied Ashton.

"The viewer is kind of done. I am not sure if it would work at this stage," said Alcyn.

"Is it possible to give it a try next time?" asked Ustin.

"If we can work on it together, it just might be ready in a couple of days," replied Alcyn.

Four Days Later.

Exhausted by the round-a-clock construction of the viewer, Ashton, Alcyn, and Ustin gave it a test.

They aimed the viewer at Earth. "Okay," said Ashton. "Earth has some very unsavoury creatures. How about we transport some of them here and then transfer them to a Draconian spaceship."

"What do you think will happen?" asked Alcyn.

"Hard to say," said Ashton who was now grinning at the possibilities. "Chaos for sure. Death maybe."

"What do you want to bring up and store?" asked Ustin.

"Hmm. We need to make glass enclosures with water pools and a heat lamp. As for the food, well we will watch and see what the animals need and bring some of that as well," replied Ashton who was now second guessing the idea.

Ustin looked through the scope. "What am I supposed to see?"

"Spiders, toads, poisonous frogs, snakes, crocodiles, alligators, jellyfish, sting rays and so on," replied Ashton.

Ustin coughed. "Educate me. What do they look like?"

"They look like... I better do this," said Ashton. He took the control chair and guided the viewer to the Florida Everglades.

"Test one. A juvenile alligator," said Ashton. He aimed the viewer at the creature. Nothing happened.

Alcyn added, "If I recall from my past life, you need to zoom in to less than five metres."

Ashton decided to step aside and let Alcyn zoom in. The vortex created sucked the creature into the air. In forty minutes, the alligator landed in the glass receiving area. As they approached the receiving area, the alligator snapped its jaws and displayed every sign of agitation. "What do we do with it now?" Asked Ustin who was terrified of the creature. The others stared at him. "Umm. We leave it there," advised Ashton. "That thing is a killing machine."

"Where do we transport it to?" asked Ustin.

"Is there a mother ship coming through?" asked Alcyn.

Ustin went quiet as he focused his attention on searching space.

"Okay, not exactly a mother ship but a carrier transporting Draconian holidaymakers. Let's see. There is a communal bath, a hot bath for Draconians but just right of that is a children's playground. It looks like an in-flight resort. Perfect."

"Give me some co-ordinates," asked Alcyn.

Alcyn adjusted the viewer. "Here we go. One very agro alligator on a cruise ship." He placed the alligator in the warm salty water.

The animal initially looked dazed. It adjusted itself to the new surroundings. Food is in unlimited supply. The alligator swam up to a female teenage Draconian. It took her by the waist in its powerful jaws. Then it went into a death roll while other girls screamed in horror. Stunned Draconians looked on while others scrambled out of the bath. Children in the playground sensing the panic, screamed as they ran to their mothers. Histeria and panic took over as the Draconians gathered their offspring and ran out of the two facilities. By then, the alligator had killed and consumed a part of the Draconian female leaving the remainder of the body to float to the surface bleeding out to discolour the water. The alligator sank to the bottom of the water before deciding to climb out to inspect the new surroundings. It eyed the children's park. It wandered over, inspected the facilities, and sniffed the ground. Food was here. Then it returned to the bloodied salt water.

The commander of the ship watched through the screen as four security guards entered the enclosure. They saw the floating body and the communal bath now contaminated with blood. They cautiously walked over to the edge. Two of the group with their laser guns drawn left the area to inspect the adjoining playground. Nothing. As they returned to the water's edge, there was a splash and a disturbance in the water. One of the guards disappeared. There was some thrashing in the water, but the remaining Draconians couldn't immediately see what the creature was.

More blood filled the spa. A guard missing an arm floated to the surface. The commander and the remaining guards retreated.

"Lock down the area. Drain this communal bath. Let's see what we are dealing with," ordered the commander.

The spa area was drained. The alligator was revealed happily munching on a Draconian.

"What in Draconia is that?" asked the commander watching the process on screen from the safety of the flight deck.

"More importantly, just how did that creature get on board?" asked the captain in a soft voice.

"Whatever it is, it has to be killed. We better not have any more on board. That thing is a nightmare. Send in two guards but don't let them venture more than a metre from the door," said the commander.

Two guards entered the closed public area. Their guns were aimed at the alligator. "Let's fire on it at the same time," said the older guard. "On the count of three. One, two three." The lasers fired. The alligator's tough skin offered some protection. Injured but not killed, the agitated alligator dropped its meal and swaggered over towards the guards. The guards ran out of the area and locked the door. Both puffed as they recovered. They looked through the glass observation window. "What is that?"

"Fuck if I know. It eats us. That is bad news."

"I hope there is no more on this ship," said the older Draconian.

"Where did that thing go?" asked the younger Draconian. They heard a few banging noises. The thin wall shook a little. The guards ran down the passageway to another of waiting pair guards. "It's trying to break out. Lock this section." The waiting guards locked the passageway. The trashing stopped. The guards waited with drawn guns. An hour passed when one guards said, "I will take a look. Cover me."

The Draconian walked nervously forward to the now cracked observation window. He couldn't see the creature immediately. He continued looking. Then he jumped back in fear but was much too late. The alligator sprung up, smashed through the glass and pulled the guard into the enclosure.

Terrified the others locked the passageway. No report was needed. All was captured by surveillance cameras. That footage would be transmitted to other vessels.

Alcyn, Ashton and Ustin drew back from the viewer, "That should slow down holiday travel," said Ashton.

"How about we place a few alligators and crocodiles around the ship? When it is bedtime for most of the Draconians we let loose with crocodiles and alligators."

Ashton, Alcyn, and Ustin collected fifty animals. The largest was no bigger than three metres. The majority were between half a metre and thirty centimetres. The small ones were liberally dumped in passageways. The larger ones were placed in the dining halls. The largest was held back for the time being. It would be transported where necessary.

The small crocodiles were hungry and irritated by the transportation process. Food was the only thing on their minds. As the passageways extended, the line of reptiles thinned out. Each was left to their own. Screams from night shift staff began to echo through the ship.

The commander was awakened from his quarters. A plague had entered his ship. He yelled orders for doors to be locked. No one was to enter the passageways. Orders were given for all passengers to lock themselves inside their quarters until further notice. Staff scurried around the ship where passageways were clear. With guns armed, they formed small groups. When they shot at the small crocodiles or alligators, the collective rays killed the animals. Over twenty small crocodiles and alligators died. Each was taken to a laboratory for examination. Thinking all was clear, an order was given out it was safe in the corridors. People left the safety of the quarters and headed in different directions, many going to the dining room.

In the dining room, the crocodiles and alligators could smell the food; chefs working in the kitchen.

The doors were locked to the kitchen area itself. The head chef did that as a precaution. The animals

had wandered the rooms and fought with each other before settling down under the tables draped with white tablecloths. Their sleep was disturbed by Draconians walking in. Dinner was being served.

When the crocodiles and alligators saw legs appear before them, the crocodiles and alligators attacked. The male Draconian was pulled under the table and eaten. The unlucky Draconian screamed out his demise, while others ran in panic through the doors and back to their rooms. This time they were joined by the kitchen staff who left food cooking on the cooktops.

The alligators and crocodiles wandered into the area. They jumped up to the overhanging pot handles. The hot pots fell over them. The burnt animals hissed their pain. Some of the unaffected attacked the injured. Other crocodiles escaped through the open dining room doors. More panic.

Guards came running in groups. Shooting multiple rays didn't seem to stop the larger creatures. The guards ran. The passageways were sealed again. Anyone caught in the passageways became history.

The remaining passengers and crew could only watch on streamed screens the carnage unfolding.

The commander gave the order for all to go to life raths. There was scoffing. To get to most life rafts, meant a perilous trip down the infested passageways. Only two full life rafts were launched. The crafts were filled with holiday makers who braved the passageways to reach the safety of the life rafts but none knew how to operate them. The trapped people waited.

Seeing nothing more could be done to stop the invasion; the commander filed a report of the infestation of creatures. It was accompanied by video clips. Then he gave the order to the crew on the flight deck, to abandon their work and enter the attached life raft.

Ashton whispered, "No you don't. Put the last crocodile at the life raft door." Minutes later, the nearly full raft had a three-meter alligator blocking the door. Those inside we trapped in the raft while others outside were trapped on the flight deck. The alligator attacked at random those nearest to him. The crew took out their laser guns. The alligator's skin burned but it didn't kill the animal. Now angered by the injury, the alligator went into a frenzy.

Injured Draconians were scattered across the control deck. The life raft disembarked taking only a few intact crew members. The alligator inspected his on deck meals. When he pulled down any standing Draconian, some of the pre-set flight controls shifted. The craft was now out of control.

It flew into the high-pressure carbon gas field emitting both heat and light. The ship fried to a crisp as the powerful rays eventually incinerated the craft.

"Now for a few more different creatures but only when we see a mother ship," said Ustin.

"Don't be a spoiled sport. A Draconian is a Draconian. They eat us humans."

Four Days later.

Ashton, Alcyn, Ustin and now Zindel were telepathically searching the Amada and Oberon. Zindel whistled. "I have found two extra-large mother ships. And from what I can see, they are heading for Xion. Let's give them something else to think about."

Ashton smiled. "We have a big collection of cane toads that are happily mating. I was informed the eggs they are laying are just as toxic as the secretion from the glands. Just transport the toads in cases with the lids slightly ajar to the main water supply of the ship. The toads will find their own way out."

The toads were dumped into the main water filter system on the advancing ship. The suction aggravated the glands of the toads. Toxins and eggs were sucked through. As the water was consumed, Draconians either dropped dead or buckled over in agony trying to vomit up the poison. But they too, scummed to the toxins. The ships on automatic navigation and no Draconian control headed for Xion.

When the Xion space controllers received no return contact with the now ghost ship, they denied the ship landing permission. Instead, the controllers watched the ship wobble and rotate, a clear sign it was out of control. The head space controller said, "Something is seriously wrong. There has been no response. Just blast the ship out of the sky."

The ship took three critical hits before exploding. In different parts of Xion, bits of rubble were found and taken to space control for examination. Nothing was found to indicate anything was wrong with the ship. No body parts were recovered for examination; obviously incinerated in the explosion.

"Nice work," said Zindel. He knew the administrators on Xion made the right decision. Most of the crew were dead from an unknown cause. A contaminated ship is best destroyed. Any surviving toad would have contaminated the planet.

CHAPTER 31

The Draconian Command Certre in Draconia.

The vacuum created by the sudden departure of the now declared fugitives, General Sanyana, General Blaze, and Colonel Yuna was quickly filled by three more eager power-hungry Draconians.

General Foth read the two reports before forwarding them to General Dota and Colonel Pardie.

He then called a meeting.

"The humans have invented dangerous creatures. One is small and carries poisons which go into the waterways to kill our population. The other consumes Draconians. The latter looks like a very deformed Lacertian; totally hideous. You have seen the pictures and the film clips." The others nodded and looked disgusted.

General Dota gritted his teeth. "Many years ago, when I was a mere sergeant, I was told how the then Prince Alcyn created monsters which wrecked three motherships. Now we know, he didn't create them but were creatures from a planet we call T71. I believe the captured humans call that planet Affen Welt. But we never discovered how Prince Alcyn was able to transport these creatures into our ships. It was like they travelled through both space and walls of any description.

I thought Prince Alcyn was dead."

"By all reports, he was dead; vaporized when a ship exploded over his palace in Daroxon. He must have shifted all his research to another planet yet unknown to us. The scientist there must have reconstructed whatever he created. We need to find the planet and the scientists," said General Foth.

Colonel replayed the film clips associated with the report. Thoughtfully he said, "These are not creatures created by DNA and genetic manipulation. They exist. The question is where?

Untamed humans have a knack for creative destruction. They are genius at it. The humans who escaped must have found a planet teaming with exotic and dangerous creatures. Over the last twenty-five years, they have learned about these animals and how to deal with or co-exist with them. Clever. Very clever. Just where in this universe is this planet? And how do they make these animals travel through walls of any description? That is more ingenious. We are totally defenceless against that technology."

General Foth tapped away at his tablet. He brought up past reports on disasters. He skimmed through them. Then he looked at the others, "Technology going through walls of any description and distance is one weapon. I suspect they have another far more sinister one. Look at the recent disasters nearly fifty mother ships were lost in a period of six Draconian months. A few who escaped said Draconians at all levels went crazy; suddenly partying, fighting each other, shooting each and deliberately leaving their posts to partake in such activities. Most of the changes of behaviour occurred just on the other side of the rip, in sector nineteen. Is there another way to enter the human universe?"

General Dota responded, "We never found an alternative entrance. We have searched for many years to no avail. Sector nineteen is it. Our scientists have been trying different techniques to bridge the two universes to create an alternative doorway. Nothing has worked. Just nothing."

"You can poo-poo this mad idea but if you can think of something better, I will be more than happy to drop the idea. Since we are talking hypothetical and basically nonsense according to our scientists, just suppose humans can do mind control. They can crawl into our heads and make us do all sorts of dangerous things. Just a mad idea," said Colonel Pardie.

"Don't be so ridiculous," scoffed General Foth. "Humans don't have the intelligence for that. Not possible. Have you ever heard of any Daconians being able to read other Draconian minds, let alone control them?"

"Just because we can't do it, it doesn't mean humans can't," defended Colonel Pardie.

"Suppose if they could. How do we protect ourselves from that?" asked General Dota who was horrified at the thought of such an intrusive weapon.

"Absolutely, no idea," said Colonel Pardie.

"We have some captured humans in the cells. Most are sentenced for consumption. We can take a few for experiments and see if this mind-control thing is true. I doubt it would be true," said Dota.

"Shall we try this crazy idea? It will be entertaining if nothing else."

Two Days Later.

Three Draconian doctors and two scientists accompanied by ten guards and Generals Dota and Foth and Colonel Pardie, watched four humans strapped firmly on surgical beds. Wires attached to their heads were tested for any brain activity. The results barely registered on the Draconian equipment.

One doctor asked, "What exactly do you want these humans to do?"

"I am going inside, and I want you to instruct them to make me jump up and down ten times. We will start with that simple task," said Pardie who was now removing all his weapons from his uniform.

He entered the room and nodded. He stood beside the closed door just in case he required a quick exit or rescue. He raised his arm. The tables were tilted for the four humans to see him. One doctor gave the humans instruction. The monitoring team studied the wave pattern emitted by the human brains. The pattern barely shifted. The doctor ordered the experiment to stop after twenty minutes.

Those monitoring the brain waves showed near flat lines. "Let's try again," said a supervising doctor.

"This time the doctor gave the same order, but this time offered a reward. "The person who can make the subject jump even once will get an extra serving of food and some wine."

The humans looked at the colonel standing near the door. Again, nothing happened. Again, it was a near flat line of brain activity. General Foth muttered, "Not even a bribe can make these inferior creatures perform. Wrap it up. Sorry for wasting your time. Take them away to their holding cells."

Back in the command centre, the trio sat down again to consider different tactics to suppress the human attacks on their ships. "Well, we can cancel out mind control. They don't have the intelligence for that. We should focus on finding this planet or planets filled with these dangerous and toxic creatures. If the apes were in sector twenty, we should focus on that sector," said Foth.

"We know for sure that planet with the mixed races of humans doesn't have these animals, but they fought back with some innovative weapons. Since the last battle, we haven't been able to get near them. They have trained their people to defend themselves well. The Lyrians have been holding out for over twenty-five years. We know for sure these toxic animals are not from that planet. They definitely have a top-secret laboratory or facility creating new powerful weapons. That facility is well hidden, and our limited intelligence seems to confirm its existence," said Colonel Pardie.

"Then the only conclusion is another planet teaming with creatures of all types; the source of human biological weapons," said Foth who was irritated at the thoughts of a hidden planet or laboratories.

Their deliberations were interrupted by an incoming report. Another attack had occurred. This time the attack was just within the human side of the rip. "How is this possible?" yelled Dota. "Bold bastards. Which teams were on duty to guard the entrance?"

A shaky voice at the other end said, "I will forward that information. They have also been attacked and their ships destroyed. The only vague message was some advanced weapon mounted on top of attack crafts entered and fired at everything in sight. No more transmission after that short one. I will play it for you.

 "I think these are modified Lyrian jets with some very advanced weapon sitting on top of the crafts. They are shooting ….."

"That is all we have. We have sent out crafts to defend the area. Shields up this time."

"Get a team to collect any debris for analysis. That includes bodies," said General Foth.

"Sir, that is not possible. Early reports indicate there is nothing to be found. Everything has been

vapourized."

Dota switched off the communication and swore. "The humans know of the rip. That has been thoroughly confirmed. Vaporization of crafts on our side is a declaration of war."

"We have more questions than answers. Who leaked the location of the rip? Were they helped by rebel Lacertians? Who is helping the Lyrians? I cannot believe they suddenly made this quantum jump in weapon technology all by themselves. The recent skirmishes on the planets using chemicals are also an insult," said General Foth. He slammed his fist on the conference table. "History is repeating itself. Fuck."

Another communication came through. The trio looked at the screen.

 "General Blaze, General Sanyana, and Colonel Yuna have been located on planet X21also known as Beta Cancari. The planet is a Lacertian rebel stronghold."

Colonel Pardie muttered under his breath before issuing an order, "Bring them back and if they resist, kill them." The two generals nodded their agreement. "Incompetent traitors," whispered Foth.

CHAPTER 32

Beta Cancari

On Beta Cancari, the two generals and the colonel concluded their planetary inspection. Satisfied most things were in order, they commandeered one of the few permanent residential huts. General Sanyana helped himself to an alcoholic drink. After downing the drink, he poured a drink for the others. "Cheers to a life of retirement." Colonel Yuna and General Blaze joined the toast. "To retirement." Yuna looked around the accommodation. "We will have to get the underlings to build better facilities to be more than base camp. I don't know why these soldiers have been so slack. Trees and other resources are abundant. There is really no excuse other than a lack of foresight and long-term planning. We should draw up plans."

The other two lifted their glasses. "To a new outpost city."

General Blaze grinned and added. "May we reign over this planet."

After three days of discussion, the trio completed a plan for a new city. Now it was just a matter of diverting the existing personnel from patrol to construction. They had no problem securing help as many knew being on construction was a much safer option than being shot at by rebels. To many, the native humans, Mammalians weren't that tasty. Chasing seconds, as many thought them to be, was a waste of time. The only advantage was that their small stature meant no leftovers, a convenient package. The flown in humans from other planets, with a bit of care, were less troublesome and tastier.

One week later, two timber buildings were erected. A new headquarters was fitted out with the best equipment removed from a series of large tents. The command centre looked impressive. The second building was equally as large. It was the entertainment centre; bars, females and electronic games all flown in after thieving such equipment from Xion and Segma. Yuna smirked at the acquisitions.

Observing from a distance, Kyrina and her small band of rebels shook their heads in disgust. "No way are you pricks going to settle in for the long haul. Tonight, we go in and add a few fireworks to their celebration." Kyrina looked at the group. Nage studied the entertainment building. "Nice. Very few exist for the size of the building. It's about fifty metres away from the other building which I assume is a headquarters or control centre. We can hit the two in one go if we just plant bombs at six locations for each building: one at each corner and two down the sides. What doesn't go up in the air will collapse inward to kill the occupants. The buildings were done in such a hurry and the workmanship is so poor, they will easily collapse and burn. We better get working on the fireworks."

Two nights later, Nage led the team into the base. A mix of Draconians and Lacertians were already drunk and sprawled out on the street or were engaging in the heated debate which would soon deteriorate into a fight. Nobody cared or noticed the strangers walking in full view. They were just a patrol of Lacertians returning.

Nage directed the team where to insert the bombs. As he was doing so, a Draconian walked by and began to question the group. Nage held up an empty bottle of liquor and acted drunk. Arika and Milo began smooching. The sober Draconian looked at Nage in disgust. "That is the new headquarters. Show some respect. Nage swayed and burped as he held up the bottle. Arika and Milo gave the Draconian the finger and continued. The finger was a clear sign not to interrupt or take away the female. The Draconian moved on.

Minutes late both buildings were laced with bombs. The team was now out of the base and ready in position. Kryina had ensured the water supply was turned off. Roni and Cerella would turn it back on as soon as any Draconian or Lacertian were seen running to the control of the water supply. They all waited in their positions. Kyrina counted as she looked at the timer. "One, two, three. Bang."

Both buildings imploded with some debris flying into the sky. Fire followed. Panicked Draconians and Lacertians ran out to the street. With bodies alight, they howled their agony. Others who were on duty ran to their aide but were frustrated as the water supply was non-existent. When Cerella and Roni saw Draconians running towards them, they quickly gave a turn of the water controls and left.

From her vantage point, Kyrina smiled at the devastation. As each of her team returned, she gave a sigh of relief. They watched for a few seconds then hurriedly left the area. Now well away and safely back at their cave entrance, they looked through their binoculars and smiled. The fire was out of control. Plumes of smoke and fire lit up the night sky as the water supply dried up. Draconians and Lacertians fled the area leaving the fire to spread uncontrolled to the surrounding land.

Kyrina said, "I wonder just how many of those bastards are dead."

Nage said rather firmly, "About ten in the headquarters and about thirty in the bar. A good hit but still too many are around." A noise was heard from above. A large personnel carrier arrived. It was circling the out-of-control fire in the base. Nage saw it land to the south but couldn't see who was arriving. Cerella left the safety of the cave and climbed higher. She was back within minutes.

"Not re-enforcements or any fire crew. Draconian government cops. They could be after us. Let's get out of here."

They went through the cave system to the location not far from the Mammalians. They observed the activities of the tribe. Kyrina and Milo smiled. "They look good. I just hope they are left in peace."

Milo nudged Kyrina. "The baby we delivered seems to have settled down, but the adopted mother is the only one going near it. The other babies seem to draw more attention. I suppose that was to be expected."

Kyrina nodded. "There is no way in this world could we have raised that child. At least it has a chance at life." She turned to Milo. "Let's keep moving. I believe we need to pester another base which has a lot of jets. Come."

Two days later they looked over another Draconian base. After hours of observation, they went under the cover of darkness to the first set of jets lined up and prepared for early morning patrols.

Cerella, Milo, Arika and Roni slipped past the only guard who was sleeping on the ground.

With hand signals only, each member approached a jet with a set vandalism actions. Each would eventually lead to a mid-air mal function. Hopefully, some would just drop out of the sky like a rock. Others would have loss of control when the jets reached a certain height or distance from the base.

Twenty jets would be downed. But another thirty would remain untouched but ready for another day. Kyrina immediately led the team away from the base. They all knew there would be search parties for the saboteurs. The group went through the cave system again to rest and plan their next move.

They emerged two days later and headed south towards the contaminated area where the Draconian ship crash landed years before. They were about halfway to their planned location which was another Draconian base. A Draconian hovercraft zoomed up beside them. "Hey, you there. What patrol group are you?"

Milo responded while the others did their best to shield their face. "Group three just coming off night patrol. No activity in our allocated zone."

The Draconian nodded. "Want a lift? No one else is on bord. There is plenty space inside for all of you.

"Sure do," said Milo with enthusiasm. The group climbed abord the near empty craft. When the moment was right, and the unsuspecting Lacertian was comfortable with the group, Akira and Milo attacked. Minutes later the driver was dead. His body was jettisoned into the tall grass outside the craft. The two other who were originally on board were shot and their bodies jettisoned beside the dead driver.

Kyrina smiled. "This will save my aching legs. Now that we have a land craft, we can move around this planet much faster. Milo teach Nage and Roni how to operate this craft. Let's by-pass this base for the moment and go to the downed ship over the old Pleiadean city."

The hovercraft reached the destroyed city withing ten minutes. The radiation alarm sounded in the craft. Milo pushed the button for the shield to surround the ship. Slowly the rebels flew over the wreckage. Cerella gasped. "Look at all the dead unburied Lacertian bodies. All appear to have died from excessive radiation. Disgusting." Her anger was visible to the others. The anger spread like a fast-acting virus. "Get out of here," said Kyrina who was now holding back a tear.

The hovercraft headed towards the mountains which once was a supposed safe refuge for the Pleiadeans. They examined each lower entrance for contamination before going around the mountain to the other side. Again, they examined each entrance until they came across one which did not emit any radiation. They parked the hovercraft as close as possible to the entrance. They were only ten metres away; the surrounding terrain gave some shelter to the solen craft.

Kyrina and her group slowly climbed out and walked across the bumpy rock surface to the cave.

There was a door blocking their entrance. "Shit," said Nage as he placed his hand over the sensor panel. The mechanical voice spoke in Pleiadean denying access. "Great," he said in a sarcastic tone.

"Arika, can you use your electronic skills to get around this?"

Arika looked at the panel. She ummed and ahred. "Stand back." She fired a single shot below the panel and one above. Then she removed the outer cover and screen. She examined the wires for a few seconds. Stuff this, she thought and ripped out all the wires with her hand. The door opened.

"Come on," she said to the others.

The alarm sounded inside the short tunnel. Roni shot the red rotating light and the sound box. The place was deadly quiet.

They came across a set of tables and chairs now covered in a layer of dust. Nage found another room full of bunker beds three tiers high. He made a quick estimate of beds. Two hundred people bunkered down here but only the lower beds appeared to have been used and then only those close to the dining area.

Cerella went in another direction, down a small tunnel. She opened the door. She gasped. In the cribs were decaying foetuses of Pleiadeans. She shut the door quickly and took stock. She wanted to unsee the sight but that would never happen. She reported back to the group who saw she was distressed. "We will not go in there," said Kyrina is a soft voice. "Seal it. We rest here tonight and then we move back."

The next morning, they were about to take off again in the hovercraft, a message came through on the communication system.

Craft ten report back your position.

Milo replied, "Craft Ten reporting. We had a breakdown. We're on the way back to the base. All is repaired."

The voice on the other ends said, "Go to sector five. We have found some people in a canyon. Go and get them since you are the closest."

"Will do," said Milo as he turned off the system. "You all heard that." The others nodded.

"Go as far as possible with this craft and then into the caves again and see what is happening there. Let's just hope there is no massacre or capturing for food," said Nage fearing the worst.

From a nearby cave, the group observed the Mammalians. "Good," said Kyrina. "They appear to be

in tack. They must have been spotted by a jet flying overhead. No one has arrived yet. We go down as close as possible and make a perimeter. Just make sure these people don't see us. They can't tell the difference between us and their attackers."

A crude perimeter was set up. Milo asked Kyrina if he could take a gamble. "I want to send misinformation back to base. I want to tell them we have searched the area, found some evidence but the people have moved on. They appear to have left in a hurry."

Kyrina nodded. "Confusing patrols will cause delays. It will give us more time."

Milo left his position. Minutes later he was talking to the base and any craft overhead. He gave the misinformation. Immediately there was confusion. Although Milo could not see any approaching craft, he could hear them u-turn in the sky and return to base. He gave a sigh of relief. He radioed to base. "Team Ten is going to search the area on foot. We will report back tomorrow morning."

The person on duty at the base gave approval and forwarded the return delay to his superiors.

The next morning, Milo informed the base, "The people have definitely moved out of this canyon area. We followed tracks heading south. They have made camp very close to base three."

"We will send jets in that direction," said the unknown voice.

Milo grinned. He stepped out of the hovercraft to make his call to Kyrina. "We have the jets heading south. The false information is the people are making a new camp close to base three."

Kyrina thought about the diversion. "Good. We will stay a few more hours here to make sure no jets fly over. We don't need a pilot reporting back that the people have returned. Then we head to base three and see what we can do to stir up trouble."

From a distance Kryina and her group checked out base three. Perched on the tallest hill, they had panoramic views of the base and the surrounding area. They could see foot patrols who leaving to search for the non-existent mammalian camp. A jet circled overhead assisting the ground patrols. Cerella noticed the base was close to being deserted. The grounded jets were being serviced by Lacertians who were supervised by Draconians. She tugged on Kyrina's arm. "We can almost walk in and plant bombs. I only counted ten Lacertians, and all were looking very bored. How about we go down and give them something to do?"

Arika did a check on the numbers. "Yep. Bored alright. Two are nodding off to sleep in the warm sun. If we approach the sleeping Lacertians, we can slip around to the administration building. From there we can access just about all the tents. We can plant mini bombs in each tent and then set them off at night when most are sleeping. They should sleep well after a full day of searching for nothing."

Kyrina watched her group enter the camp. They went in and out of the tents planting mini bombs.

The last place was the administration building where Roni surrounded the building with larger bombs. As he did so, he looked through each window assessing the contents. There was no one in the back room. A door to that room was ajar. He looked around for a possible Lacertian or Draconian who may have stepped out. No one was around. He slipped inside and helped himself to some medical supplies. Pleased with the haul, he left the building with a full bag.

When he and the others arrived at the hideout, he displayed the goods. Smiles beams across all their faces. "Very nice work," said Kyrina. "Now let's get some shut eye for a few hours and then let's see the fireworks."

At eleven at night, Kyrina woke each member of her group. "Show time," she said as she walked around the group.

Below, the camp was quiet. Only a few Lacertians were on patrol. Milo noticed no one was near any of the jets. "Can we delay this for thirty minutes. I want to add a few to the jets. I think every second jet should suffice. They are so bunched up, any jet going up will damage the one beside it. Anyone want to come?"

Milo nodded. "Let's get this done a.s.a.p."

When Milo and Roni returned, the group sat down with a small selection of food and drinks. They each had their cup filled. "Ready for the entertainment," asked Kyrina. The others nodded. She pushed the buttons on the remote control. Bang. Bang. Bang. More followed. Milo said, "Now for the grand finale." Kyrina handed him the controls. "Be my guest." He pushed the button. The jets went up. The fire raged towards the jets with no bombs. Panic in the base set in. Those on night patrol didn't know where to start. Fires, screams, explosions appeared in all the tents and then the jets went up. The fire equipment for the surviving Draconians and Lacertians was inadequate. All they could do was run away from everything; they didn't know what was going to explode next. The fires from the jets raged out of control aided by increase wind.

Kyrina's group looked on. "I think we did a good job on that base. Let's start moving. That wind is directing the fire in this direction," said Arika. The group went to the hovercraft and drove back to the Mammalian settlement. They just arrived when Milo received a message. "Team Ten, we have reports of a fire coming close to the location of base three. Go and investigate."

Milo replied, "We just left the area and barely escaped the fires. It was an attack by Mammalians. They were obviously in the base while patrols were searching for them. We did a quick search for them. We couldn't do much due to the fires. However, we did see some Mammalian bodies. They got caught when the wind fanned the fires."

"How many died," asked the unknown voice.

"At the base, it is easier to count the survivors; between ten and twenty. We had to get out before the hovercraft went up in flames. I think most of the Mammalians died in the fires as well," lied Milo.

"I will send someone to assess the damage and look for survivors," said the voice.

Milo just turned off the radio. "Let's keep low for a few days."

Milo and Arika moved slowly away from the camp. Arika voiced her concern in a soft voice hoping no one would ear. "I am worried about Kyrina. Her injuries are slowing her down."

"She is still mentally as sharp as ever. I agree we need to keep an eye on her as much as possible. I will have a chat to her. I know she will deny everything."

"No let me do it," said Arika. "Female to female is much better. I will get around it with idle girl talk."

Arika slowly approached Kyrina. They chattered about the past, the present and the future. The conversation was punctuated with feelings now newfound capabilities. Arkia ended the conversation with time to sleep before the next set discussion of future attacks.

The next day Roni turned on the Draconian radio. He heard a generalised message regarding three Draconian fugitives: the two general and a colonel. He smirked and whispered to Cerella who was also listening. "Good luck finding those bastards. If they were in the base with the nice wooden buildings, the scavengers will have fun piecing together their parts, that is if the runaways were on base and inside the buildings."

Cerella nodded. "Watch the greed spew out. The reward isn't very high but enough for some to leave their posts. In the early stages of this war when Prince Alcyn was alive, the bounty for his capture was astronomical. Hundreds of Lacertians left their workstations in all walks of life to try to find Alcyn. Most went bankrupt trying to locate him. The ship that hovered on the roof of the main palace building blew up. Prince Alcyn must have vaporised in the explosion. I was told that Prince Alcyn ordered all staff out of the palace, but he stayed behind. I wonder where most of the palace people escaped to."

"Kyrina mentioned the two galaxies were in a mess. Those in Amada didn't have enough crafts to evacuate that many citizens. Where they went is unknown. The people in Oberon had more crafts and started evacuations much earlier. This place was once a Pleiadean refugee planet which was gifted to us by the Pleiadeans. Kyrina is hell-bent on keeping this planet for Lacertians, namely, rebel Lacertians. "

"I saw Kyrina writing in her small laptop. I think she is chronicling the history of the place. At times I see her very deep in thought. She has guarded that computer with all her power. I think she will hand it over on her death bed.

Speaking of which, can't be that many months away. Her condition is really declining," said Roni.

"The others have noticed it too," said Cerella.

Three days later they were about to move onto the next Draconian base. Arika went to get Kyrina. Kyrina didn't budge. Kyrina had died in her sleep. Arika ran to the other and told them of the news.

They dropped their belongings and went to see Kyrina. Tears flowed. The mission was delayed. They divided up her belongings, all precious items for a resource scarce group. Arika found Kyrina's small laptop and read the contents under different files. She read the file names to the others but only opened a few to read out. The first of these was the trade agreement between Xion and Segma.

They wondered if that could be honoured since the Draconians took over the planet.

The next file contained notes which had no embellishment. Just a list of planets in Oberon, Amada and their co-ordinates. Then there was with the planet Tiamat. After Tiamat was three question marks: no galaxy listing, no coordinates just three question marks. Underneath was another planet name with its name crossed out as several times as if she couldn't work out the spelling. After each deletion were another set of question marks. The information puzzled the group.

If they were planets or even bases, where were they? Just how did she know about these places.

Nage slipped the small laptop into his backpack. "That is precious cargo. It must never fall into the hands of the Draconians."

The group began to dig a grave near the entrance of the cave. They placed a maker, a Lacertian honour's marker and inscribed her name. Nage said, "She deserves a much better burial than this humble place and marker. When we get rid of the Draconianas, we will begin a new civilization and the capital will be called Kyrina.

CHAPTER 33

Earth.

Same Time Period.

At Daraxon Technologies, the board was in a meeting. Hammond gave an account of the finances and how much the cost of their share of funding the interplanetary war had cost. It was beginning to drain the company.

Tayee followed with a report from all the astronomy centres. All types of signals to gain information about any star or exoplanet was halted. Earth was in shutdown. The risk of a Draconian ship picking up the signal was too high. They didn't want a beacon to guide them to Earth. Tayee followed his report with another. Most of the countries had donated something. He smiled as he read the list:

biological waste, human waste, stockpiled banned chemicals, old stocks of biological laboratory bacteria and viruses, confiscated narcotics, toxins from snakes, eels, and other assorted animals....see appendix, weapons of all ages and descriptions, including nuclear weapons. To Tayee and the rest of the board members government seized the opportunity to clean up their part of the planet. He chuckled when he read out, "Some park rangers in the US saw alligators fly into a vortex. I bet they were wondering how they were flying into space and why."

Jed looked alarmed when he recalled being sucked up by a vortex many years ago. "Hold on a second. The viewer has been reinvented?"

Tayee looked surprised. "It could have been. Alcyn, Ashton and a few other people are on Genesis. They obviously transported that creature for a surprise attack somewhere in the other galaxy."

Hammond was deep in thought. "It may have been an experiment. I heard cane toads were on the shopping list. Only Ashton would know about such animals, and he had adapted them for warfare. Smart. It saves human lives. Smart move. I believe the government of this country is having a major cane toad issue. The creatures are poisoning the waterways and killing other animals which mistake them for common frogs they normally eat. I don't think the Australian government will mind if these poisonous introduced creatures are used in war. I wonder if they will permit wild boar and wild buffalo?" he wrote the animals down on his notebook.

Cassie looked up from her notepad. "Price Alcyn said the Lacertians were sound sensitive. Loud sounds made them go insane."

"So what?' asked Lenax who wanted more information. "

We send recordings of heavy metal music. Err I would like those bands to go off planet and never assault my ears again," said Cassie.

"Now, Now," said Hammond. "The music recordings will suffice and the biggest speakers possible will do. Musician going to war? Not really. The suggestion is good if we can get a group to enter a shopping mall or to a stadium with lots of Draconians who go there for entertainment. Blasting their eardrums and making them go crazy for a while will help create disorder. The more I think about it, the more I like it."

"Add some feedback whistle now and then to make things interesting," said Sue. "How many speakers do we need? I can arrange them."

"No. We use what the Draconians have. It is just a matter of organising a concert. In the middle of the concert, we get them to play heavy metal and anything else that makes the Draconians and Lacertians freak out. It is mind control stuff again to get the music heard. Is Ashton and Alcyn up for that?"

Jed reflected on the events years ago and the information Prince Alcyn gave. "Add some supersonic jet flyover in the recordings. That will make the Lacertians and Draconians panic as well. The reverberating boom sent them crazy and made them do all sorts of self-harm or they harmed others. If they harm themselves, then we can save our own people from battle. Another idea I have is a free toys samples or sample of something which attracts teens. The items over time breakdown to release a toxin of some kind. The food went well but we can't reuse that idea. Food from the sky is now used up. The authorities will ban them immediately and the public is aware of gifts from heaven. We make packets for sale in shops. That would be much harder."

Tayee smiled. "Ashton and Kora are in touch with rebel humans. The rebels need to get in contact with rebel Lacertiains. The Lacertians do the drop off as products on consignment. That should work."

Lenax asked, "Where are Ashton and Alcyn now?"

Hammond replied, "On Genesis. Well, I think they are. This Zindel person like to divert their attention to other parts of the universe. Have you seen the set up in the room next door? They sit there with cranial neuro-transmitters for a few hours and mind travel through space. They cause havoc on Draconian mother ships coming through the rip. Actually, they said the rip is more shaped like a hole." Hammond went to the whiteboard behind him. Ashton said it was roughly circular shaped with the bottom half with very visible electro-magnetic fields running across the bottom half. The top half is where the Draconians enter."

Tayee asked, "Do you know how many ships they knocked out?"

Hammond had to think for a few seconds. "About twenty. Give or take a few."

"How do they do it?" asked Cassie.

"Mind control to find a ship. When they find one, they somehow enter the heads of a few Draconians and control them like puppets," said Hammond.

"Wow. That is some serious stuff," said Sue in complete awe.

"We better get back to the agenda. We have to clear out our warehouse of all the donated toxins and whatever else we have stored. From Genesis it goes to another planet for distribution and usage. I was informed it is called Lyria. Where is Lyria?"

Lenax grinned. "Here it is a constellation. There must be a liveable planet hidden in that constellation. It is somewhere up there." He jokingly pointed upwards.

"We should wait for requests from Genesis before we send things at random," said Hammond.

"They better start asking for stuff, we can't receive any more items," said Tayee.

The meeting continued for another thirty minutes with a focus on product manufacturing for Earth.

It was close to closing time when intel accompanied by Ustin appeared as holograms.

"Hello everyone. It's me again. Just in case some of you have not met a good colleague, my name is Ustin. We need some really cool items. Guns with lots of ammunition, more mustard gas, more agent orange, more narcotics. We need as much as you can send."

Tayee invited them. "Come to the warehouse and help yourselves. We have come up with a few new ideas."

This is the captain speaking.

The area of turbulence is now behind us.

You can now unclip your seat belt and resume other activities.

Thank you for co-operating.

204

CHAPTER 34.

The Planet of Shardon.

"Shardon has so far avoided rebel attacks. The latest attacks have been incredibly affective. I think we can put that down to two things. One is the planet is smaller than the others and being over to one side of the Amada galaxy. It is a bit out of the way for rebel Lacertians. Any dissenters are quickly found and done away with," said one of the Sahrdonite administrators. He continued after taking a sip of water. "The youth are getting bored. They never see any of the entertainment that appears on other planets. They travel to other planets, and a few have never returned due to attacks. Because this is a safe planet, I think we can consider having a rock concert here. There is no risk. No history of attacks since Prince Alcyn blew up major facilities at the start of our occupation. That was over twenty years ago. It would make the teens realize we are not in a backwater of any kind, but a progressive and safe planet zooming ahead in all ways."

A female administrator agreed with most of what was said. "As a parent, one of the few parents who have lost a child to attacks on another planet, I second the motion for a major rock concert to be held. Two groups for sure will come to entertain our teens. How many more is debatable. Even if just two groups are present, I think the teens would love it."

The first administrator replied. The best and biggest venue is the open-air amphitheatre. It has the ability to seat fifteen thousand teens. Those who fail to get in, can see the performance from the surrounding hills and watch the large screens. All inside and out will have their usual headphones as each can alter their volume to suit their ears."

A month later of the news of the music festival, teens from Shardon and a few from surrounding planets poured into Shardon's amphitheatre. It was a sell-out. Every available space in the surrounding hills were taken days in advance by those who camped to secure their spot.

Zindel advised the Earth people the show was on. He took the pre-loaded recording of a heavy metal rock group and some of the loudest speakers to Shardon. Acting as a Lacertian labourer, he slipped the recording with its own separated equipment and power supply behind the regular stage equipment. He connected everything via remote control to his ship. He waited.

On the ground and disguised as Lacertians, four rebels handed out dolls of the two performing groups. The teens took the offerings, a very limited edition novel promotional idea that many believed would be worth a fortune in the future.

The first Draconian group played their music. The crowd adjusted their headphones to what suited them. They smiled, swayed, and danced along with the music. All was going well. There was a gap in the music flow as bands change over.

Zindel took control of a band member from the first group. He announced, "Did you like our music?" The crowd yelled, "Yes!"

"Do you want to hear more?"

"Yes," The crowd was stamping their feet. "More. More! More."

The solitary musician picked up an instrument and began playing. A happy crowd. Then he stopped and announced, "I have a recording of a brand-new group. They couldn't come but they sent me this incredible new style of music. We liked it and we hope you do too."

The musician turned on the recording. The heavy metal music began to flow. Zindel took control of the equipment. He turned up the volume. No matter what adjustment level the teens made to their headphones, the music was constantly loud. Even when they removed the headphone, they could hear the music. The crowd went into a frenzy and mental breakdown. The sound of feedback and supersonic jets blasted their ears rendering many instantly insane. They attacked each other with anything. Many killed themselves. Total carnage. The very few sitting on the hills escaped for a while. Zindel turned on the loudspeakers nestled under his ship. He flew over the escaping teens. The sonic boom and the loud music made them stop. They either dropped dead or attacked each other. The surrounding streets were littered with death and untouchable bleeding bodies. They attacked anyone who tried to assist to add more to the carnage.

The recording of the music was played again with the mix jets, feedback, and any other high-pitched sound. The reverberation in the flyover in the surrounding area which included apartment buildings did its work. Windows shattered. Any Draconians and Lacertians fell to their deaths or became mentally unstable and attacked each other. Just to be sure, Zindel dropped bombs of assorted gas and assorted drugs over the neighbouring areas. He disappeared as fast as he came.

Back at the stadium, the only surviving item thing were the dolls, waiting to do their deadly deed.

Time passed. The clean-up of the dead teens and the deceased in the surrounding areas were hampered by the lingering assorted strange powder and the lingering gas which made the cleaner ill and mentally deranged. Draconians and lacertian thought the smell of the bodies were to blame. As time progressed, they realized the wind distributed the superfine powder through the gas masks. The clean-up crews fell ill or died. The Lacertians did the bulk of the cleaning and succumbed to the toxins and bacteria from rotting bodied. The air became more foul as the days moved on. All bodies were cremated regardless if they were identified or not. The risk of further delays was too great.

The stadium was one of the last places to be totally cleared of dead bodies. The advance decaying bodies of teens fouled the air. The administrators noted these bodies were not covered in fine powder like the teens who camped on the hills. One by one, grieving parents who were still alive or not seriously ill after the aerial attack of fine powder and gas identified their teens. On other parts of Shardon, anger, and hatred spread through the communities.

The novel promotional dolls took on a sinister and macabre reminder of the tragedy. They were collected. Many of the younger siblings took them for their sentimental value, not for their future monetary value. About two months later, the dolls began to deteriorate. Gas leaked out to kill any Draconian within a five-metre radius. More deaths. More anger. More hatred. Broken families.

The Shardon administrators were furious and at a loss. So many precautions were taken to ensure the event was safe. All failed. The Shardonites realized they were not immune from attack and their attack was the most lethal of all. It was like a grand finale.

The Shardon administrators counted their losses. Over thirty thousand teens, and thousand more adults and young Draconians died within months.

Reports started to come in from other Amada planets. In Centari, Daraxon and Centari toys sold in any shops began to break down. A strange powder lightly blanketed the cities. Gas seeped out of the toys. The same kind of dreadful event had occurred there as well. It was a near total decimation of a generation, over one hundred thousand more Draconian lost their lives.

The surviving Draconians contacted Draconia of the news. Samples of the toys and the persistent strange white powder were flown to Draconia.

The news of the attack spread throughout the galaxies. The resistance groups celebrated. The ruling Draconians were at a loss. They became fearful of the Lacertians. Who were the traitors? Who collaborated with any resistance groups? And who were loyal, become blurred. Lacertians were treated more harshly. That only added fuel to the fire of distrust.

The price of human meat collapsed as Draconians were now suspicious of the quality of human meat. If humans were immune to the toxins and consumed them, the toxic matter locked in the tissues of the flesh would build up slowly in their own bodies and eventually kill them.

Readers.

This is the captain speaking. We are heading into major turbulence.

Please return to your seats. Remove any trays of food and drink.Please take them to the kitchen. please stow away any loose items in the compartment above your head.

Place your seatbelts on.

The turbulence may cause us to redirect the craft to another planet for safety checks. If that occurs, you will be permitted to leave the craft and proceed to the space terminal. Refreshments will be available in the main area. A movie for delayed passengers will be screening in lounge two. You will be advised of the length of time of the delay should we have to detour.

Thank you for your attention.

CHAPTER 34

The Lords of the Universe.

Thuma studied the results of the attacks in sectors nineteen and twenty. There was a noticeable Draconian statistical spike in the culling of Draconianas and to a lesser extent of Lacertians since Earth ideas were added. Thuma thought to himself, *earth people have some very dangerous creative ideas. I am beginning to think, they may not be as primitive in all aspects of life. They are scary. It may be worthwhile to go there myself and take a closer look.*

Thuma went to his one-person craft and flew to Earth. He hid his vehicle on the dark side of the moon. He examined the moon bases. Then he teleported himself to the south pole. He turned himself invisible as he inspected the scientific work being carried out. He nodded his approval.

He travelled to Australia. Daraxon Technologies site caught his eye. Invisible again he examined each room and each manufacturing aspect. He grinned. Daraxon technology was being created. Price Alcyn's transporter was there. He examined that. Only one destination was in the system, Genesis.

There were buildings of concern. One contained drugs and assorted weapons all confiscated by various law enforcement bodies from around the world. It was heavily guarded. Thuma noted, well that over half the stockpile had been moved out. The supply for the galactic wars had come from here.

The next heavily guarded building contained a stockpile of chemicals. Thuma walked down the aisles, garden chemicals, disinfectants, and containers of gas. He read the list; mustard, capsicum/pepper, hydrogen, carbon dioxide, nitrogen, helium, and carbon monoxide. He smirked when he read the anaesthetic. He left the complex.

He made a whirlwind inspection of different space stations and space observatories. He noted they were only in observational mode. He nodded his approval at the precautions. He saw their potential when working to capacity. Then it was a quick inspection of large corporate medical laboratories and various research centres.

Finally, he crisscrossed the planet to find the vast inequalities of human health, service, and wealth, planetary degradation, and attempts at restoration. He shook his head in dismay at the battle zones. However, he studied the tactics. He noted their weapons would defy detection if used by advanced civilizations. After all the detection systems were designed for advance weaponry, not deadly effective 'primitive' ones. Perfect.

He went back to his craft and flew home. He wrote a report for the others: The Unbalanced Progress on Earth. He sent a copy to each other Lords.

Azna contacted Thuma. "Thank you for the report. Interesting. What a mixed-up planet. Earth humans still have potential if they don't wipe out each other or their own planet first. What made you visit the planet?"

"I had to see what they were up to in all forms of development. As the title says, it is unbalanced."

Azna said, "I have all the information regarding the closing of the rip or hole in the universe. It can be done but some galaxies will be impacted in a negative way. Others may have positive impacts. It is unclear what could happen where. Some may just have a time shift rather than a planetary disturbance. It is hard to tell what gravity, dark matter, dark energy, gases, various light rays, radio, and electromagnetic fields will do. If we study each variable, we will add a minimum of two years of time. We have to make a choice. We go in and attack within a few weeks or wait until all the variables are studied. That will allow Draconians to penetrate further into our system. More human lives will be lost. If we go now, we still lose lives, but we end the problem. Read the report. We will take a vote in a few days. Happy reading." Azna clicked off.

The joint meeting saw the debate about the variables nutted out. Preparations were considered for the worse outcomes in the affected galaxies. Jose said, "It is settled. We attack next week. I will alert all the emissaries in all sectors. They can have their assistants and students monitor everything. Let's just hope we are not annihilated in the process or send all the planets back to the stone age or some ancient stage of development."

"We only have one chance at this. If we stuff up, it is a big bang," said Sigma.

"Oh, please don't remind me of that," replied Jose. "That was one spectacular mess that took forever to clean up."

One week later, the craft built by the Lords of the Universe sped towards the hole in sector nineteen. "Let's do a final study of the hole's behaviour. No one fires unless instructed. Let's be sure when it is the best time to close this thing up with the least amount of damage," said Azna.

Two weeks later, the series of assorted measurements were complete. "The hole explodes every three days. Then it settles again to allow crafts to pass through." Xetron looked at the old data and compared it with what he had now. The energy of the hole had dropped to near zero levels immediately after an explosion. The explosion didn't travel far in space but covered the entire circle to block any entry. Xetron surmised, any vehicle trapped in the explosion would vapourised instantly and the matter would increase the power of the explosion exponentially. He ordered, "Team one. Set up the hexagon carbon crystals all around the ship. It must cover all parts and all vehicles in the wings."

The pilots went to work setting up the matrix of the shield. A massive net formed over the craft.

They all flew back to their stations. "Team Two, Three, and Four. Get ready to fire the red laser beams and the long distance all frequency ultra-sound. Just a reminder. Make sure you are wearing protective helmets for high-intensity light and sound waves. Make sure the light shield on your craft is activated. There is going to be an intense light; status twelve." Xetron could hear a series of clicks coming through the system.

Xetron waited until he was given the confirmation that all safety procedures and equipment were in place. He could see in the central control the stages of powering up. "Begin combining the ultrasound waves." He watched the dial in the control room. "Add the red laser beam and light rays." The ship's arms began to glow with the red light. "On the count of three fire through the carbon shield. One. Two. Three. FIRE!"

The red beam combined with the ultrasound waves formed a matrix of light and sound sub-atomic particles. The projectile hit the centre of the hole slightly above the newly forming electromagnetic waves. After two minutes, Xetron ordered, "Stop firing. Stand by for other orders." Nothing appeared to happen.

"Repeat the procedure. This time aim lower and into the forming electromagnetic field." After one minute of firing, there was a spark. "We are leaving the area. All engines on. Do not disengage. Central control will override all individual crafts."

The mother craft at maximum speed out of the area. The spark was growing fast behind them. There was a shattering sound that rocked the ship. The ship was engulfed by the blast. Xetron looked at the exterior temperature. It was hot, much hotter than predicted. The cooling system was activated.

Emergency lights came on. The ship continued at maximum speed to escape the ever-engulfing blast.

Xetron looked at the data. The ship was still going too slow to outrun the blast. He ordered,

All craft engines to maximum speed on. Do not disengage from the mother ship." He looked at the new data.

The extra boost coming from the fighter jets increased the mother ship's velocity by fifty percent. They escaped the blast. Now it was the aftershock of shifting gravity and time. Dark matter and dark energy surrounded the ship to form a dense blanket. Xetron looked at the new readings and he sighed. There was no choice but to ride out the situation. He looked at his watch and noted the hands madly spinning backwards. "Uh-oh," he muttered to himself. He glanced at Azna. She too had a worried look. He guessed; she had already noted time was spinning backwards. Just how far back could only be assessed when they returned home.

Minutes passed but it seems like an eternity. The ship entered a corridor that came out in sector fourteen. Slowly the ship began to cool down. Xetron ordered a check on all parts and functions of the ship.

While this was happening the time-gravity continuum warped and twisted in sectors nineteen, eighteen, and twenty. The missing planets of Elkondite, Salutre, Pleiades, and Sirius reformed and were in the same state before they disappeared. The missing people were there. They were none the wiser. Isobola, the one prison planet that was converted to a holiday resort for Draconians returned to its orbit. Buildings and prisoners intact, back to pre-Draconian extraction levels. The people worked the mines as before. Nubia was back to normal. and Genobola A and B were in essence, the planets in Oberon were back to their glory days.

In the galaxy of Amada, the planets were back to normal. Again, many of the people were none the wiser. To them, nothing had happened. The palace of Price Alcyn was intact, the only building fifty kilometres into the edge of a desert. The people in the palace were at their normal workstations. Everyone looked the same as they did just over twenty-five years ago.

The Lords examined each sector. Jose grinned. "Not too bad considering what could have happened.

All other sectors have not been affected. The dark energy and the dark matter with all their other bits and pieces are intact. They will continue in their normal expansion. Only sectors eighteen, nineteen, twenty, and a tiny bit of twenty-one, show a time progression lapse."

"Excellent work," said Azna.

"I think his calls for a celebration," said Thuma.

"A big one. Not just for us, but for all who contributed," said Azna.

Readers,

This is the captain speaking.

We will be diverting to the planet of Daraxon. This is a precaution check.

You will be permitted to enter the space port. As mentioned before refreshment will be available in

One lounge and a movie will be screened in lounge two.

However, we all do have a problem.

You are now twenty-eight years younger than what you were when you left Earth.

For many, it won't be an issue. Unfortunately, younger passengers maybe effected and are now you

Young children of babies. A nurse will assist parents with babies and young children under the age of

Three.

Sorry.

CHAPTER 35

The Planet of Daraxon.

 A nurse knocked on Prince Alcyn's door to his private quarters. "Sir, the man who was sucked up in the viewer in Portal 106 is awake. He is still a bit dazed." Alcyn placed the glass of water down and hurried with the nurse to the small hospital in the palace. Alcyn slowed his pace when he entered the room. He slowly leaned towards the man. He said as he pointed to himself, "Alcyn."

The man looked blankly at Alcyn. He said nothing. "My name is Alcyn," said Alcyn.

The man's eyes wandered around the room to observe the others watching him. He tried to lift his hand to point to Alcyn, but the pain raced through his arm. His finger barely lifted as he directed his gaze towards Alcyn. He said, "Alcyn. Surfie." Alcyn frowned and pointed to himself. "Alcyn."

The man nodded ever so slightly. "Alcyn."

Alcyn smiled and confirmed the man's response. "Alcyn."

As Alcyn turned away, ready to leave the room, the man whispered, "Alcyn. Surfie."

Aclyn shook his head, gave a slight grin and left the room. The others followed.

Alcyn went to the portal centre. He met with his most trusted assistances, Beathkin, Vestale, Amo and

Hammond. "The man in the medical centre is called Jed. He doesn't know, I already know his name. When he recovers, we will give him limited movement around the palace, always with an escort."

Hammond nodded. "What makes you believe he is going to be important?"

"I just know. His people and he will be instrumental in winning the impending war.

When is the next election on Lacerta?"

"Next week," said Amos.

"Amos I want you to do the following. Organize a flight to Lacerta. I want to leave tomorrow.

Vestale, start closing down all portal travel to all planets. Just give the excuse, maintenance. Then

Get all the presidents to give me an inventory of all crafts of all sizes and all pilots."

Vestalel was about to ask why but changed his mind. Alcyn always had a good reason which always made sense minutes later. Alcyn picked up on Vestale's thoughts. "The next elected president will be

Kyros. Despite him being a Lacertian, he is a good lizard. His life is in danger."

Alcyn turned to Hammond, "Get me Zanthe. I want her to do pilot training. She gets pulled from all other duties. She starts like yesterday. Get commander Patrum. He is going to train Zanthe in more advanced techniques. It will be a huge jump from small crafts to larger ones. It has to be done."

"When you have done that, get me all the presidents in the Oberon galaxy. Include the administrators on Isobola."

Hammond looked at Alcyn. "I think you know something is going to happen. Am I right?"

Alcyn nodded. "Let's just say a premonition of war. The key is saving Kyros. He is in danger."

9 781963 209860